THE LYING SEASON

HEATHER CHRISTIE

Black Rose Writing | Texas

The author grants the final approval for this literary material.

First printing

This is a work of fiction. Names, characters, businesses, places, events, and incidents are either the products of the author's imagination or used in a fictitious manner. Any resemblance to actual persons, living or dead, or actual events is purely coincidental.

ISBN: 978-1-68433-755-2
PUBLISHED BY BLACK ROSE WRITING
www.blackrosewriting.com

Printed in the United States of America
Suggested Retail Price (SRP) $19.95

The Lying Season is printed in Traditional Arabic

*As a planet-friendly publisher, Black Rose Writing does its best to eliminate unnecessary waste to reduce paper usage and energy costs, while never compromising the reading experience. As a result, the final word count vs. page count may not meet common expectations.

For my mother,
Suzie Christie

Also by Heather Christie

WHAT THE
VALLEY
KNOWS

THE
LYING
SEASON

CHAPTER 1
THAT NIGHT

The light was fading as Piper Rose pulled her family's black ten-year-old Honda Accord into the Millington Valley High School parking lot Saturday evening. The cooler of Miller Lite and Noah's and Cooper's shotguns in the trunk, plus the weed in the glove compartment, made her feel like a fugitive.

She wore ragged denim jean shorts, a pink tank top, and her white high-top Converse sneakers, no socks. Waiting for her brothers, Noah and Cooper, and their friend, Little Ryan Hartline, she checked her reflection in the rearview mirror and fixed her auburn hair, pulling it up into a messy bun with a clip and expertly arranging a wisp to fall against her jaw. She had replayed the smoky eye You Tube tutorial five times. The tiniest smudge of brown eyeliner accented her light blue eyes, and she hoped it didn't look like she was trying too hard. Her stomach was a little jumpy.

"Ready for a good time?" Cooper banged the hood. His cheeks, still flushed from the hot shower, made his blue eyes look even brighter. "You're the designated driver tonight, but I'm the pilot for the first leg of our adventure. Scoot over."

"Really? I thought you said it was fine if I drove now."

"Move over. It's my prerogative according to Mom and Dad. You don't want me to fail my driver's test next month, do you?"

She sighed. "Okay." She hated the twitch of disappointment in her chest. The privilege of the driver's seat dangled in front of her, then snatched away. It was stupid, to be upset over this, but it was how it was in their family. She hopped over the center console, caving, like she always did. They were only letting her come because she had agreed to drive Little Ryan home at midnight. Despite the freshman's varsity call-up and tag-along to the bonfire, he wasn't invited to camp out overnight and hunt the next morning.

Freshly showered from soccer practice, Noah and Little Ryan tumbled into the backseat. Noah's gelled blond hair resembled a porcupine's and Little Ryan reeked of Axe body spray. He was always trying too hard to impress everyone. Like me, Piper thought and then dismissed it.

Cooper moseyed through town, then gunned it when he turned onto RT 74. They passed the old gristmill, went through the red covered bridge over the Manatawny Creek, and weaved their way deep into the valley until they saw the faded, old red and gray sign: Stone Haven Quarry. A long gravel lane ended at the dilapidated entrance, a KEEP OUT sign on the padlocked metal chain-link gate. Hopping the fence wasn't a problem. The twenty-minute hike to the lake, laden with party paraphernalia, posed more of a hindrance. The trick was to bring as few vehicles as possible and not draw attention. Most kids carpooled and hid their cars in the brush along this section. Others parked in the roller rink's lot on the far side of the hill and trekked in along the creek. They were the first to arrive.

"Get that dead branch." Noah pointed. "Prop it across the bumper when I'm done."

"You're paranoid," Cooper said. "The cops won't be out here tonight. It's almost dark. They're lazy." He dug into his pocket, pulled out a joint, lit it, and took a big hit.

"Shut up. A little camo is good. All we need is Sheriff Mismo sniffing around." Noah popped the trunk. Before Little Ryan could see, Noah handed Cooper the bulky sleep bag roll that concealed their guns and said under his breath, "I'm not hiking down in the morning. Hide them good when we get up there. Nobody needs to know our plans." Then he shouted to Ryan over the hood. "Come here. Grab the soccer balls and the badminton net. Time for a soccer tennis lesson—the beer bong version."

Piper snatched the chips, pretzels, Doritos, five-pound Sour Patch gummies bag, and the sole two-liter Coke bottle from the back seat as

Little Ryan snuck around the side of the car. "I've got it." He bounced on his toes, a conspiratorial smile on his face. "The good stuff, too." He opened his drawstring bag to reveal a Smirnoff vodka bottle.

"Great. Your brother hooked us up." Piper set the bags and Coke on the ground and took the bottle. "Hey, Noah."

"What's up?"

"I've got a little birthday gift for you." Piper walked toward Noah, the vodka hidden behind her back. "Special present for a special birthday. You're officially an adult."

"Not till tomorrow."

"Close enough."

Piper handed him the loot.

He turned it, marveling as if it was a museum artifact. "Glad I'm not driving tonight."

"At your service." Little Ryan bowed awkwardly as he was carrying two soccer balls, one wedged under each arm. "Mr. Well-connected, that's me."

Noah ignored him. "Pretty cool," he said to Piper. "Thanks." He gave her shoulder a gentle jab.

Warmth spread through Piper at that one simple word. She looked up. An entire universe of stars poked tiny holes against the night sky.

"That shit will make you sick," Cooper said, a blunt between his lips, a tiny orange glow on its tip. "I'm sticking with the medicinal herbs."

"Fucking pothead." Noah put the vodka inside the duffle. "Onward."

"Somebody pull up their flashlight." Cooper motioned for Little Ryan to pass the ball. Cooper first touched it with ease and juggled, dexterously clenching the joint in his mouth, the sleeping bags under his arms.

Piper collected the sacks and Coke and then awkwardly dug out her phone. Any deeper into the woods and the cell service got spotty. Her heart raced, and she dropped the Coke bottle. The Tisch audition email was there. Fingers trembling, she doubled tapped the message.

September 30 at 10:30 AM

Four weeks away. Yes. Perfect. Tonight was turning out to be even better than she imagined it could be. She scooped up the fizzing Coke bottle and then leapt, the bags banging against her thighs. "Guys," she yelled. "I got my audition notice."

"Wow, great," Cooper said with none of the enthusiasm she felt. "Big fucking deal."

"It is, asshole." Piper smiled anyway. She was tired of her family dismissing her accomplishments. Tisch was a big deal. Finally, everything was falling into place.

They lumbered toward the lake, walking along the narrow path. The stones crunched underfoot, announcing their passage in the still night. Dense foliage and tall trees flanked them on both sides. Every once in a while, Piper spotted a lonesome late season lightning bug and, pretending it was a shooting star, she made a wish.

Let us beat Concord.

Please let me get into NYU.

Make something happen with Ethan.

The full moon was low on the horizon, a huge silvery globe beckoning them. At the clearing on the bluff, the lake spread out below, like a sheet of black glass. Huge logs sat in a sloppy semicircle around an abandoned fire pit. An osprey squawked and swooped down to the water, then rose with a fish in its talons.

Noah hid the gun bundle in the brush and then took charge. Collect wood. Set up the net. Arrange the snacks. Piper tied a trash bag to a nearby tree. Cooper and Little Ryan got the fire roaring and erected the badminton net. Within minutes kids arrived with more party accoutrements. Mostly alcohol. Piper kept glancing at the trailhead. Where were the Horn brothers? If she was honest, the prospect of seeing Ethan was the only reason she was here.

The soccer tennis tournament began with Cooper as the main referee. The idea was to keep the ball in the air and get it over the net, like volleyball or tennis, except the players could only use their feet. Anytime the opposing team scored, the other team had to drink. About forty minutes into the party, Piper spotted Mia Diaz, the pretty drama club president. Her hair was wavy and jet-black and her lips shone with an iridescent pink gloss. Piper caught Noah checking her out more than once. Grabbing two Solo cups filled with vodka and coke, Piper approached Mia.

"Hey, I'm sorry I got the soccer manager position." Piper handed Mia the drink. "I know you wanted it." She took a tentative sip. "I think Noah and Cooper coaxed Coach into it. Go figure. Most of the time they act like they hate me."

"Thanks, and no biggy. I'll be super busy with the play. I bet I can get Mr. Franks to give me extra credit." Mia said, her chocolate eyes cool, and Piper wasn't sure she believed her. Then Mia pointed. "Guess the party can get started now. Look who's here."

The Horn brothers, Ethan and Jacob, carrying two cases of Old Milwaukee, appeared at the clearing. Piper's stomach fluttered. The crowd parted as they entered, everyone was awed that Ethan, a college kid, had graced them with his presence. He was going Division 1 to Temple University—a big deal. He'd only come home between preseason training sessions to see his brother and former teammates play. Piper forced herself not to look at him. In the last year, he had the terrible effect of making her heart spin and her cheeks redden on sight.

Maybe it was the moonlight, but Ethan was more handsome than usual. He wore a red Temple shirt pulled tightly over his muscled chest, and his jet-black hair was combed back and gelled into place. His eyes were a soft, warm brown, and when he scanned the crowd, his gaze stopping on Piper, she almost jumped. Jacob, Ethan's younger brother and Piper's best friend since forever, caught the moment and rolled his eyes. She shot him a don't-start-with-me look and turned her attention to the soccer tennis match. When Noah offered her another drink, she took it. Why not? Two couldn't hurt. It was time to celebrate.

Her Tisch dream was falling into place.

As the night deepened, the party broke up because most kids had junior driver's licenses. By midnight, only the Rose siblings, the Horn brothers, and Little Ryan remained. Piper sat on a log next to Ethan as the fire warmed her bare legs, and she slowly sipped the vodka and Coke, the alcohol barely detectable in the soda's fizzle. She peered into the flames. The surrounding chatter was a soft din; she half-listened to the guys' conversation, and every once in a while she stole a glance at Ethan's profile. Thank God the vodka had slightly calmed her jack hammering heart. Otherwise, she wasn't sure she could be this close to Ethan.

"Coach O was a pro. It was before Major League Soccer came here," Cooper said. "It was the indoor league." He swigged the last of this beer and then stepped on the can, crushing it. He'd broken his pot-only rule.

"I saw the trophy in his office—Defender of the Year."

Jacob handed Ethan another beer, but held Piper's gaze as if he had picked up the vibe pulsing through her body. "I also heard he played in the Premier League for a year."

"It's true." Noah poured Grey Goose into a Solo cup.

Piper wasn't counting, but she was certain Noah had drunk a lot. He sure seemed to like her gift. She had lost count of her own sips, too, though she didn't think she was drunk, just warm and fuzzy. She never filled her cup. It took little to blur things.

Noah was still talking about Coach. "He's the real deal. Concord doesn't have a former pro for their coach. We need to crush those assholes. One hundred sixty-five straight wins. One hundred and sixty-six after today. Well, screw them. If it's the last thing I do as captain, we're beating them."

The fire cracked and popped, sending a burst of light into the darkness. Piper's cheeks grew hotter. The alcohol that coursed through her body made everything tingle. Maybe part of it was sitting next to Ethan. Yes, of course. She let her leg touch his ever so slightly. The heat of his skin sent a shiver down her back. She traced her index finger in the loose dirt by her feet and then immediately wanted to wash her hands. She glanced up to find Jacob watching, the annoyance on his face undeniable. So what? She wanted to say. But then she softened. Piper knew Jacob liked her the way she liked Ethan. Poor guy. She sighed as she dug for an open mini Purell from her pocket, squeezed the last drop, and then threw the empty bottle onto the beer can pile.

"Yeah, man. Pro, D-1 college, played in Europe." Little Ryan gulped his drink and swayed. "I only have one question. What the hell is he doing in Millington?"

"He's a bit of an asshole. Maybe dickheads don't last at that level," Jacob slurped his beer.

"Coach just likes to take the piss out of you," Noah said.

Jacob waved, imitating Coach's Scottish accent, and beer sloshed out of his can. "You're so fucking slow, laddie."

6

Piper giggled, and then she noticed Jacob looking at Ethan.

"You're just a pussy," Cooper said to Jacob. "And you are pretty slow."

"Fuck you, too." Jacob plopped down on the other side of Piper, and his knee nudged her leg. When she pulled away, Jacob glowered and said, "Isn't it time for you to take Ryan home?"

"Not yet," Ethan said, turning to Piper. He stood up. "Let's walk down to the lake."

Maybe she was drunk. Ethan was asking her to do what? Things were awful confusing and Jacob was about to blow a gasket. She just had to get herself and Little Ryan home later. But first she could take a walk with Ethan. What could that hurt? She took a deep breath.

Jacob was practically in her lap, leaning against her.

"Oooh, Jacob and Piper sitting in a sitting in a tree," Cooper sang.

Little Ryan joined in, "K.I.S.S.I.N.G—"

She scooted away from Jacob. Ethan put his hand out to help her up.

Rebuffed, Jacob rose and stomped toward the woods. "Got to pee. Have a nice fucking walk."

God, Jacob. *Why do you have to be like that?* Piper thought. She hated whenever someone was mad or disappointed.

"No taking advantage of my little sister. You know she doesn't drink." Noah winked at Ethan.

The guys laughed. Piper set her cup on the ground and squashed it with her sneaker. She would have been mad at them, if she were fully sober. She knew that. But they didn't matter.

Prickly raspberry stalks and low-hanging tree branches lined the path. Ethan walked ahead of her, holding the trailing plants out of her way and pointing out the rocks. Piper's head swam with a pleasant buzz, making the world softer and the outlines of the trees indistinct.

It was a steep incline and as they got closer to the lake, the air cooled with the hint of water, and Piper's heartbeat ratcheted up a few ticks. She had dreamed about a moment like this—her and Ethan—alone. Now it was here and she wasn't sure what to do.

"Do you want to sit down?" she offered.

"Sure," Ethan said, and pointed to a rock bulging near the shoreline.

They parked themselves on the crag. Piper pulled her knees to her chin and wrapped her arms around them. Her nerves caught in her throat and she blanked on what to say. Instead, she focused on the lake and how the moon sprayed a cast of glitter on the calm surface. Her stomach flip-flopped with each passing minute. Finally, Ethan broke the spell by picking up a small rock and skipping it across the water.

"Five. That's good," Piper said, her voice higher than she would have liked. "You're lucky that you're out of here this week. I can't wait until next year." She leaned back on her hands and extended her legs, crossing her feet, feigning confidence, but was sure Ethan could see straight through to her jittery soul.

"Temple's good. I hope I get some playing time."

"You will." The conviction in her reply startled her, and she flushed.

They took turns skipping rocks and they talked more about Temple. Then they were quiet and watched the lake. The silence bloomed with little electrical vibrations, and then Ethan turned and the purr zipping between them increased to a roar. For a moment she couldn't breathe, and there was no doubt she wanted him. "Why did you ask me to come down here?" she squeaked and then cracked her knuckle, the pop embarrassingly loud.

"To show you the lake?"

"That's it?" She was pretty sure he was lying. Something was happening here.

"The guys were getting too loaded. I wanted to get away." He inched back to his spot.

"It's just. I hoped that—" Her heartbeat quickened. Say it now. Do it. "I thought, maybe, you wanted to be alone with me." There. She let the words come out of her mouth.

He tilted his head as if prodding her to say more. "I'd never take advantage of you."

"What if I wanted you to?"

Ethan studied his black and white Adidas Sambas, slumping ever so slightly. "Piper—" his voice trailed off. "It's not as if I haven't thought about it. But there's—"

"I want you to." She touched his cheek brazenly, surprising herself with her boldness.

"We can't. You know Jacob is hopelessly in love with you."

She didn't talk, but leaned toward him and rested her hands on his chest.

There it was again—a momentary flash of pure desire in his cinnamon eyes. He reached for her and she let her lips connect with his in a hungry, frantic sweep as they melted against one another. Abruptly, Ethan broke away and Piper almost tumbled off the rock. His face was guilt-stricken. "Sorry," he said. "It's just that Jacob—"

"I know," she said as both longing and regret whipped through her. She hopped up and then stumbled. "So sorry. You're right. We can't—" And then she ran. Terrified. Embarrassed.

*

At the quarry entrance, Piper dragged the branch away from the Honda bumper and threw it into the woods. It was pitch black and her head swam, making it hard to keep her balance. She bent over, propped her hands on her knees and sucked in a big gulp of fresh air. Her white Converse sneakers were caked with mud and grime. She had run up the trail, through the woods, brambles tearing at her legs, and then cut over onto the quarry lane, steering clear of the bonfire. Sweat ran down her temples into her eyes. Her legs stung from the long, red scratches left by the brush. She'd made a fool of herself. Stupid. Stupid. Stupid.

Was she drunk? Maybe she shouldn't drive. Then her phone pinged, detecting she was back in the service area. She pulled her cell from her back pocket. The 7:27pm text read: *We are headed to Philly for a night out. We'll probably get a hotel. Don't forget to lock the doors. Come straight home after you drop off Ryan Hartline. Tell Copper and Noah to have fun. They're not texting back. Dad ;-)*

Of course, Dad had texted the boys first. Well, at least now she wouldn't miss curfew. Her stomach churned and leaning on the car, she saw a knee through the window. Little Ryan was passed out on the back seat. She knocked on the glass, but he didn't stir. The time on her phone read 1:17am. How long had she and Ethan been at the lake? She readjusted her bun, and then opened the door, climbed in, and rested her forehead on the steering wheel. The car was hot and smelled like

9

sweat and beer. She spotted a still-wrapped stick of Wrigley's spearmint gum in the change holder and dug it out.

Dance. That's what mattered. She didn't need Ethan Horn. Or Millington Valley. Or an idiotic normal senior year liked Mom and Dad harped. She needed to stay focused. NYU. Right now what she desperately wanted was her hand sanitizer, but she had left her extra bottle in her pack at the campsite. Her skin itched and the longing to purge the invisible, sticky film of dirt and sweat was overpowering. Coming to this party was a silly idea. It had been humiliating. It was the alcohol. That's what she'd tell Ethan before he left for Temple. She would apologize. Or maybe she'd pretend it had never happened.

Little Ryan groaned.

She found the key under the crusty floor mat and started the engine. Tomorrow she'd disinfect the entire vehicle. The headlights shone into the woods, illuminating the tree trunks. She slid the vehicle into reverse, and stones spit against the undercarriage of the car.

"Stop!" There was Ethan, suddenly pounding on the back window. "Open up."

Piper jammed on the brake and rolled down the window. "What?" she said.

"Hey, I'm sorry." Sweat dripped from his forehead. "You're a pretty fast runner for a dancer," he said, his expression earnest, and for a split second she wanted to lecture him about athleticism and dance. Then he said, "Maybe if things were different. Jacob just complicates things too much."

"I get it. You're right. The vodka was doing the talking for me." She lied, her mouth saying one thing and her brain and body meaning another. "Actually, I'm embarrassed."

The muscles around Ethan's lips stiffened, but his eyes softened. "Man, I'm sorry. I shouldn't have sent you such mixed messages." He pulled at the door handle. "Get out for a second."

Pointing to the back seat, she said, "I've got to get this little drunk home."

"Just for a second."

She opened the door, but Ryan didn't stir. She stood and her head swam. Ethan reached for her hand, and his warm fingers encircled hers.

She hesitated, making herself believe she didn't want him. Then he pulled her close. Tentatively, she laid her cheek against his chest and felt the thump of his heartbeat in her ear. "It just can't be," he whispered. "Maybe when we're all out of the valley and Jacob gets interested in someone else." He tightened his arms around her and she felt his longing. "Not now. We can't hurt my brother like that."

Piper gently pushed him away. "Like I said, I didn't mean it." The thick summer air pressed against them and they stayed like that, close enough to feel each other's body heat, but apart enough to ache. The sounds of the forest and the soft hum of the car engine were background music. In a movie, maybe Piper would know what to say.

The bloody little gashes on her legs throbbed and her heart pounded. She stepped back and took a deep breath. "I'll see you around, okay?"

In that moment, when she turned to get into the Honda, she heard the undeniable crack of a shotgun blast.

PIPER'S JOURNAL ENTRY
SUNDAY, SEPTEMBER 4

We really screwed up.

I can barely hold this pen. My hands are shaking bad. WE ARE DESPICABLE! Monsters. God forbid someone finds this journal. I can't keep it inside much longer—I am literally about to break. I need to STAY CALM. And I can't even think about what would happen to the guys if this got out.

SOOOO

Things to do instead of panicking:
Start reading Schindler's List (AP History is going to be tough this year)
Figure out dance schedule for next three weeks
Unravel how I feel about Ethan (Does that even matter anymore? Does anything?)
Chop up leftover broccoli and make swan soup for Bert and Ernie
Buy Purell (one bottle left)
???
Screw it. It's hard to think about anything but "the situation." I feel horrible and ugly inside. My life is falling apart. This is NOT how I thought senior year would start. And I can't believe I'm even worrying about myself right now. If there is a hell, I'm going there. It's made for people like me who've done the sort of thing I've done. The thing we've done. Satan better make room for Noah, Cooper, Ethan, and Jacob, too. They're just as guilty as I am.

Maybe more. A lot more.

CHAPTER 2
THREE DAYS EARLIER

The Wednesday before Labor Day, at the Millington Valley-Concord scrimmage, Piper sat at the scorekeeper's table scribbling in her journal, itemizing her to-do list while vaguely listening to the soccer game. It was a stretch for her, taking time away from dance and studying, but she needed the extra-curricular activity credit for graduation. Though she wouldn't admit it to Noah and Cooper, she liked how soccer had clear winners and losers, the neatness of it all. It wasn't the same with ballet. That was art—open to interpretation, filled with a vagueness that made her feel like she could never get it perfect, no matter how hard she tried. Plus, the team desperately required her organizational skills. Even though she was on the sidelines, it gave her a reason to be part of a team. She had ditched everyone and everything for ballet since she was twelve.

She tucked her hair behind her ear and traced her pen over the name Ethan Horn she had neatly written across the top of the page. She allowed herself a glance at him—just one—standing with his mom and dad at the eighteen-yard line. Anything more than that and Jacob would bug her about it.

What could she say to him without sounding like a complete moron?

"What the—!" Head soccer coach Christopher O'Connell yelled and threw his sunglasses. Piper jerked up to see Coach's shades land next to the mangled blue and white umbrella he had pitched moments earlier. He always carried his umbrella. *Lest me fair Scottish skin crisp like fried bacon.*

Out on the field, the referee whipped a red card from his front pocket and thrust it at Jacob. "You're out!"

"What?" Jacob pretended to stumble. "Me?" He pantomimed disbelief, and he then mumbled something under his breath, which enraged the ref.

"Jacob's fouling every goddamn time." Coach raked his hand through his thick, salt and pepper hair as sweat dripped from his sideburns. Then he turned toward his assistant coach, Mark Morgan, a graduate student and former MVHS player, affectionately known as Coach Marky. "Screw me back to Scotland! We need him!" He coughed and wiped his forearm across his mouth.

Piper braced. A red card meant Millington Valley would have to play a man down. This wasn't how they were supposed to be SENDING A MESSAGE TO THE LEAGUE! Not at all.

"Bullshit! That wasn't a foul," Ethan shouted. "The guy dove. There was nothing there."

"Hey, Ref!" Dr. Horn, Ethan and Jacob's dad, stepped over the sideline. "Get off your knees! You're blowing the game."

Noah charged toward Jacob, followed by Cooper, who always followed in Noah's tracks, and several more players.

"Out," the ref shouted at Jacob's back. "That was your last warning!"

Noah slapped Jacob's shoulder. Jacob shrugged, turned, and ran toward the bench, glancing at Piper as he passed her. She gave him a thumb's up, and he grinned. But his bravado was for Ethan's benefit. It was as if Jacob was working his entire life to be more like Ethan, and she understood. She wanted to be as good as her brothers, too.

By default, the Horn brothers, Ethan and Jacob, and the Rose kids, Noah, Piper, and Cooper had fallen into a group when Piper's mom and Jacob's dad became partners in their medical clinic: The Rose–Horn Medical Center. Where Millington Valley Stays Healthy! Ethan had always been their leader and Piper their distant, unwelcomed fifth member.

The scorching August sun baked Piper's tan shoulders as she turned away from the Horns' outburst and glanced at her phone. Where was the Tisch email? If she had to wait one more day, she would burst. She sat up straighter and flicked off a speck of dirt from her shorts. Like her brothers, she was an athlete. She was! Getting into Tisch would prove it.

"Direct kick," the ref shouted. Millington Valley sideline erupted in groans and boos. Feet stomped. Inappropriate hand gestures flew.

"Need glasses? I'll write you a prescription!" Dr. Horn dropped his water cup and trampled it viciously. Piper stifled a nervous laugh and resisted the urge to pull out her phone again to see if the Tisch email had popped up in the last two seconds.

The ref pointed at Dr. Horn as if holding a sword. "Another word and you're out of here." Mrs. Horn tugged fiercely at her husband's arm, and standing on her tippy toes, her pink Vineyard Vines polo shirt rode up as she hissed into his ear.

Millington Valley liked victory, whatever the sport. The soccer team's golden season was to begin today with triumph over their archenemy, the perennial powerhouse of the Concord Tigers. Their fair-skinned, Camel-smoking, umbrella-carrying, former professional Scottish soccer player, Coach Christopher O'Connell, believed this preseason scrimmage was the beginning of something big. He had coached these boys the last three years (after winning the position over the twenty-four-year-old Coach Marky) and that was long enough to know the state championship was destined.

Only today wasn't going quite according to plan.

Relax, Piper wanted to say. It's just a practice game. She slipped off her flip-flops and pointed her toes, pressing her feet against the dry, prickly grass and immediately thought better of it. Half-drunk Gatorade bottles were scattered about, and only God knew what lurked in the mess. She had the itch to grab a bag and collect the trash, but it would be weird to do in the final, hectic minutes of play.

Coach grew still and studied the ruckus on the field as Jacob plopped himself on the bench. Jacob's light brown curly hair was dark with sweat and his cheeks were red. Mrs. Horn shot an apprehensive look their way, her bosom heaving as she smoothed the front of her top. Coach would be mad at Jacob, and Mrs. Horn had a hard time accepting any fault in her boys.

Piper had to admit the excitement was a little contagious. Magical, almost. She checked the official timer. Ten minutes left. Please, please don't let Concord score! Despite all his cockiness, Jacob would blame himself if they lost. Plus, she couldn't endure her brothers' anger about another Concord loss, especially on this last weekend of summer.

Coach ignored Jacob as he untied his cleat laces, rolled down his socks, and plucked out his shin guards. Jacob looked at Ethan for his approval and Ethan nodded. Then Coach turned around for a moment. Sweat ran down his face in rivulets. "How are we supposed to win without a full squad on the field?" he demanded.

Jacob stayed silent, but lifted his chin.

"That's right. Hang your head," Coach said to Jacob. "See how much help you are to your teammates on the bench." He cleared his throat and spat. "Fouling in the back? Stupid. Stupid. Would Ethan do that?" Jacob's shoulders sagged.

Piper cringed. Jacob hated comparisons to Ethan and she would never hear the end. Jacob talked about Ethan non-stop, and if she was honest, she wanted to ask him a million questions about his brother. But Jacob tensed up at her slightest mention of Ethan. Still, she couldn't stop thinking about Ethan. How he looked, how he walked, the way his hair bounced when he ran. What he thought of her.

If he ever did.

Jacob didn't approve of whatever was brewing between Ethan and Piper. Why did he care?

Coach Marky nodded and stooped to pick up Coach's glasses and the mangled umbrella. He handed the shades to his infuriated boss and then attempted to straighten the bent umbrella spokes. Piper fiddled with the timer. Perspiration dripped down her neck. A gasp from the crowd forced her to look up in time to see the Concord shot.

Gooooooal!

Coach flung his sunglasses into the field for a second time. "Goddamn-it!"

"Are you happy now?" Dr. Horn shouted at the ref. "Want a silver platter? Serve us up to Concord in high fashion?"

"Out!" The ref shouted at Dr. Horn. "Play will not resume until that man leaves the field."

Coach kicked an air ball. "Well, fuck me," he said under his breath. The ref glanced at Coach, unsure of what he'd just heard. "Sorry," Coach said and jammed his hand into his front pockets of his crisp white tracksuit. Piper was sure Coach's bark was going to get him into trouble if he didn't watch it. He had a total disregard for political correctness.

The din of the angry spectators quieted. Mrs. Horn grabbed her husband's elbow and guided him toward the parking lot, their pace agitated, every fan watching their departure. Ethan stepped back a few feet and crossed his arms. The sole Horn left to support Jacob. Piper would've felt bad for Mrs. Horn, but she had it coming. She was always overbearing with Jacob, poking her nose in where it didn't belong. Forever saying things she shouldn't. It served her right to have a taste of her own medicine.

Piper spotted her dad across the field. He would laugh at dinner tonight when Noah and Cooper told Mom how her normally gentle, soft-spoken partner, Dr. Frank Horn, had conducted himself. Again! It was like he turned into a different person at a soccer game. She and Dr. Horn took turns trading shifts to keep their clinic covered during matches.

Piper watched Jacob, who sat ramrod straight, his forehead furrowed, and his attention on the field. Jacob waited until his parents disappeared into their car, then he approached Coach. His shorts were wet with sweat, the white fabric translucent against his husky thighs, and his hair curlier than usual because of the humidity.

"What? What is it you want?" Coach turned around again and then pressed his lips together to stop whatever further insult attempted to escape. "Back on the bench."

"It wasn't my fault. The guy jammed his elbow into my ribs and then dove. Didn't you see that? Ref's fucking blind."

"Watch your goddamn language," Coach said, and settled his I-dare-you-to-say-another-word look.

"Me?" Jacob frowned and dug his cleat into a patch of dirt. "Maybe you're right. I shouldn't have fouled this late in the match."

"That's the smartest thing you've said all game." Coach gently punched Jacob's shoulder. "Just don't do stupid shit, eh?"

Jacob nodded, a small smile flickering on his face. "Right, Coach."

"Nothing to be happy about. We're going to lose this game. And tell your dad to keep his mouth shut."

Ten minutes later the bullhorn sounded and the game was over.

Concord 2. Millington Valley 1.

Piper groaned. This was not good. Not good at all.

"I need a cigarette," Coach muttered, wiping his forehead. He retrieved his sunglasses and Coach Marky handed him his umbrella.

As the crowds cleared, Coach called the team to center field. They formed their usual semi-circle screen around him as he stood in the shade of his lopsided umbrella, puffing a cigarette. Tobacco on campus was forbidden. If Principal Unger caught Coach with a smoke, it would screw the team. Piper made a beeline for the trash bag and headed toward the small hill that overlooked the soccer field to clean up the mess. She worked until the sideline was free from every discarded wrapper and water bottle, then glanced at the parking lot where the band was practicing and looked for Ethan's familiar frame among the cars. Had he left without saying goodbye?

She checked her phone, scrolling through her emails again. Zilch. Coach's voice ricocheted off the hills as he lectured on and on. Satisfied that order had been restored, Piper eased herself onto the ground and leaned back on her elbows, waiting out the tirade for her ride home.

"Oh, we're so fucking great. The goddamn Millington Eagle's article went to your heads, I'd say." Coach twirled his umbrella, looking like an angry male Mary Poppins. Piper wouldn't be surprised if he burst into a song and levitated, spewing insults as he floated away. "Now don't go blaming Jacob for that foul. Remember, we win as a team and, goddamn it, we lose as a team. And don't fucking forget that!" He paused. "Man for man we should beat Concord." Coach dropped his cigarette and flattened it with his Adidas Samba. "Well, that didn't happen today, did it?" He raised his eyebrows at Coach Marky.

On cue, Coach Marky said, "No boss, no it did not." He nodded and then squinted at the green hills beyond as if they might explain the loss.

"We were every bit as good. Just unlucky. Concord didn't have a wrong kick. The bear ate us." Coach rubbed his nose. "Fuck me. It's that goddamn smell again."

The guys chuckled. Cooper belly-laughed. "The pig farm. The sweet scent of hog shit only us country boys can truly appreciate."

"The wind changes and we're under a goddamn olfactory attack." Coach sighed. "Maybe this is good. Teach you not to be too cocky. Every game will count. We're going to beat Concord if it kills me."

"That's right, boss," Coach Marky echoed, a flash of irritation in his expression.

Always the showman, Coach took a big breath and looked around for dramatic effect. "I know you guys have some stuff going on this weekend with Noah's birthday. Don't do any stupid shit. I'll not be losing any of you for underage infractions. Text me if anybody needs a ride." He heaved and waved his arm in a sweeping gesture. "Get out of here."

Piper checked her phone again before slipping it into her back pocket. Nada. Ugh—another long weekend of waiting. Thank goodness for Noah's party. At least that would be a distraction. She grabbed her bag, stood, and dusted off her shorts. One more school year and then she would be in New York. But for now she was here and it was time to live a little, right? She stifled the voice in her head telling her no. Parties had never been her thing, but this year was going to be different. Noah was turning eighteen and the entire school would be at the quarry, including Ethan.

A thrill ran up her back.

Maybe it was time to tell him how she felt. Or, if she couldn't come right out and say something, she was pretty sure she could work up the nerve to hint at it.

Piper strolled across the field, stopping to retrieve Coach's still smoking cigarette butt. She pushed the end into the ground and then tucked it into a small Tupperware container she had learned to carry in her bag for these necessary clean-ups. Then Piper found her Purell and squeezed a quarter-sized circle into her palm and rubbed her hands together, then worked the hand sanitizer up and down the inside of each finger, around the half-moons of her cuticles, under her nails, and over the tops of her hands.

Then she did it again.

CHAPTER 3

In the passenger seat of the Rose Honda, Piper adjusted the vent so cold air blew across her neck. She watched the locker room door labeled BOYS and willed it to open. Mia Diaz stood with two field hockey players near the snack bar. Piper smiled and waved to which Mia half-smirked and turned away. Piper wished she could hear what they were saying. The urge to apologize for getting the soccer manager was strong. Instead, she slid down in her seat and propped her feet on the dashboard and refreshed her email again. Nil. Her toenails were polished royal blue with perfect white stripes for a little MVHS school spirit. Leaning back against the headrest, she closed her eyes. There was a knock and she jerked up and pressed the window open.

"Noah and Coop'll be out soon." Jacob wiped his hand across his forehead, pushing his wet curls to the side as his gaze lingered on her long, tawny legs.

"You played well. It was a bad call." She straightened up and lowered her feet to the floor.

He dropped his gym bag. "It sucks losing to Concord."

"It wasn't your fault." Piper glanced over his shoulder as Mia and her crew disappeared. "Don't be so hard on yourself."

"Actually, it was. The blame falls on me."

"Win as a team. Lose as a team, right?" Again, she scanned behind him.

"Who are you looking for?" Jacob said, irritated.

"Nobody. I wish my bozo brothers would hurry."

Just then Ethan rounded the corner of the locker room. "Hey, bro," he called and started toward them. Piper flushed a bit and hoped Jacob didn't notice.

"Tough one, buddy." Ethan slapped Jacob's back. "It was a questionable call. But you've got to be careful in the back."

Jacob stiffened. "The guy tripped over his own foot."

Ethan had Jacob's same light brown eyes, but he was six inches taller than his short, stocky brother—a sore point with Jacob.

"So, what's up with this big party I'm hearing about?" Ethan squeezed Jacob's neck. "My last high school blowout. You going?" Ethan asked Piper. But before she could answer, the locker room door banged open. With gym bags slung over their shoulders, their hair shower wet, and soccer flops on their feet, Noah and Cooper tumbled onto the parking lot.

"Here they come." Piper pointed, and both Jacob and Ethan turned in the commotion's direction.

Noah lumbered toward the car with a slight limp. He was big, the tallest kid on the team at 6'3", and he was the oldest since he had been held back in kindergarten. He had always been physically more mature than his classmates, being a full year older than most of them, and this had given him a certain confidence. Noah and Piper were both seniors, born only twelve months apart, and sometimes it got weird, but mostly they stayed out of each other's ways. Noah wore his blond hair in a super short flattop with a ring shaved an inch above his neck. Piper hated that he didn't shave every day. A few days' growth of beard produced several centimeter-long blond hairs on his chin, making him look like a billy goat. All the professional soccer players were wearing beards, and this was his poor attempt at one. If Piper had to listen to him talk about his D-1 offers anymore, she would go crazy.

Cooper didn't resemble his tall, blond sibling. He was short and brawny, with dark brown hair. Their mother said Cooper inherited a recessive Greek gene that ran through her side of the family. But all the Rose kids, including Noah, had clear, ice-blue eyes.

Noah rested his hands on Jacob's shoulder and Ethan's back. "Flirting with my sister?"

Jacob's cheeks turned a little pink as Noah pulled him into a half Nelson. "Next time, break the guy's leg if you've got to foul and piss the game away." Cooper laughed and released his grip on Jacob's neck. Then he opened the driver's side door and slid into the Honda. "The Coop is driving home. Got to pass that driver's test next month."

"I'll put on the air," Jacob said to Ethan. He picked up his bag and headed toward the red Ford pickup truck he shared with Ethan, a truck that would be 100% his when Ethan left for college on Tuesday.

"Get in the back, Pipe." Noah popped the passenger side door. "Mom wants me to be shotgun since I'm the adult." He made air quotes with his hands and rolled his eyes. He threw his gym bag in the backseat. Cooper plugged his iPod into the adapter and Meek Mill's *Dreams & Nightmares* erupted. The team loved the hardcore Philly rapper.

"Okay, okay." She wouldn't let the snub bother her. "The backseat is the safest place when the lunatic is driving." Piper got out of the car and found herself face to face with Ethan. The sun caught yellow flecks in his light brown eyes and her breath hitched. For a moment, they stared at each other, Meek Mill throbbing around them.

"You going to the party?" Ethan asked.

Her heart skipped a beat, but she said yes, trying to keep her cool.

"Are you camping out and hunting in the morning, too?" Ethan winked.

Piper's tongue caught in her mouth and she couldn't fake indifference, and her cheeks turned hot. Say something, she warned herself. He going to think you've lost it. "I am," she managed to say.

Jacob beeped the truck's horn. "Let's go," he called across the parking lot. Cooper revved the engine and tapped the horn. "Yeah, let's get out of here."

"Later, buds," Ethan said to Noah and Cooper, and then he stepped closer to Piper and tapped her arm. "See you there."

In the Honda ten minutes later, Piper clutched the armrest.

"Slow down," Noah said with uncharacteristic maturity as they passed the Suds & Go and neared the stop sign by the funeral home on Main Street. Even Mr. I'm–not–afraid–of–anything phantom–braked whenever Cooper drove.

"Okay, Sir Traffic Inspector." Cooper slowed to two miles per hour. "Is this okay?"

"Both of you, stop it," Piper said from the back seat and tested her seat belt strap. She stared out the window at the pretty container of red geraniums hanging from the funeral home's light post and thought, *This kid should not be permitted to get his license.*

"Turn there," Noah said. "Dad wants you to practice spaces in the alley."

Piper pulled out her phone. Nope. No Tisch email. She clicked on the original notification and was rereading when the car lurched to a stop.

"Fu-u-u-uck," Cooper said as Piper's seatbelt snapped across her collarbone and she jerked up.

Ned Walker, the village drifter, had both hands planted on the Honda's hood. His unkempt brown hair was long and straggly, and his curly beard was speckled with gray. The deep ridges across his broad forehead were etched with dirt, and his face was a wizened, leathery tan. Despite the heat, he wore a hat made from squirrel fur and a deer hide cape. His eyes were the color of wild moss. He pointed at them and mouthed the word SORRY, and then he threw back his head and let out a maniacal laugh and pounded his fists on the hood.

Everyone knew Ned.

For generations, he had haunted the imaginations of valley children. He was a drugged-out Vietnam Vet who slept outside in the cornfields and hunted in the quarry. He shuffled along the rural roads, venturing into town from time to time. Some nights, when it got too cold, he'd sneak into detached garages in the alley off of Main Street. Sheriff Mismo had cited him plenty of times for trespassing, vagrancy, and hunting without a license. One time, their Grandmother Adele Rose found him slumbering under her back porch, sprawled on her lounger. She fed him lunch and then called Ned's elderly sister, Wanda, to retrieve him. He was crazy; all the kids knew that. To adults, he wasn't so scary, just an eyesore and a nuisance, but to kids—including those in the car Ned was leaning on, still grinning wildly—he was an unknown threat. You couldn't know what he might do.

Ned pounded the hood with his fists again, twice. He was having fun.

LSD. Acid. Rumor said that was what fried Ned's brain. Piper had never seen him this close up. He held her gaze through the windshield. Though she saw he was just a grimy old man one degree away from total homelessness, his stare sent a chill down her spine.

"Back it up," Noah whispered.

Cooper shifted into reverse, the car wheels spinning in the gravel before gaining traction. As the car reversed, Ned stumbled but quickly regained his balance. He waved at them, his arm high, like a friendly old codger, before he shuffled behind the Delong's Candy Shop storage shed. It took a few minutes for Piper to lose the feeling of him looking straight at her. What had he been thinking?

"Man, that guy is creepy," Cooper said as he slowed to make the turn off Main St. onto route 663.

"You've got to be more careful, Coop," Piper said. "You could have hurt him."

Noah tapped on the window. "Everybody calm down."

"You two don't have to tell Mom and Dad about it, okay?" Cooper said. "They'll have a shit fit."

They drove in silence. Cornfields and scattered farms flanked the road that led out of town. A mountain ridge in the distance stood dark against the blue sky. Though the hills appeared far away, it was only a five-mile drive to the base of the hillside where their dad had purchased a twenty-acre parcel. On it sat a dilapidated old stone farmhouse—their home—a building that was in a perpetual stage of renovation. Her bedroom included. She was waiting for Dad to finish the bookshelves he promised her a year ago.

Cooper stopped the car at the end of Rose Tree Lane, which was just the tip of their long, dirt driveway. Their Dad had installed a little green street sign, making their lane appear like its own road. "I'm serious. Don't tell them I almost flattened Ned."

Up ahead, they could see Bert and Ernie, their two swans, floating on the large pond. They had adopted the birds a few summers ago from the Yellow Creek Fowl Rescue and Piper loved them. She planted duckweed and wigeon grass around the pond's perimeter and helped her dad build a winter shelter. The swans recognized Piper and swam nearby whenever she delivered her special medley of lettuce, broccoli, and carrots.

"No worries," Noah said. "It's cool. Keep driving."

"I don't mean you." Cooper glared at Piper in the rearview mirror. "Can you be quiet about this?"

Piper gazed out the window. The farmer next door had sown soybeans instead of corn this year. "I'm not like that anymore."

"Really?" Cooper exhaled.

"I didn't tell them you guys are having a huge banger at the quarry this weekend." Piper paused for effect. "And I didn't tell them I'm going with you."

Noah sighed. "Come on, Piper. It's not your scene. You know it's a party, right?"

"Of course." Piper nodded. "How stupid do you think I am?"

"This is ridiculous. It's your senior year and now you decide to hang out." Cooper twisted around. "There's going to be mar—i—juan-a," he sang, pulling the syllables apart, "And alcohol."

"Like it or not, Cooper Allen Rose, I'm coming." Then she mimicked her mother's voice and said, "Piper's just so involved in this year. I'm so glad she's experiencing everything." Immediately, Piper felt bad for making fun of her mother.

"God help us." Noah chuckled and rolled down the window. "We've got Miss Goodie-Two-Shoes as our guest. Coop's right, though. Don't say shit about Ned. We don't need Mom and Dad freaking out on us. I can hear her now—'You could have killed him!'"

They needed to relax.

She was a member of their club—their team. She would not monitor their behavior and report back to their parents. Besides, she didn't see the boys as some kind of inseparable group anymore. Ethan was about to leave them all, and the quarry party was most likely her last chance to say something to him. To let him know she wanted to be more than a friend.

JOURNAL ENTRY
WEDNESDAY, AUGUST 31

I think Ethan is interested. I'm pretty sure he's flirting. He practically asked me to sleep out at the quarry. That's not something you say to just anybody, right? There's this pulse bouncing between us. I don't think I'm imagining it. Now what to wear to the party? A romper? No, that's too dressy. I need to be cool, but casual. Maybe denim? Or leggings with a tank? I don't want it to look like I'm trying too hard.

Cooper almost mowed down that scary dude, Ned. Freaked me out.

Excited for school to start. Senior year! I'm almost out of here. YES!!!

Bert and Ernie are mating. It's beautiful the way they entwine their necks and synchronize their movements. I'd be so excited for cygnets! It's late in the breeding season, but I'm praying. They are super protective and squawk whenever I get close to the nest. Might need binoculars to see inside.

Goals:
Straight As
Dance 6x/week
Nail Tisch audition
Tell Ethan how I feel (OMG!)
Fix things with Brittany

CHAPTER 4

The pianist was a young hipster, probably a student from The University of the Arts fulfilling his extern hours. His fingers glided across the keys and *Swan Lake's* allegro filled the room. The dance studio smelled of flowery deodorant and sweat. Bright sunlight fell through the old factory windows, illuminating shafts of dust particles. Piper leaned against the rear wall and watched Brittany Bonner leap across the floor. Her former best friend was small, muscular, and powerful, built more like a gymnast than a ballet dancer. May it was this arbitrary difference that had unraveled their friendship. Maybe Piper just looked more like a dancer.

"Higher. Reach." Madame Sylvie tapped her stick against the wooden floor as she studied Brittany's every move. Madame Sylvie wore her usual uniform: a baby pink sweater wrap, knotted at her tiny waist, a long black chiffon dancer's skirt, and her signature bright red lipstick. Her gray hair was shellacked with hairspray and pulled tightly into a ballet bun. Her voice rose and her French accent grew more pronounced. "Now jete . . . and, next."

Brittany landed and then hurried out of the way. There was no searching glance in the mirror for Piper, and with that snub Piper felt a pinch in her solar plexus. For years, the two girls had relied on each other for moral support. A brief nod. A small smile. Piper inched forward, her leotard plastered to her back, and waited in fifth position for her cue. Alone.

Madame Sylvie signaled and Piper flew across the floor.

"Yes, yes. That's what it should look like." Madame Sylvie's fire engine lips broke into a smile.

Piper flinched with the compliment. Please don't make it worse, she tried to convey with her eyes as her gaze locked with her teacher's. She landed and circled to the end of the line, the girls' steely glares bouncing off her back. She knew what they were thinking. After the American Ballet Theatre auditions last spring, when Madame Sylvie announced to the entire level five assembly that Piper had won the only spot in the ABT summer intensive, the atmosphere changed. Everybody knew Brittany had auditioned, too. Now, despite the thick humid air in the studio, a chilly silence followed Piper. She was the one who went to New York for the summer.

She wanted not to care, but she missed them. Deep down, she wasn't sure she deserved the award. Brittany was a stronger dancer in a lot of ways.

They used to be friends—the four of them: Piper, Maya, Allison, and Brittany. In ninth grade, each of them had been accepted into The Rock School Pre-Professional Program. It was an honor and they all felt special. Within two weeks of entering the program, they became The Squad—the fabulous four. But everything was different since Piper had been labeled the best. Now, dance was pure work. Hard work. The fun vanished with The Squad's cold shoulder. Piper had to get into Tisch— an acceptance would show them that the ABT selection had not been a mistake.

Piper slid forward in line, her hands on her hips, her spine perfectly straight, her eyes focused on no one. The music filled her, and again she rocketed into the air. This time, she looked in the mirror. They were watching her, a wall of black and pink, their hair pulled into tight buns, their bodies too stiff. In mid-leap, Piper held herself airborne for a fraction of a second—enough time to hope the extreme height of her jump registered.

Later in the changing room, Piper closed the curtain across the stuffy cubby and in privacy peeled off her damp bodysuit and tights. She jumped into the shower, then dried off, dropping the damp towel on the ground to create a barrier between her bare feet and the grimy floor. She slipped into her sundress, unzipped her ballet bag, and found her flip-flops. The conversation on the other side of the screen made her pulse quicken.

"I don't know why Madame allows it," Brittany whispered. "We're here all the time. And she only shows up when she can."

"Special treatment for special dancers," Allison mimicked Madame Sylvie's French accent, her voice a nasally buzz.

"What's so special about Miss Universe? It doesn't take talent to be pretty." Maya chimed in. "She's not as good as everybody thinks she is."

"You're right," Brittany said matter-of-factly. "But she has the body those snobby companies like."

"I'm not saying she's a poor dancer," Allison said. "It's just that it's not fair. Why should we sweat it out every day, and she's only here on Tuesdays and Saturdays?"

"It is a double-standard," Brittany said. "I'd never be able to get away with that. Madame Sylvie excused her because of a school requirement. She's in charge of her brothers' soccer team or some stupid shit like that." Brittany paused, then imitated Madame Sylvie, too. "Now, now ladies, Piper has a soccer game." She sang the last two words. "A soccer game? What the fuck?" Then it was quiet, the silence pulsing, waiting.

Piper paused, her heart pounding, then whipped open the curtain. "And Thursdays. Today is Thursday, you know." She stared at all of them—Brittany, Allison, and Maya. "And I train at home the days I'm not here."

Brittany nonchalantly popped a breath mint into her mouth. "I thought you'd left." Allison and Maya didn't say a word, just stood with their arms crossed and tight expressions on their faces.

"So, it's okay to talk about me as long as I'm not here?" Piper's voice cracked. God, don't let me cry!

For an instant, Brittany's expression softened. "No, it's just that we are dedica—"

"What? I'm not?" Piper's mind whipped, searching for a quick comeback, but came up empty. She bit her lip and stared at them. Then she heaved her bag over her shoulder and muttered, "Excuse me."

Brittany moved aside and Piper slid past Allison and Maya. She fled down the hallway, rammed her shoulder against the emergency exit door. The alarm blared and Piper's heart leapt. Quickly, she checked over her shoulder and then bounded down the stairwell. Pushing open the street exit door, she squinted against the bright sun and searched for her mother's white Nissan Pathfinder parked down half a block. Piper rushed, her cumbersome bag whacking her back, and pinched the bridge of her nose, careful not to step on any sidewalk cracks. Mom sat hunched over her phone, scrolling. Her dirty blond hair was pulled severely away from her face into a tight ponytail, and she wore one pair of reading glasses on the bridge of her nose and a second pair on her forehead. She was pretty once, Piper thought, with her sparkly blue eyes, but now she was too stressed out and she looked like she was always frowning. So much so that deep lines were etched permanently across her forehead. Piper knocked on the passenger's side window and her mother startled, then hit the unlock button. Piper opened the door, threw her bag on the floor, and climbed inside.

"The clinic is crazy hectic." Her mother tapped her phone and slipped it into the cup holder. "I'll drop you at home, but I've got to get back to help Frank." Straightening up in her seat, she turned the key in the ignition, and pulled onto Broad Street, then as afterthought said, "How was class?"

"Great." Piper gave her best fake smile and fastened her seatbelt. "We worked on a super hard piece. Brittany and I partnered. Madame Sylvie wants to showcase us as a duet in the winter exhibition since this is our last year dancing together." Her voice pitched, but she was sure her mother didn't notice.

"How did Maya and Allison feel about that?" Her mother flicked a quick, concerned glance at Piper.

"Oh, they're fine. It's no biggy." Piper unzipped the front pouch of her bag and dug her hand inside, hunting for her Purell. "They'll get a feature in the spring show, I'm sure."

"You have such a pleasant group of friends." Her mother smiled. "I can't believe this part of your life is going to be over soon. Just think, next year you'll be at Tisch." Her mother tapped the horn and slid into the left lane.

"Traffic isn't too bad." Piper said, changing the subject. "Maybe I should drive. You know, start getting some Philly experience." God forbid if her mother knew that her perfect daughter didn't have a single person she could call a friend at the studio. Her mother expected a lot. Perfect grades. Dance five days a week. Normal social life. Help at home.

Taking care of the swans. And now, the soccer team manager position. Piper was forever trying to please her and always coming up short.

"I'll drive. This road is treacherous." Her mom raced through the yellow light. "I'm not sure you're ready."

No doubt, Piper thought and pinched a huge dollop of Purell into her palm. As they cruised up Broad Street, the scent of the clean alcohol filled the car and a spider of calm spread through Piper's chest as she rubbed the gel over her hands once. Twice.

Her mother pointed at the Temple University sign. "Ethan will be there next week."

Yes, Piper agreed. On dance days, only twenty-eight blocks will separate Ethan and me. She counted them whenever they left the city.

CHAPTER 5

By the time Piper and her mother turned onto Rose Tree Lane, it was dusk and the air was thick with humidity. Piper opened the window and the hot air filled the car along with the hum of chirping cicadas. Inhaling the sweet summer night, she pushed The Squad's rebuff out of her mind. She waved to Bert and Ernie as they swam toward the driveway to greet the car like puppies. She went indoors, took another quick shower, and jotted a few lines in her journal so not to break her write-every day streak.

Clean and changed into a fresh outfit, Piper hid in the house's shadow, and watched Noah, Cooper, and Coach chatting on the patio. The scent of roses, charcoal, roasting chicken, and cigarette smoke made a familiar and oddly comforting aroma. She ran her fingertips over the top of the mauve-pink Cardinal de Richelieu roses staked along the walkway. The blossoms were six inches wide and would turn deep purple as they matured—prizewinners for sure. Piper was pleased that despite her mother's busy schedule, she always found time for her flowers. She bet Mom would enter this one in the Millington Valley Fair.

Piper emerged from the darkness.

"It will be done. I'm telling you." Coach inhaled his cigarette and paused for dramatic effect. "Concord is not invincible. I refuse to live in a world in which Concord cannot be beaten."

"Right, Piper?" Coach motioned to the wrought-iron chair. "Our tiny dancer is home." Everyone stared at him. "What—nobody gets the reference? You know, Elton John's song?" Off key, he dramatically bellowed, "Blue jean baby, LA lady. A seamstress for the—"

"Oh my goodness, you are butchering it." Piper laughed and sat down, the metal cool against her bare legs. "Concord is soccer royalty. And we're the peasants. Even the lowly manager knows that." She pulled the chair forward, and a foot dug into the crumbling patio grout. Resetting the flagstones was one of the many projects her father was working on.

"Now lassie, I'll have none of that talk," Coach said.

"No one in the county's beaten them in the last ten years." Noah swigged a water bottle and then rubbed his thumb and forefinger over his want-to-be goatee.

"They're just used to winning." Cooper said. "They walk the walk, talk the talk. They believe they're winners, but those pansy red Tigers are going down next time."

"Really, Cooper? You can't use the word pansy anymore," Piper said. Coach's political incorrectness was wearing off on him.

"Give it a break, Pipe," Noah said, and Piper shrunk into herself a bit.

"I think he meant weak." Coach winked. "Remember, that's why soccer is the beautiful game. It's unpredictable. Any team can beat any other team."

The topic never changed: how and when Millington Valley would defeat Concord. Under the porch overhang, the long picnic table was set with plates, napkins, and silverware. Dad had even lit two citronella candles and placed them at each end. The brownies he'd baked rested on a side hutch, and there was a huge tossed salad of lettuce, green peppers, onions, and carrots fresh from his garden in the center of the table.

Coach's wife, Jennifer, chatted with Dad near the grill, each with a beer in hand. The chicken sizzled. Intermittently out on the pond, Bert or Ernie squawked and pounded their wings.

"Almost ready." Dad pointed his barbeque-crusted tong toward the door. "Tell your mother."

There had been a lot of these nights this summer. Coach and Jennifer came over at least once or twice a week for dinner. Piper liked the way they would sit around and talk. Her parents didn't shoo the kids away like in years past. It was as if their elders wanted them in the conversation, almost as if they'd joined a new exclusive club. Adulthood. And she was a member, just like her brothers.

"Hope the weather breaks so it's not this damn hot for practice this weekend," Coach said and tapped his cigarette on the armrest. And then, as if just noticing somebody was missing, he asked, "Where's Jacob? It'd be nice to have both my captains here."

"He's cramming his AP English summer project," Piper said. "It's a six-pager due the first day of school. He only started reading thirty minutes ago." Piper knew this because she had had texted Jacob, telling him to stop by with the ulterior hope that Ethan would accompany him.

"Saturday we're doing a 6 pm practice," Coach said.

"Saturday night?" Noah said. "You kidding?"

"Yeah. Why, do you have other plans?" Coach shook his gin and tonic, and the ice cubes clinked against the glass.

"No, no. Just that a couple of us might go hunting this weekend." Noah gave Piper a nasty don't-say-a-word look. Piper held Noah's gaze for a moment and then smiled at Coach. She reached for her napkin.

"Hunting? Not some big banger?" Coach winked. "Not a partay?"

"Yes, sir. I mean, no. No party."

"Man, can't you leave those poor animals alone?" Coach swallowed his drink. "Might surprise you, but I'm a card-carrying member of Green Peace. It's madness that Pennsylvania allows a sixteen-year-old to hunt without an adult."

"Time to eat." Dad set the tray of barbequed chicken in the center of the picnic table. "We've never been too enthusiastic about the whole hunting hobby."

Mom set down the lemonade pitcher. "I agree with Coach. I never should have let Doc Horn take you guys hunting as kids. This male-bonding pastime has gone too far. Guns make me nervous."

"We're thinning out the deer over-population," Cooper said matter-of-factly.

"It's not even deer season," Piper said.

"We're practicing on muskrats," Cooper said. "Think of it as our public service."

"Sure it is." Coach pressed his cigarette stub into the gray stone, went to get up, and lost his balance. Stumbling, he braced the chair and slipped back into the seated position.

"You okay?" Piper said.

"Fine."

"What's that?" Piper's mother walked toward them.

"I've just got this sore spot on my lower leg. Bites when I make a quick movement."

"Let me look," Mom said. Dad and Jennifer drew closer, creating a small huddle.

"Sit," Jennifer said to her husband.

Coach plopped on the seat. "Really, it's nothing." He pulled up his gym pant and eased his hand down his shin. "I think it's a bruise from a whack at practice."

Mom bent down and ran her fingers over Coach's shin. Then she pressed and Coach winced.

"That's it," Coach said. "It's hot to the touch, eh?"

"How long has it been like this?"

"Couple weeks maybe."

"Feeling okay otherwise?"

"Fine."

Jennifer crouched next to Mom. "He's been exhausted."

"The damn heat makes me drag." Coach chuckled, but the uncertainty in his voice was noticeable.

"Mind your language, love." Jennifer sighed and rolled her eyes.

"My Scottish blood can't handle the brutal humidity. What do you think it is, Doc Amy?"

"I'm not sure." Mom pursed her lips and unconsciously twisted her finger into her braid ponytail like she did when she was in deep thought. Then she made eye contact with Coach. "It's probably nothing, but an ultrasound won't hurt. Stop by the clinic in the morning. I'll have Frank check it, too."

"Now, I can't be rushing into the doctor's office over a wee bruise," Coach said.

"We'll be there," Jennifer said, using Coach's knee as an aid to stand up.

"What a way to ruin my appetite." Coach rose and headed toward the house.

Noah raised his eyebrows, and Piper shrugged. Their mother was not an alarmist. They had to be almost dead before she'd take them to the clinic. One time, Cooper had complained about stomach pain, and it wasn't until he collapsed on the kitchen floor that she took him seriously enough to feel his abdomen. Thirty minutes more and his appendix would have burst.

Piper dumped her lemonade on the grass and then couldn't help but rearrange the plastic cutlery on the picnic table, placing the remaining forks, spoons, and knives neatly together in their own Solo cups. Though nobody said anything more about Coach, there was an unvoiced shift in the atmosphere—an invisible awareness of a trespasser who did not belong.

CHAPTER 6

Les garcons sont stupides, Piper wrote on the side of her French notebook. She sat at the soccer manager's table, growing more and more anxious as she watched the team on the other side of the field. This was their last Friday morning practice of the summer. Next week school would be in full swing. She had already organized the guys' duffel bags, and the Gatorade bottles were in perfect formation under the bench. Tapping the French translator on her phone, she searched for the equivalent of moronic. *Debile. Stupide.* Then she checked the parking lot, hoping Coach would show up soon. Or maybe Ethan would stop by to watch the last practice before he left for Temple in Philadelphia.

"Knock him down!" Cooper's voice echoed as he pounded the four-foot foam pole vault mat, aka the pit. "That's it!" It was a chicken fight. The eventual winners' ransom lay at Piper's feet in neat piles, lines, and stacks. Full Gatorade bottles. A couple dollar bills. A four tin tall tower of chewing tobacco. The guys had stashed their "bets" with her for safekeeping, which she'd promptly arranged into satisfying symmetrical piles.

Cooper was the ringmaster, or as her parents labeled him, the instigator, and he'd organized the wagers, too. Noah wobbled in the deep pit with Little Ryan on his shoulders. Ryan battled in a fierce tug of war with a JV player perched around Jacob's neck.

The problem was they weren't playing in a pool. The field was on a plateau that abruptly dropped twenty feet down a hill a few yards beyond the pole vault area. Guys had their cell phones out, recording the melee.

Noah stumbled and sunk deeper into the unwieldy foam. He corrected his footing and then lunged forward, a huge grin on his face. Noah and Jacob jostled from side to side, the thick foam a spongy quicksand. Their teammates were delirious with excitement as if they were ringside at an Ultimate Cage Fighting match.

Piper reached for her phone to call someone who could stop this. There it was—her you're-no-fun personality being too cautious. Who could she call? Then she stopped and coated her hands with Purell instead of phoning anyone. They probably wouldn't get busted. The soccer pitch and surrounding track were tucked into the back of Millington Valley High School.

Piper's phone buzzed with Coach's number flashing on the caller ID.

"Hey, Coach," she said.

"I'm stuck in traffic on the Schuylkill. Does Marky have them running?"

"Coach Marky isn't here."

"That's right. He's away for the long weekend." A horn sounded in the background. "Shove off! Yes, you—sorry, Piper. These people don't know how to drive. Well, are they practicing?"

"Sort of."

Piper looked up and grimaced as Little Ryan toppled from Noah's shoulders. He rolled off the pit, hit the ground with a thud, and then sprang to his feet, thrusting his hands in the air, a wad of Jacob's hair clenched between his fingers. The guys went wild. Jacob yelled, and Piper was pretty sure it was the word *fuck*. He had both hands on his head.

"Let's say they're getting a workout." Piper pressed the phone hard against her ear to muffle any incriminating background shouts.

Ryan danced in a circle with his hands tucked into his armpits, flapping his arms like a victorious chicken. The other guys joined in, shouting, "Ryan! Ryan!" It was like a rave gone horribly wrong. Noah jumped down from the thick foam and slapped Ryan on the back.

"Put Noah on the phone," Coach said.

Piper shouted for her brother and waved. Noah jogged across the field and Jacob followed him. "It's Coach," Piper whispered, and handed him the phone. Jacob turned back toward the team and pantomimed to quiet down, but no one noticed. Noah moved out of earshot, and Piper noticed the blood dripping from the side of Jacob's head was more than a trickle. "I hope there's no permanent damage to your hair follicles."

"Me, too." Jacob swept his curly bangs over the bare patch of bloody scalp at his right temple. "Don't you feel honored that we make you privy to our unique team bonding activities?"

"I feel so special." Piper tucked her hair behind her ear and then stuck her hands in her short pockets. "Really, you guys are—"

"Being co-captain, I have a responsibility to maintain team morale." He deadpanned. "How's your AP paper coming along? Want to meet and proof each other's essays?"

Piper's chest tightened with the hopeful lilt in his voice and the flush that crept across his cheeks. Why must you do this, Jacob? We're just friends.

"I already submitted in on Classroom Connect."

"Oh." Jacob's voice fell. "I was thinking—"

"How about the next assignment?" She said not able to help herself. "We'll work together on the English one."

Jacob's eyes brightened. "Sounds good."

Piper nodded toward the hill as the first cross-country runners popped over the top. "Better make everybody look like you're doing something productive. Coach is on the phone and the cross-country assistant will bring up the rear on that bunch."

"No, it's worse." Jacob pointed behind her.

Piper's heart leapt when she turned around and saw the Horn's silver BMW. Maybe Ethan was stopping by. Instead, Mrs. Horn got out of the car. She spotted Jacob and hurried toward him, a small brown paper bag in her hand.

"You forgot this." Mrs. Horn was out of breath and her cheeks had a thin film of sweat on them. She opened the bag and handed a Cliff bar to Jacob. "You don't want to get hungry." She inhaled deeply, catching her breath, and then straightened the front of her precisely ironed bright pink Lilly Pulitzer linen shirt. "Hi, Piper."

Jacob blushed. "Mom, I don't—"

"Where's Coach?" Her gaze darted behind them, searching. "What's going on here?"

"He's caught—"

"Oh my God, what happened?" she said and touched Jacob's bloody temple.

"Nothing. I'm fine."

Mrs. Horn cupped her hands to her mouth and shouted, "Boys! Everybody over here." She put her hands on her hips. "That's right! Get your butts over here!" Then she said more softly to Jacob, "Your father will look at your injury tonight." Piper heard her say, even more quietly, "This is not how you earn a soccer scholarship. Your brother would never have allowed this when he was captain."

Jacob recoiled just enough for Piper to notice. Noah spotted Mrs. Horn and quickly got off the phone and walked toward them. "Coach is about forty minutes away." He handed Piper the cell. "I have his instructions."

"Unbelievable." Mrs. Horn's nostrils flared. "Good thing I showed up to get this session going." Her hands waved, directing the team to move closer.

"Mrs. Horn, Jacob and I've got this." Noah crossed his arms preparing for a blow. "We'll take care of training until Coach gets here."

"Everything's under control, Mom," Jacob said, his hand balling into a fist around the paper bag.

"Obviously, that's not true. I don't see a practice happening. Do you think this is how Concord trains?" She stooped and picked up a tobacco tin. "And this is outright unhealthy." Her eyes narrowed. "And illegal."

The rest of the team jogged into a semi-circle around them.

"Mom?" Jacob pleaded under his breath.

Slowly, Mrs. Horn turned and looked at each player with a sharp gaze. The guys grew quiet and serious. Then she pointed at a couple of underclassmen. "You two, set up two rows of eight cones. We'll run some dribbling exercises." She turned to Jacob. "Count off by twos."

Nobody moved.

Jacob's face blazed fire-engine red. "Come on. This isn't cool."

"I don't care what's cool. Now count." She glared at Jacob who was about to burst.

"One," Noah said and stepped forward. In solidarity, Cooper slid into line next to Noah and said, "Two." The rest of the team followed.

One. Two. And so on. Jacob was the last player to line up. "One," he spit through clenched teeth.

The mountains in the distance touched the sky, deep green puffs against the blue heavens. As Mrs. Horn commandeered the MVHS soccer practice, Piper was sure she saw Jacob's pride fly clear over the far ridge and out of the valley. For a moment, she wanted nothing more than to wrap her arms around him.

CHAPTER 7

On early Saturday mornings, without the hustle and bustle of dancers, the studio's locker room was a lonely place, heavy with the underlying stench of dried sweat. Piper never let her bare feet touch the grimy, brown carpet, terrified that she would end up with a fungus. Perched on the bench, she rummaged through her freshly laundered leotards and tights in her duffle bag and found her pointe shoes. She had arrived a few minutes early to hide a Mason jar filled with petite pink tea roses in Brittany's locker (she had not forgotten the combination). No note. But Brittany would know the gift was from Piper's garden. She had been to the farm plenty of times. The flowers were a test, a feeling-out, a secret way of communicating, *Let's move on. I'm sorry.*

Last week's hipster pianist was already at the piano practicing his scales, and she wanted to be at the barre before the other girls arrived. She swaddled her toes with lamb's wool and then wiggled her feet into her pointe shoes, the right and then the left, the way she always did. Wrapping the pink ribbons precisely, she made a perfect crisscross that climbed up her ankle. At the sink, she turned on the water and let it run until it steamed. Two squirts of liquid soap. Rub front of hands. Palms. Between fingers. Under nails. Lather and count to twenty. Rinse. Repeat. The door opened, and Piper jerked away from the sink.

"When's the Tisch audition?" Madame Sylvie said, her face an expressionless mask, her lips deep red. The woman never came into the dressing room.

"Soon, I hope. My audition time should be in the next couple weeks."

"Are you anxious?"

Piper nodded and pulled down a paper towel from the dispenser, careful not to let her damp hands mar it before tearing it free. "Yes, it's scary. I hope I don't mess up."

"You won't. Try to enjoy this part—the before. You're going to have a long dance career, but nothing will ever be quite this exciting again. The first validation of your craft is thrilling." Madame Sylvie tightened the knot of her sweater. "Listen to me, an old woman. What I'm saying will make sense someday, my dear. You'll see."

Piper warmed at the my dear. "You make perfect sense," Piper said, and rose. "I want to be accepted into Tisch. I want it more than anything." Saying it aloud made it real. Piper's stomach fluttered. Maybe she was good enough. This was her chance to prove it to herself and everybody else.

Madame Sylvie pulled a tattered strip of baby blue ribbon from her waist. "It's from the costume of my first performance with the American Ballet Theatre. Swan Lake. I was only in the corps, but I felt like a star." She placed it in Piper's hand.

The worn ribbon was still smooth and soft. Piper rubbed it between her thumb and forefinger.

"Perhaps it will bring you a bit of luck." The old woman's lip quivered. "You've worked hard. The studio is proud of you. I'm proud of you."

A small lump lodged in Piper's throat. Madame Sylvie was a woman of few words. Most of the time, she acted as if she didn't even like her dancers.

"Thank you," Piper said, swallowing. "I will treasure it. Always." Then, without hesitation, she wrapped her arms around Madame Sylvie's frail frame. "Thank you." She squeezed. "For everything."

The door flew open and in walked Brittany, her phone glued to her ear. She stopped cold when she saw Madame Sylvie. Piper stuffed the ribbon into her sports bra. Brittany was dwarfed in an over-sized green Philadelphia Eagles sweatshirt. She gave a tentative smile as if to say,

What's going on? Loud and laughing, Maya and Allison tumbled into the room, saw Madame Sylvie, and they, too, went silent.

"Girls." Madame Sylvie dipped her chin and left.

"Good afternoon, Madame Sylvie," they said in unison.

Piper grabbed her bag and scurried behind Madame Sylvie. Brittany's eyes bore into her, but Piper smiled anyway as she headed to the barre to warm up. If they knew that Madame Sylvie had given such a gift to Piper, their jealousy would compound. The ribbon would have to stay a secret.

Within ten minutes, the room filled with dancers. In the movement and distraction of the crowd, Piper watched Brittany through the mirror, looking for a hint that she had seen the flowers. Brittany's muscles made hard lines under her bodysuit. And she was pale. Maybe her meanness was ruining her appetite. Piper moved through the barre routine, willing her mind to clear and her body to mesh with the music, but her thoughts returned to tonight's quarry bash. Noah so wouldn't expect it the vodka from her. Maybe she would even try a little herself—that would surprise him—it gave her a thrill to think about doing something so unexpected. Still during floor exercises, she pushed herself until her face burned and her heart pounded. Sweat dribbled down her spine, her moist leotard sticking to her back. Exhilarated. The Tisch audition was right around the corner and she would be ready.

After class, Piper changed in a hurry, and when she went to scrub her hands again, she spotted pink petals poking from under a crumpled paper towel in the trashcan. Her heart tightened. Okay, Brittany wasn't ready for a truce. Piper was sure that if the tables were turned, she'd be happy for her friend.

Coach's red Jeep was parked in front of the dance studio's door. She peered over her shoulder, then crossed the sidewalk, and jumped inside, throwing her bag in the back seat. She felt like a two-year-old, not being able to drive.

"Hey, kiddo," Coach said as he flipped his turn signal and pulled onto Broad Street. "How was class?"

"Good." Piper fastened her seatbelt and then checked her phone. A text from Little Ryan telling her he'd successfully secured the vodka.

"Not much traffic. It should be a quick drive home." Coach reached for the pack of cigarettes in his shirt pocket.

"Thanks for the ride. I know it's a pain." Piper checked her phone again. "My parents are terrified I'm going to crash if I ever drive on the Schuylkill Expressway."

"Worked out great. I dropped off a new battery sample at a client on Reed Street. Now I won't have to come down during the week with the insane traffic. Plus, with the emergency at the clinic tying up your mom, and your dad already committed to taking Cooper to club tryouts, it was Noah or me."

He lit the cigarette and took a deep drag.

Piper cracked the window. "Noah wasn't too excited about spending his morning chauffeuring me. He's got a lot of nerve asking you to do it." She hated smoke and turned toward the fresh air. Loose wisps of her hair blew against her neck. "Just drop me at the clinic. I need to do some filing for Mom."

Coach opened his own window. "Wish I could quit these damn things. Want to get something to eat?"

"I'm fine. Don't we practice again at six?" Piper said.

"So, we'll be a little late."

"Mrs. Horn will have a fit. She was in rare form yesterday."

"The nerve of that woman. Bet she's told the whole valley I was late. Oh, and her poor son got a wee scratch. Damn gossip she is, and always running people down. If she knew what was best, she'd keep away from my soccer pitch." Coach tapped his cigarette on the ashtray and coughed. "How about Geno's Steaks? We can get takeout for Noah and Cooper, eh?"

"It's fine, really. I'm not hungry." Piper glanced out the window and stifled a cough. She wanted to get home, flee this smoky car, and take a shower. She could feel dirty, microscopic tobacco particles sticking to her skin and settling into her still damp hair. Mom was going to have to let her drive herself. This was ridiculous having Coach pick her up.

"Okay, whatever suits you." Coach switched lanes, veering to the left, passing under the I-76 W sign, and Piper relaxed. That was the way back to Millington. He chucked his cigarette onto the expressway and they made small talk until the familiar mountains came into view. It was

3:30. She'd have plenty of time to get ready. The guys wouldn't finish practice 'til at least seven. Coach pulled in front of The Rose-Horn Medical Center in the strip mall off Rt 74. It shared the space with Four Sisters' Pizza and a State Farm insurance office. She hoped Mom's emergency was resolved and she was ready to head home. The filing could wait.

"Thanks for the ride." Piper opened the door and the scent of the pizzeria's roasting garlic hit her.

"Much obliged." Coach winked at her. "Don't have too much fun tonight."

"What?" Piper said, dumbfounded.

"At Noah's birthday party out at the quarry."

"How do you know about it?"

"Camp out, my ass. Those boys believe they're sneaky and smart, but they're damn loud." Coach laughed and coughed. "I'll give them a short practice this evening. Just keep everybody in line. I don't want to lose any players to an underage. Remember, a team is only as strong as its weakest link. Take care of those bozos."

Piper grabbed her bag from the back seat. "Aren't you going to tell?" She searched Coach's eyes for a hint of reprimand.

"Who?"

"The parents. The principal."

"Like that would stop you. Well, it might for tonight, but there'd be another night. Just be careful." He tapped her nose. "I was a kid too once, you know." He froze. "Good God, it's our favorite busybody."

Piper turned to see Mrs. Horn and jerked back. Standing inside the glass entrance door of the Horn-Rose Medical Center lobby, Mrs. Horn's gaze was sharp, her head tilted as if mentally weighing the scene before her, trying to reconcile any scenario that would explain why Piper was in a car with Coach, and why Coach had touched Piper's face.

CHAPTER 8
THAT NIGHT

"What the hell?" Ethan whipped around as another shot cracked the night in two.

Piper willed herself to take a slow, calm breath. Whatever had been going on between her and Ethan before the shotgun clap definitely was over.

"I bet they're shooting beer cans," Ethan said.

She tucked her loose hair into her hair clip and readjusted her bun again. "Maybe they're prepping for your male-bonding animal slaughter in the morning."

"It's the middle of the night. Those assholes are going to get in trouble."

"Not like they'll wake anybody out here."

A third blast cut through the quiet.

"I'm heading back. Sounds like they need an adult on the scene." Ethan winked, which made Piper involuntarily crack a smile. He glanced at the forest and then cleared his throat. "We good?"

"Sure," she said. It was hard not to be charmed by him. Then her expression cooled. "I think I should come with you. Just to make sure everything is okay."

"Let's go then."

Piper checked the backseat. Little Ryan was still curled up into the fetal position, sound asleep. He'd be fine for another thirty minutes. She reached across the steering wheel, took the keys out of the ignition, and dropped them on the floor mat.

In silence, they trekked side-by-side, traversing the four-foot wide path, their strides quick and growing faster. Ethan hopped over a briar branch, and Piper did the same. The flanking woods were dark and eerily hushed. The closer they drew to the party site, the harder Piper listened, straining to hear her brothers' or Jacob's chatter or even another gunshot. They came upon the deserted campsite and found the bonfire, now a fraction of the height it was a couple hours ago, with no hint of where their brothers had gone. Cold, hard goose bumps popped on her skin despite the humidity, and she rubbed her palms back and forth on her forearms.

"Here's the shotgun." Ethan picked up the firearm and opened the stock, his breath heavy. A few empty green casings were scattered on the ground along with an exploded Old Milwaukee can. Three empty beer cans sat on the cooler, waiting to be blown away. "You're right. It looks like they were popping a few cans."

"Well, where are they?" Piper's chest tightened, and she wasn't sure if it was from the physical exertion or the needling apprehension that her brothers and Jacob were in trouble.

"They probably went for a dip in the lake." Ethan tapped the soccer ball next to a heap of sleeping bags, and it rolled a few feet and stopped in a divot.

"That's not too smart in the state they're in." Piper picked up the fallen can and placed in on the cooler in line with the others. "We better check."

"Count on Miss Worry Wart to want to make sure," he said jokingly, but Piper noticed an uneasy sharpness in his brown eyes. Both of them were concerned.

With the unexpected quiet, a clove of dread bloomed in her gut and a chill snaked up her back. They weaved around a bend and ducked a low-hanging branch and jogged, trying not to trip over tree roots. Something wasn't right—she could feel it in her core. Ethan sensed it, too, and he took off sprinting, passing her with ease. They were halfway to the lake when a blood-curdling howl cut the stillness. Piper lurched and Ethan caught her arm before she went down. "What was that?" he said.

"Maybe an animal?" Sweat pooled in her armpits and along the nape of her neck. The cry sounded human—a person in pain. She took a deep breath and reflexively pulled out her phone. The tiny *No Service* warning displayed in the upper left-hand corner of the screen.

"It came from that way." Ethan pointed into the woods and headed into the thicket. Trudging behind him, Piper's mind raced. Her earlier desire and foolishness about Ethan seemed distant and trivial. She needed to see her brothers right now, to know those assholes were okay. Imagine if something had happened. What would she tell her parents?

The heavy brush made it hard to move quickly, and the dense woodland played with their internal compasses. Finally, the forest cleared, and an overgrown meadow spread out before them with a clear demarcation of where something had trampled through the overgrown grass and weeds. The night sky was dark and the stars brilliant against the blackness, the moon small and high in the sky. For a moment, Ethan and Piper paused and listened carefully, letting their eyes adjust to the luminescence. Piper's gaze followed the downtrodden trail through the unruly meadow and there in the distance where the forest started again, she saw them.

Cooper and Jacob were on their knees hunched over a large object. Maybe an animal. Piper ran, the tall grass lashing her already cut-up legs, and Ethan followed. As she drew near that she realized Cooper was crying, heaving—his face was blotchy and red. A furry lump was on the ground between Cooper and Jacob.

But it wasn't an animal.

It was Ned Walker.

Piper's stomach heaved and her head spun. She forced herself to take a deep breath and to clear her mind. Think. Stay calm.

The town vagabond lay crumpled, a pool of blood seeping from his abdomen, his tattered white shirt turning crimson. His grimy fur cape was tied with a piece of twine at his neck like a noose.

"What happened?" Ethan's voice faltered.

"He's hemorrhaging," Jacob said, his voice strangled and keening, hysterical. He ripped his shirt over his head, rolled it into a ball, and pressed it against Ned's stomach. "We thought he was a deer."

"It was an accident." Cooper heaved and pinched his eyes.

Piper fell on her knees beside her brother. "You shot him?" Her heart thrashed as the thick night pressed against her, making it hard to breathe.

"Jesus-fucking-Christ! There's no service anywhere." Noah crashed through the woods with his phone in the air.

Ned was sweating profusely, his breath labored, and his green eyes unfocused. In a panic, Piper forgot about the germs a homeless person might possess and reached for the old man's wrist. His pulse hammered and Piper pressed her fingers firmly against his skin to be sure she felt it. She had no idea what to do.

"We've got to get help." Cooper's eyes were wild.

Jacob leaned forward, using his body weight to apply pressure to Ned's abdomen. In an instant, his knotted shirt was soaked through with gore and his hands were red with Ned's blood.

"We'll have to carry him down to the cars." Ethan crouched by Ned's feet and gently lifted the man's combat boots. "You two." He nodded at Jacob and Cooper. "Slide your hands under his back. Noah, support his head. Lift on the count of three. One, two—"

Ned gurgled and a tremor shot through his body and then he then was still, his mouth falling open, his eyes rolling back in his head. Everybody froze.

"Okay, back up a second," Ethan said. "Maybe we shouldn't move him."

Piper bent down and felt for his pulse again. But this time she couldn't feel anything. Please. Please. Please. Let me find it. She tried his other wrist. Nothing. Then she pressed her fingers against his neck, hoping to detect the thrum of his carotid artery. Please, she silently begged as sweat broke out on her forehead. Beat. Beat. Beat!

"What the fuck? Is he dead?" Cooper screamed and raked his bloody fingers through his hair. On his hands and knees, Noah crawled around Ned and pulled his little brother into a bear hug, gripping him as if trying to squeeze away his panic.

HEATHER CHRISTIE

"Shut up." Jacob's face drained of all color as he stood and stepped back, wiping his hands down the front of his shorts and bare thighs. "He's not dead. He can't be dead." His chest and legs were covered in sweat, grime, and Ned's blood.

Ethan looked at Piper beseechingly, the injured man a gulf between them. "I can't feel anything," she said under her breath as her heart banged against her ribcage. Hopelessness penetrated every atom of her being. For a moment, nobody spoke, and then Ethan moved next to Piper and checked for Ned's pulse, too. They waited, each hoping Ethan, the de facto leader, would miraculously locate Ned's heartbeat— that he'd save them as he had so many times on the soccer field. Ethan dropped his chin and sighed, and fear splintered in Piper like a fissure radiating through thin ice. He made eye contact with each one of them before saying anything.

"He's dead."

"Fuck. Fuck. Fuck." Cooper heaved and pushed Noah away.

Jacob dropped to his knees and pressed his bloody hands against his face. "Holy fucking shit," he whispered. One by one, they each slumped to the ground, forming a circle around Ned, their heads bowed. Piper kneeled between her brothers, her mind ping-ponging between panic and paralysis. Had someone been standing on the other side of the meadow, he would have thought they were praying. They stayed like that for a long time, the moon high above them, casting a pearly spotlight on the five friends.

"What the fuck? We're in a shitload of trouble," Noah finally said. "I guess we can kiss college goodbye."

What about Ned? Piper thought. "It was an accident," she said, staring at the dead man in front of her. "Wasn't it?" A strange calmness overcame her and her mind cleared. It was as if they were in a surreal art film or a grisly nightmare from which they would soon awaken. "We just have to explain what happened. We can make it right."

"How did it happen?" Ethan asked.

Cooper wiped his eyes. "We were—"

"Shut up," Noah said. "It doesn't matter now. The guy is dead. Nobody say anything." He glared at Cooper and Jacob.

"Don't you trust me?" Piper said, hurt.

51

"Honestly, no," Noah said. Then his voice softened. "It's just better if you guys know nothing more. It was target practice gone wrong. We thought we'd hit a deer and followed it when it took off. That's it."

"What do we do?" Jacob looked at Noah and then Ethan—the two guys who had always made decisions for him in high-pressure games.

But it was Cooper who spoke. "We hide him for now. Then we'll come back and bury him and give him a proper funeral."

"You mean not tell anybody?" Jacob's voice was shrill.

Noah stood and rubbed his temples. "Cooper's right. Ned's dead. There's nothing we can do about it. We'll never be able to carry him all the way back to the entrance. And if we could, what are we going to do? Drive to the police station and deliver him to Sheriff Mismo? Hey, we're drunk and high and we killed this guy, but we're sorry."

"Let's think this through," Ethan said.

Jacob fell eerily quiet and slumped forward, his elbows digging into his thighs as he sat cross-legged.

Piper brushed Ned's ratty hair from his forehead. "He's a person. We can't just leave him."

"Yes, we can and we will." Noah's jaw was hard, set with determination. "What, are you going to give up New York so you can go to juvy?"

"Who says we'd go to juvy? It was an accident," Ethan said. "And Piper wasn't even here!"

Noah glared at Ethan. "You're right, you wouldn't go to juvenile detention. A nineteen-year-old is an adult. You'll go straight to jail. Goodbye, Temple." He checked the time on his phone. "I guess I am eighteen, too. Happy fucking birthday to me. And Cooper and Jacob, you guys can forget about any soccer scholarship offers."

Ethan held up his hand as if warding off something. "There's got to be—"

"It's the only solution," Cooper said, his voice heavy with resignation. "It was an accident. No one is to blame."

Noah pinched his eyes and took a deep breath. "No good can come from us saying anything. We have to—well, arrange Ned, and leave him. We'll come back tomorrow with shovels and bury him."

Numbness had seeped into Piper's soul and she saw the situation with more clarity. Noah was right. They had been here together, and each one of them had too much to lose. Ethan's first official college season started in three days. Noah had a full verbal commitment from Penn State. With a good season, an offer should come in for Jacob. Cooper was the youngest with the brightest soccer future. He'd already had interest from five top soccer schools. And she had New York. Ned had terrorized the town for years. It might be weeks before anyone noticed he was gone. She brushed her hands together, wishing she could plunge them into a vat of hand sanitizer. The guys were quiet. With great care, she leaned closer to Ned and tucked his hair under the furry hat he wore. She didn't know who had shot Ned, and she realized it didn't really matter. It was done. It was over.

Jacob spoke first. "Okay." His voice was hollow and unsure. "Okay, that's what we'll do." Bloody hands on his thighs, he looked up and his eyes held a sadness Piper had never seen before. Ethan went to him and extended his hand. Jacob grabbed it, and Ethan pulled his brother to his feet and yanked him into a messy embrace.

So, they decided it. They found a dry gully a couple of feet inside the tree line and carefully placed Ned in it. They covered him with fallen branches, gingerly laying the camouflaging vegetation across his body so as not to allow it to poke or prod him. Jacob and Cooper, the most soiled, went down to the lake to wash. They marked a spot just outside the tree line with a small pile of rocks so they'd know where to turn into the woods and find Ned. Piper double-checked the site to make sure they didn't leave a trace. The hike back to the party site was long and it felt like morning would never come. Nobody spoke. A dreadful cavity opened in Piper's abdomen. She didn't allow her eyes or mind to stray from the dirt path. She was an unintentional accomplice in a night gone horribly wrong.

The campfire was still smoking when they arrived. Piper poured a can of Old Milwaukee on the embers to extinguish the fire. The last thing they needed was to set the woods on fire and draw the fire company and Sheriff Mismo to the quarry. They stuffed bags full of debris, leaving not a single beer can, shell casing, or forgotten potato chip. Noah rolled the sleeping bags around the shotguns and then strapped the bundle into his duffle bag to carry like a backpack. By 2 AM, they were on the return trip to the quarry entrance, with five bags of trash, their soccer balls, and the cooler. There wouldn't be a camp out tonight. Before they left, they huddled.

"This stays with us," Noah said. He placed his fist in the middle of their circle.

"Not a word." Ethan set his hand on top of Noah's. Cooper and Jacob followed suit.

Piper hesitated for a moment. What were they doing? Then, with a shaky hand, she reached into their jumble of arms and positioned her palm upon their stack. "I promise."

With each step, their vow of silence grew stronger. The farther they went from the meadow, the more it seemed it hadn't happened. Tonight had occurred in an alternate universe.

"Shit," Noah said under his breath as they crossed the trail entrance. Coach's red Jeep was parked next to their black Honda. Little Ryan hustled toward them, blocking Coach, who lounged on his bumper, a cigarette in his hand, its glowing tip like a beacon.

"Coach showed up," Little Ryan said. "I was trying to stall him. I'm sorry. My mom called him when I didn't come home. I've been texting and texting you guys."

"No service up here. You know that." Jacob draped his arm over Little Ryan's shoulder. Without a word, Ethan and Cooper stepped in line with Jacob to shield Noah and his suspicious duffle bag. A perfect screen. Piper ran ahead and popped the trunk. Noah hid the reprehensible bedroll in the Honda. Coach was pissed, but the guys were apologizing like crazy. They claimed the fun just got ahead of them.

All anybody wanted was to get out of there.

CHAPTER 9

Piper remembered the actual day—the very moment—when the Horn brothers became a part of her life. Her mother and Dr. Horn were partners in a new clinic; her mother expected the kids to be partners with the Horn sons.

"I'm counting on you to make them feel comfortable," her mother had said. "They don't know anybody yet. Think how hard that is."

Even now, ten years after, Piper recalled the tiny American flags embroidered on her mother's light blue scrubs. And how she was sitting at the head of the table, reigning over them all as she dished out Eggo waffles.

"They play soccer, you know," she said. "You'll have a lot in common."

And Piper had groaned and stabbed her waffle. Two brothers, plus two other brothers.

"Do they have to come to Grandmom's house every day?" Noah asked. "This could like totally ruin our summer."

"Be nice. Frank Horn is one of my oldest friends from medical school. Until we have the clinic up and running, Grandmom is going to watch all of you. We need Dad and Mrs. Horn at the clinic to help us."

Noah sighed and Cooper huffed. Piper thought they were just acting for the sake of the show. She was sick of boys. And now there would be two more.

They saw Jacob and Ethan that very day. Piper was sure one of them was adopted. At eight-years-old, Ethan was already four inches taller than seven-year-old Jacob. His limbs were long and lean; Jacob's were thick and stubby. Ethan had a short, black buzz cut, Jacob a mop of sandy brown curls. Ethan squinted all the time, and said, "Go ahead, make my day." Jacob, hooked on the old Bugs Bunny Cartoon Network reruns, was forever asking, "What's up, doc?" Piper thought, okay, a cowboy and a bunny. Maybe they'll grow up.

What the boys had in common was their love of soccer. They carried balls with them wherever they went. That first summer together, they played hours and hours of soccer, sowing initial seeds of comradeship that would grow into deep, unbreakable bonds. Piper was part of their soccer love story by unlucky, sisterly default. She wouldn't have cared if God flattened all their soccer balls.

One day in late July, weeks before soccer practice would start at the Youth League, the kids found themselves in the alley behind Grandmom Rose's house, contemplating the dormant cornfield that abutted the back street. The Giant grocery store bordered the field and a forest thick with prickly bushes. Scrub trees lined the far edge of the tract.

"Come on," Noah said and headed toward the tree line. The others fell in behind him. They hiked over heavy earthen ruts. They snapped dried cornstalks and fashioned them into swords and swatted each other.

At the demarcation of the field and the woods, Ethan, their natural leader as the oldest and bravest, said, "I'm going in." He lashed his corn spear against a wild raspberry bush and pushed its thorny branches out of the way.

Jacob said, "Eh, sniff, sniff, what's cookin', doc?"

They all followed Ethan into the woods.

The air turned cooler under the canopy of trees. Spiky twigs lashed Piper's calves, and her white sneakers quickly caked with dirt. Oh, how she hated when her shoes got smudged. Boys! If only the Horns had a daughter. About forty yards into the woods, the trees cleared to reveal a small river. A long time ago there must have been a dam because there was an enormous slab of concrete that jutted halfway across the creek.

"Woo-freaking-hoo!" Ethan kicked off his shoes and peeled his sticky T-shirt from his chest. "Time to go swimming."

"Man alive," Noah said and followed suit.

"You should get out of there," Piper said and crossed her arms. "We're not allowed to swim without an adult."

"It's not deep." Ethan splashed. "Plus, who's going to tell?"

Piper glared. Ethan glowered Eastwood-like, hand on hips, cool water running between his legs. Noah stepped to the edge of the water, digging his toes into the mud. Jacob pushed him, and all the boys erupted in laughter. The water wasn't higher than anybody's waistband; even short Jacob's thighs were visible. Soon the four boys were standing in their underwear. Sunlight danced through the trees overhead and shimmered on the ripples in the stream. The situation made Piper's heart pound. Boy, were they going to get into trouble.

"Come in, scaredy-cat," Cooper yelled. "It feels good."

"Nope," Piper said. She watched Ethan make his way to the chunk of concrete. Little rapids formed around its base. "You better be careful," she called. "We'll be grounded for life if you drown."

"Stop being a party-pooper!" Cooper yelled as he hit the water.

Ethan gripped the side of the concrete, slipped, and fell back into the creek. For a moment he went under, and Piper screamed. Then he popped up, a huge, wild smile plastered on this face. In an instant, the other three boys moved toward the old dam.

"That's it!" Piper yelled. "I'm getting Grandmom. You guys are going to kill yourselves."

Jacob sprang out of the water, and in true Bugs Bunny fashion, hollered, "Of course you realize this means war!"

"Yeah!" Cooper echoed and chest-pumped Jacob like a crazy WWF wrestler.

"Tattletale! You're out of the gang!" Noah shouted. "You can't use the secret handshake anymore."

Piper felt her face blazing. "I don't want to be in your stupid club." She caught Ethan's gaze.

"Go ahead, make my day!" Ethan said, and the boys jeered.

Piper took off through the woods.

And so began a pattern that had endured for a decade: the boys did something stupid, and Piper told on them. It was just the way she was. They had all come to accept that they should keep her in the dark as much as possible.

But that was about to change, because Piper now had a secret that was unspeakable. A secret they all shared.

CHAPTER 10

Piper woke in a haze with a dry horse throat. The window AC was spitting cold air into her attic bedroom. Scraping her teeth against her tongue, she was startled by the cakey film of her mouth. Sunlight poked through the sides of her Roman shade and she rolled over to hide from the brightness. She was still dressed in her cut-off jean shorts and her pink tank top. Her muddy Converse sneakers laid haphazardly on the floor. Why hadn't she bathed last night? Her heartbeat quickened, and she reached for her phone as if it could explain things. Then the horror crashed through her consciousness.

A soccer ball flying over the badminton net.

Laughter. Vodka. The sweet smell of marijuana.

The bonfire's orange tentacles climbing into the night.

Jacob watching her and Ethan leaving the bonfire.

She squeezed her eyelids together and shook her head. Her first impulse was to wash. Scour. Expel. The alarm clock on her unpainted bookshelf read SUN 9/4–9:48 am. She swung her legs over the side of the bed and took a deep breath. *Settle down*, she told herself. Think. The images and sounds grew sharper, pummeling her from all directions.

A shotgun blast.

Running through the woods.

Another crack.

Blood.

Panic.

The monster. An old man. Ned.

Coach. Fleeing the quarry.

What had they done?

The flashback that bashed against her memory again and again was of Ned—his stale, rank breath, his filthy, decrepit animal pelts, and warm blood gushing from his stomach—the picture blared like a screaming bullhorn. No. No. Please don't be true. She dry-heaved and then leaned against the bedpost.

Breathe.

She opened her door as the knot in her gut doubled. How had it happened? Who had pulled the trigger? It probably wasn't Jacob. He tagged along on the hunting trips for the camaraderie and so as not to disappoint his dad and Ethan, but he rarely hunted, hating the sport. That left Noah and Cooper. One of her brothers had killed a man. Cooper was reckless and stupid—it was likely him. Her little brother was an asshole, but he didn't deserve this sort of bad luck. He would never hurt someone on purpose. But he was the one who said they should leave Ned.

Dear God, none of this made sense. She didn't want to know what had really happened. She inhaled, attempting to swallow the wooziness. The house was quiet, and Noah's door was ajar, his room empty, his bed made.

"Mom?" she called. "Dad?"

She went to the hall window. A dozen folding chairs lay on the grass, and a red and white–checkered tablecloth was draped over the boxwood bush. The Honda sat a bit askew in the driveway. She remembered little except dropping off Little Ryan.

Touching the warm windowpane, she whispered, "Dad." Already back from Philly, he was in the garden pruning the roses, and Mom was setting up an extra card table. There were bunches of blue and white balloons tied to the chairs, bobbing in the gentle breeze. Piper had forgotten they were having a Labor Day open house picnic for Noah's eighteenth birthday.

A blast of chilly air blew into the hallway, and a deep uneasiness washed through her again. She wrapped her arms across her chest. Last night's atrocity seeped into her core and settled.

Thankful for the empty house and a few private moments, Piper went down the steps to the second-floor bathroom. She brushed her teeth and showered—for a long time, systematically washing her face and scalp, then her arms, fingers, and nails, soaping her legs three times, cleaning her feet and toes repeatedly. The water stung the cuts on her legs and the suds turned pink as she ripped open the dried bloody nicks that crisscrossed her calves and thighs. Drying off, she rubbed the towel hard enough to chafe her skin, creating raw, blotchy, bloody patches. Then she poured isopropyl alcohol into the open wounds and let it burn, which made her feel the tiniest bit more human. She found a couple band-aids, covered the throbbing slashes, and then put on clean clothes.

In the kitchen, she opened the fridge and found it packed with tin-foiled dishes. She straightened the lowest tray and adjusted the wrap. She snatched a cold bottle of water and drank it all without stopping. The screen door slammed, and she whipped around.

Noah dropped his bag on the table hard enough that the water sloshed in the Mason jar that held a bouquet of lavender roses. His eyes were bloodshot and he wore the same rumpled shirt and shorts from last night. They stared at each other for a long time. Finally, Piper said, "Where were you?"

"I couldn't sleep." He ran his hand over his stubble. "Went down to the creek fishing. Then over to Grandmom's house and cut her grass."

"How about Cooper?"

"Still snoozing, I think."

Piper waited for him to say something, to acknowledge that they had left a dead man in the quarry—that they now had to bury him. He slumped into a chair and rested his elbows on the table. "Fuck," he finally whispered. "What a mess."

"It's horrible." Piper slid into the seat next to him and touched his hand. "How are we going to get back?"

"I forgot about this stupid party." Noah's face was stricken. "Mom and Dad will shit a brick if we're not here for the whole thing." He brought his elbows to the table and put his forehead into his hands. "Goddamn it, maybe we should have carried him out of there."

"You're right." She went to the fridge again. "But we didn't." She turned around and locked her gaze with Noah's. "Why didn't we?"

61

"Shit. I don't know." Noah blotted his eyes. "Too late for blame now. We've got to be fast. Text Ethan and Jacob. Tell them to meet us in thirty minutes."

She threw Noah a water bottle and then turned back toward the fridge. Hidden by the door, she took a deep breath and let the coolness envelop her. What had they done? A sudden flash of Jacob covered in blood and dirt and Cooper's hands awash in red made her tremble. It had been a terrible, terrible accident. They had done all they could to save Ned. Hadn't they? Now nature needed to take its course. They would return him to the earth. He would be at rest. Piper had to protect her brothers. They had a future. It had to stay a secret, what had happened at the quarry; it would ruin all of them and their families. Mom and Dad could never know. It was a secret she had to keep. One stupid moment, one senseless misunderstanding in the woods, one terrible shot at a fleeing animal. Ned.

It would always be there among them, though. How would they ever look at one another and not remember? Life stretched out before her. How do people live with guilt? How can they be happy? They weren't evil; they had hearts and consciences. She couldn't put it into words, but she had a sense of the burden they would carry from now on.

If you can't change something that happens, you live with it. You can't undo what has been done.

CHAPTER 11

Piper squinted and wished she had not forgotten her sunglasses. The trail was ablaze with color, and she couldn't believe they had been on this same path a few hours ago. The green tree leaves were vibrant against the cloudless blue sky, and red raspberries dotted the verdant foliage. They had to be fast. The goal was to dig the hole, get Ned into it, cover him with a couple inches of dirt, and get back to the party before their parents got suspicious. Tomorrow, they'd finish the ghastly task. Her stomach churned with unsettled nerves and the foul gastric acid of a hangover. There was no turning back now.

"It's just up ahead around that bend at the oak tree." Noah carried a hoe, digging it into the ground every other stride like a walking stick. They made a long, single file line with Jacob and Cooper lugging shovels about twenty-five yards in the lead. Ethan hauled a big, awkwardly folded tarp and Piper toted the branch clippers and a water bottle.

"I see the pile of rocks," Jacob called over his shoulder and disappeared around the curve. Cooper followed him.

"Man, this is surreal," Ethan said.

"I second that," Noah said. "You think this is the right thing to do? I mean, seriously, what could we say at this point?"

"We're out of options," Ethan said. "What's done is done. Let's get this nastiness over."

Piper's heart bashed against her ribcage with each step that drew them closer to the deceased man. They were going to bury a bloody, decaying dead person—a human being. She swigged her water, swished it in her mouth, and spat.

They weaved around the corner and found Jacob and Cooper motionless, their shovels fallen at their feet. The branches and debris that had covered Ned were tossed aside.

They stood motionless, reeling at what they saw.

Jacob wheeled around. "He's gone." He jerked his hands up in disbelief.

Noah rammed the hoe into the barren ditch. "What the—"

"Where is he?" Ethan dropped the tarp. "This shit just keeps getting worse."

Piper moved closer and stared into the empty gully. Panic splintered through her core.

"Maybe he wasn't dead." Jacob brought a shaky hand to his forehead. "Maybe he crawled away?"

"His heart wasn't beating. I'm sure of it." Ethan touched Piper's arm. "Right? You didn't feel a pulse either, did you?"

"No, no." Piper's eyes welled and she swallowed hard. "There wasn't any heartbeat and he wasn't breathing. I'm sure." She inhaled deeply. "Okay, let's think."

There was a rustle in the woods.

"Shh—" Noah pointed in the sound's direction. For a moment, everyone froze, then a branch snapped and a deer bolted through the trees.

"This is a fucking nightmare." Jacob turned away and then yelled, "Fuck, fuck, fuck!" He kicked the air as if rocketing a ball into the net, his entire body thrusting with the effort.

"Fuck, is right." Noah looked at his watch. "We've got to find the dude." He gripped the hoe, his knuckles white.

"And what are we supposed to do if we find him?" Cooper said, his voice full of dread.

"I'm not sure," Noah said. "I guess it depends if he's dead or alive."

They searched as long as they could and couldn't figure out what had become of Ned. With each passing minute, Piper feared he was clinging to life, a shotgun hole in his waist, and by failing to find him they were even guiltier. Or she imagined he was dead and that animals were feeding on him. Both scenarios ended with Sheriff Mismo on his way to arrest all of them. Maybe that would be for the best.

*

Twinkling white lights hung from the tree branches, and flaming Tiki torches lined the driveway. Bowls were scattered on the picnic table. The party had thinned out, leaving Coach and his wife, Dr. and Mrs. Horn, and Piper's mother and father congregating in a semi-circle. Noah, Cooper, Jacob, and Ethan played soccer bounce-back against the barn wall, their energy explosive, their laughs nervously too loud. Piper forced herself to recline on the chaise lounge on the patio's far side and tried not to choke on the lemonade she sipped. With each thud and crack of the ball against the stone, she flinched.

Ethan glanced at Piper a few times, but she was afraid to hold his gaze lest Jacob notice. His muscles showed through his sweat-drenched T-shirt and her longing to touch him returned. And this repulsed her.

God, how could she even think about him like that after what they had done?

Thousands of stars sparkled against the dark canvas of sky, and the sight made her question how the last thirty-six hours fit into the order of the universe. Tomorrow they had to go back to quarry—they would search until they found Ned. The warm night air, as gentle as a soft blanket, provided no comfort, and though her stomach had calmed and her headache was gone, Piper feared she would never feel normal again. She rolled to her side and closed her eyes.

Piper's back tingled. Were the adults staring at her? This is it. They know we're hiding something. In quieter tones, they continued, and Piper strained to hear, catching the words Sloan Kettering and blood clots and the phrase rule out cancer. Thank God the chatter was about Coach's health and not their hideous deed. And then she felt bad for thinking only about herself. Still, she relaxed a little and feigned sleep.

"Man, I don't want to turn into someone who complains about his every ailment." She opened her eyes to see Coach parked in the closest chair. He was wearing another one of his green and white Celtic jerseys. He took a long drag of his cigarette and set his beer on the ground by this foot. "This damn health scare has everybody up in arms. You don't look like you're feeling too great yourself. Tough night, eh? That's what the poison will do to you."

Piper wiggled into a better sitting position, adjusting the recliner. "I'm fine. Just tired."

Coach raised his right eyebrow and nodded toward the guys. "What about them, eh? They party too hard? It was late by the time we met up at the quarry. Everybody was in a goddamn hurry. Weren't the boys going camping and then hunting this morning?"

"You'd be proud. Everybody took it easy with preseason and all. You know, you shouldn't curse so much." She swung her legs around and slipped her feet into her flip-flops, ignoring his questions. "So, is everything okay? With the tests and stuff?"

Coach smirked. "I believe so." His eyes were deep brown, almost black, and unreadable. It was as if he peered into her mind and could tell something wasn't right. Maybe she was paranoid. She saw Ethan go to the food spread, and she got up. "I'm going to try the macaroni salad." Fleeing Coach and his inquiries was the best thing to do; otherwise she might buckle and accidentally say something she shouldn't.

Ethan handed her a plate and then leaned closer. "Noah wants us to meet at the pond in ten minutes to go over logistics for tomorrow."

Piper scooped a dollop of pasta onto her plate.

"And no texting. Don't mention the quarry or anything in writing."

She took one bite of the salad and then promptly dumped the plate and her spoon in the trashcan. "My appetite is shot, since—"

"I know, mine too."

"Okay, I'll see you over there in a few minutes." As Piper crossed the patio, she batted Coach's smoke out of her path, and then went into the house to make her exit appear like she was going to the restroom.

Five minutes later, Piper crested the bank that rolled toward the pond and saw Ethan already waiting. He sat on the dock, leaning against a piling. The moonlight hung over the still water like a silvery balloon. She made her way down the hill and onto the small pier her dad had built when they had first bought the farm.

"Where is everybody?" In the middle of the pond, Bert glided soundlessly behind Ernie, a slow gentle ripple in their wake.

"Still kicking around." He stood and watched her as she drew closer. "I wanted to talk to you alone." His eyes filled with yearning.

Piper paused, searching his face to make sure she wasn't misreading him. "Now is not the time, plus I thought you said—"

"I know." He stepped toward her and brushed her silky hair behind her ear. His touch sent a shudder through her body. Just then, a soccer ball fanned overhead and crashed into the pond with a wet whack. The swans hissed and snorted.

Ethan broke away instantaneously and turned to face the water, his back to Piper. "Man, I'm not thinking straight," he said under his breath as Noah, Cooper, and Jacob popped over the top of the hill. "Let's get through tomorrow. We'll figure out what to do about us later. And Pipe, you know you can never tell anybody what happened at the quarry."

"I know." Piper's voice cracked.

Jacob was the first to the pier. Wet with sweat, his hair kinked into ringlets. He wiped his brow. "What are you guys doing?"

"Waiting for you, asshole," Ethan said, the joke falling flat.

Jacob looked at them questioningly as if he didn't want to consider why Ethan and Piper would be together, and alone. Noah joined Jacob, followed by Cooper, and they made their plan for the morning. If they found Ned alive, they'd haul him out of the quarry, make an untraceable call for help, and leave him by the side of the road to be found.

If he was dead, they'd bury him.

CHAPTER 12

Piper climbed the steps two at a time. The moonlight poured through the window and shone on the hardwood floor landing. Noah's door was closed, his iPod speakers turned low. She placed her hand on the knob and felt the soft, driving thud of the bass in Mill's *Last Breath*. She wanted to talk to him, to share honestly how scared and confused she was. Would the weight of regret and self-reproach ever go away?

Instead, she turned and crossed the few steps to her room. The cool air from the window AC unit hit her when she opened the door. In bed, Piper pulled her light down comforter to her chin and closed her eyes, shifting her leg from under the blanket so the AC blew on it, soothing the welts. She wanted to linger in the tingly memory of Ethan's touch and to think about what it meant, but she couldn't erase Ned's weathered face from her mind. Then she realized—that day in the alley. His hands on the dashboard, his hair disheveled. His sad smile. The way he'd mouthed *sorry*.

She bolted upright.

Were Ned's fingerprints on their car? Would that connect them?

The kitchen was full of shadows and smelled clean. From beneath the sink, she found the wash bucket, pine oil, a sponge, and a few rags. With great care not to wake anybody, she put the bucket in the sink, turned on the faucet, added soap, and let the water bubble and foam. She paused before heading outside and noticed the blue numbers on the microwave clock read 1:47 AM. It had been less than twenty-four hours since the accident, but it felt like a lifetime ago.

The night seemed even brighter now—the full moon like a low watt light bulb. She walked to the driveway and set down the bucket in front of the Honda. Then she fished out her phone and turned on its flashlight and slowly made her way around the car, illuminating the old vehicle's dings and dents. She dipped the sponge into the warm soapy water and started with the hood—the spot where Ned had touched their car— scrubbing it and then wiping it dry with a paper towel. Bit by bit, she cleaned each section of the car and then she washed the hood again. Her fingertips grew white and fingers waterlogged.

"What are you doing?"

Piper froze, her knee digging into the hard driveway. The hair at the nape of her neck lifted as she looked up to see Noah. Deep rings had formed under his eyes. "I'm washing the car." She squeezed the sponge.

"I see that." He walked over to the car and ran his forefinger across the window shield. "Why?" They stared at each other, the night quiet and thick around them.

"It's dirty." Piper dipped a rag into the cold, grimy water, rung it, and tossed it to Noah. "And . . . Ned touched it, remember?" Noah nodded and wiped the hood in careful broad sweeps.

"I can't sleep. My mind won't quit racing." Noah wrung the cloth and rubbed the metal once more. "I just want it done."

"Me, too," Piper said. Maybe it had been Noah, maybe he'd accidentally shot Ned and that's why he had insomnia.

"Thank God, it'll be over either way tomorrow. Man, I hope we find him alive." He dumped the bucket and collected the wet rags. "Let's go." They walked back to the house together, put away the cleaning materials, and then climbed the stairs side by side. A ribbon of light fell from Cooper's room into the dark hallway. Noah nudged open Cooper's door and Piper peeked over his shoulder.

Cooper, on his knees at his bedside, his hands clasped in prayer, looked up apologetically. He unfolded his hands. "I was just—"

"Hey, no need to explain," Noah whispered and backed out. "See you in the morning."

The sun rose the next day and with it the announcement from their parents that the entire family was leaving immediately for a two-day

Pocono Mountains white water rafting trip to celebrate the start of Noah's and Piper's senior year. Shit.

"Some good quality time, that's what we need before this crazy year starts." Her dad filled a cooler with water bottles.

"I can't believe our last first day of school with you two is here." Mom draped her arms over Noah's shoulders and gave him a quick hug.

"I have so much to do before school starts," Piper said. "Really, today is not a good time."

"I've got stuff, too," Noah said. "Can you be away from the clinic?"

"Too bad," Mom said. "Hand over your phones."

"I guess if it's convenient for you, it's okay," Noah said, his voice hard.

"Calm down, buddy," Dad said. "You've got the entire year to be busy. This is not a negotiable vacation. We need some family time."

"I've decided on an electronic detox for the next forty–eight hours." And with that, Dr. I'm-so-busy Amy Rose pulled her iPhone from the wall charger, kissed the screen, and put it in the junk drawer, laughing. "You guys are in screen rehab, too." She gave them her don't–question–me look.

Panic filled Piper. Noah didn't look too calm either, and Cooper almost fainted when he bounded into the kitchen and heard about their impromptu but mandatory, electronic-free, two–day vacation. Piper fired off a quick group text to Ethan and Jacob: *Meeting must be postponed. 911. MOS. Go without us. If no luck, we'll go back.*

"We're leaving in thirty minutes." Dad cleared the table. "Pack light, but don't forget your fishing rods."

"You'll love the cabin we rented," Mom said. "There's a stream."

They pulled away from the farm phoneless. When they returned Ethan would be at Temple, but they had no choice but to go with their parents. A steady, low decibel panic vibrated in Piper's gut. There was no way to turn it off.

JOURNAL ENTRY
TUESDAY, SEPTEMBER 6

We have to get back to the quarry! No ifs, ands, or buts. Ethan and Jacob looked all day Monday and found nothing. Not a clue. I feel sick that we cut out on them. Mom and Dad's little trip screwed us. I called the hospital from the old pay phone at Boyer's Junction. "No gunshot wounds the last few days," the receptionist said, but then she started asking too many questions so I hung up. I keep second-guessing myself. We did what we had to do. We couldn't have done anything different that night, right? I hope there isn't a stench. It's been sooo hot. This is surreal, like one of those nightmares in which you know you're dreaming, but can't wake up. Only, I'm not dreaming. This is real. I feel like I am constantly about to vomit.

HOW DOES A DEAD MAN DISAPPEAR????

School starts tomorrow. Not sure I can do this.

CHAPTER 13

On Wednesday, the first day of school, the temperature soared to 95 degrees. The small oscillating fans the teachers brought from their homes did little to assuage the situation. The only relief came with the occasional humid breeze blowing in through the half-opened windows. Piper sat in Mr. Franks' homeroom, her legs sticking to the plastic chair, her anxiety mounting about the heat and what it would do to Ned. Flyers for the school musical, *Bye Bye Birdie*, were being passed around. She collected her hair into a ponytail. Noah was behind her as he always was in homeroom. Slipping her hands into her book bag, she stealthily squeezed an orb of hand sanitizer and rubbed, scouring for the fifth time.

This was it. Senior year—the last first day of school—she should feel something, right?

And she did. She felt like she was in a true-life horror show. Noah barely slept the whole time during the "family-bonding" trip, and Cooper found a Gideon's Bible and started reading it—reality was becoming more bizarre by the minute. Today they had a soccer game, which made tomorrow, Thursday, the first day they could get back to the quarry. The plan was they'd meet after practice to search for Ned before it got dark.

That morning, her parents had taken their annual front porch picture. Noah and Cooper posed on the top step and Piper on the one below like they had done for every first day of school photo for the last thirteen years. They'd each held a sign: twelfth grade for her and Noah and eleventh grade for Cooper for the scrapbook. They went through the motions. Fake. Fake. Fake.

"Hey, Coach just texted." Noah tugged on her ponytail.

"What?" Piper turned around ready to slug him.

"There's an emergency pre-game meeting. Coach wants everybody dressed and ready by 2:45. You're supposed to send a group text."

"Guess that's a manager duty." She made air quotes with her fingers.

"Sure is." Noah smirked. "The captain has to stay free for more important shit."

They were doing their best to act normal, but Noah was antsy and looked like shit. His blond stubble was three days old and the bags under his eyes pronounced. Piper shot off the text about Coach's meeting and then pretended to pay attention to Mr. Franks. He finished his morning announcements then zeroed in on Noah.

"Tough loss to Concord, but it's okay. Let them think they can win." Mr. Franks wiped the sweat from his forehead. "This is going to be our year. I can just feel it. You'll get them next time."

"We'll try, that's for sure." Noah nodded.

The bell rang and Piper startled. Smiling weakly, she said, "Thanks," as she passed Mr. Franks' desk.

At lunchtime, when Piper spotted Noah in the cafeteria, she knew something was wrong—well, everything was wrong—but something else was amiss. Jacob and Cooper were sitting with him, but they were apart from the team at a quiet table in the back. Noah waved to her and she headed toward him, her stomach roiling at the scent of hot dogs and sauerkraut, Millington Valley's traditional first day of school meal. Noah's face was ghostly pale, and he didn't have any food. Jacob's elbows were on the Formica table on either side of this tray, his hot dog half-eaten and the pickled cabbage untouched. Cooper had five wrapped chocolate chip cookies stacked to his right and a pile of wrappers to his left.

"You guys need to act more like yourselves. People are going to talk." Piper lugged her bag onto the bench and slumped next to Cooper. Mia Diaz sat three tables away and Piper locked eyes with her for a moment and then Mia instantly looked away. Did she know something?

"You hear?" Noah glanced up at the ceiling and then squarely at Piper.

"What?" she said.

Cooper took a cookie off the tower and slid it to her. "Someone found him," he said under his breath.

"What?" Her heartbeat slowed.

"Ned," Jacob whispered and stirred his fork in the sauerkraut, releasing a pungent whiff of sour vinegar. "A hunter found him."

If Piper hadn't been sitting, her knees would have buckled. Instead, she leaned on the table. "What state was his body in? I mean, was it obvious he'd been shot?"

"Piper—" Noah took a deep breath and closed his eyes. "He's alive."

Piper's stomach lurched. She was going to be sick.

"Unconscious," Jacob said. "He's at Millington General on life support."

*

By 2:40 pm Noah, Cooper and Jacob, along with the rest of the team, lagged under the locker room's overhang in the shade waiting for Coach. Meek Mill's *Shine* echoed from someone's iPhone. They were doing their best to pretend that it was a normal day. The temperature had dropped, and though it was still sunny, dark, low rain clouds capped the mountain ridge in the distance. The afternoon had been a blur, Piper moving from class to class in a haze barely containing her panic. She leaned against the brick wall and scrolled through her old texts until she found Ethan's goodbye message from Monday morning when she had informed him about her parents' last-minute adventure trip, and the message she'd sent from lunch: *911 about IT. Call ASAP.* The little grayed out letters still read *Delivered*, and she waited, watching for them to turn to *Read.*

Coach's red Jeep flew up the hill and slid into a spot beside the bus. He got out of the Jeep, threw his cigarette on the asphalt, and stepped on it. He strode toward them, his hands jammed into the front pockets of his white sweatpants. For a fleeting moment, Piper feared Coach had figured out their transgression.

"He's pissed," Cooper said. "What'd you do now?" He punched Ryan's shoulder, feigning normalcy.

"Me?" Ryan pointed to his chest. The rest of the team gathered around him.

"What do you think? Your shit doesn't smell? I can't even go in the effing locker room. A stink bomb exploded in there."

"Both of you, shut up." Noah gestured toward Coach and then crossed his arms. Coach landed at the opening of their semi-circle.

"What's up?" Noah said.

Coach lifted his sunglasses onto his sunburned forehead; then his eyes tightened, his gaze moving around the squad, and then pausing for a split second on Jacob. "This morning I had the good fortune to receive an email from Principal Unger. He dug a crumbled paper from his pocket. "This letter—" he hit the paper with his hand, "—was written anonymously." He raised his eyebrow. "Let me tell you a person who doesn't sign his or her name is a coward with a capital C."

The team was quiet, but they looked at one another, wondering what this was about.

Coach read:

Dear Principal Unger,

I am writing on behalf of the families of the Millington Valley High School Soccer Team. It has come to our attention that several soccer practices have been unsupervised and that boys have been injured during this unregulated time. Furthermore, the head coach, while he might have been an excellent soccer player in his day, does not know how to deal with impressionable young men. His language is abhorrent and abrasive. There is a great fear that our boys will be scarred for life from his verbal abuse. It is also suspected that he uses tobacco on school property. Winning is important, but providing suitable role models is paramount. Coach Christopher O'Connell needs to be corralled. Otherwise, we will be forced to make the school board aware of these unfortunate circumstances.

Signed,

A Concerned Parent

"Now, I'm no fucking horse." Coach ripped the paper in half, then quarters, and threw it on the parking lot. "My advice is to let your parents know that if they have anything to say, they best say it to my face. Tell them to shove their letters up their arses." Coach pantomimed drinking a cup of tea with his pinky finger in the air. "Oh, excuse me. Pardon me. Did I hurt your feelings, eh? Aww, I'm sorry. Well, fuck off. This team is about winning. If you can't stand the heat, get out of the kitchen." The guys parted and Coach walked into the locker room, letting the door slam behind him.

Piper flinched. It was silent, and then, one by one, the guys meandered over to the bus. The vehicle's door creaked open. Mr. Robinson, the bus driver, lumbered down the few steps of the bus, his heavy frame unsteady. He circled the vehicle and cranked the rear door ajar. The guys threw their gear into the back and climbed inside. Jacob lagged behind the group, and Piper deliberately trailed him. He stopped and opened his bag. Piper was close enough to see that a flush had crept across his neck and his ears reddened. Piper was sure Mrs. Horn had been the author of that letter, and she knew Jacob knew it too. But this was the least of their problems.

The ride was hushed, without the usual rough housing and trash talking. Perched in the seat directly behind the bus driver, Coach stared out the window at the passing cornfields. No one dared to provoke him. Even Assistant Coach Marky was buttoned up, sitting by himself in the seat behind Coach—there wasn't the usual scribbling on a white clipboard or strategizing about the match. Piper occupied the front-row seat opposite Coach. The warm air whipped through the open windows, and she twirled her ponytail into a messy bun to stop it from flying around. Piper wanted to ask Coach how the ultrasound had gone, but now was not the time. Instead, she checked her phone again to see that her message to Ethan still hadn't been read.

They had better win today. More importantly, they had better figure out what to do about the Ned situation. And fast.

JOURNAL ENTRY
WEDNESDAY, SEPTEMBER 7

Ned is alive! Thank God. He's unconscious, but what if he wakes up? Will he remember us?
This article was in the paper this morning:

Millington Valley Army Vet Found Wounded in Quarry
Ned Walker, 70, was found by small game hunter Rolf Stouffer early Wednesday, September 6 in the Stone Haven Quarry near the west bank of the lake. Walker was unconscious and suffering from a gunshot wound, which did not appear to be self-inflicted. Walker, sister to Wanda Walker, is an Army Veteran, 23rd Infantry Division, Vietnam. Anybody with information about the shooting of Walker is asked to contact Sheriff Anthony Mismo at 610-987-3726 or smismo@millington.twn.pa.us.

I agreed with the guys we should leave Ned there and come back. Why did I go along with them? I really, really, really don't know what we should do. If we had somehow lugged him out of the quarry that night, would things be different? I should be happy Ned is alive, but I am terrified, and now part of me wants him to . . . die. Does that make me evil? Yes, I'm rotten, pure and simple. This is my fault. The guys are right. We have too much to lose.

P.S. Ernie laid a couple eggs. She sits on her nest all the time. Bert won't let me get close.
P.P.S. On the outside, I look normal. But on the inside, I am freaking out!
P.P.P.S. I have to do something about this!

CHAPTER 14

Sitting on her bed, Piper shook the turquoise nail polish and twisted the cap. Her toes needed constant pedicures; otherwise, a tiny hangnail or a jagged bit of skin could create an excruciating pain in her pointe shoes.

"Shit, that stuff stinks." Noah threw a Nerf soccer ball and it bounced off Cooper's shoulder. "Open a window."

"Sure, why don't I throw the air conditioner onto the yard so you can get some goddamn fresh air." Dressed in only his royal blue practice shorts, Cooper lay on Piper's bedroom floor, clutching his stomach. "I can't take this. I think we ought to tell somebody what happened."

"What, exactly, would we say?" Piper's hand was unsteady as she brushed the polish over her big toenail. "Maybe you should report that to the West Chester recruiter who called tonight . . . Hey, Coach, could you use a nice murderer? I'm a great center mid-fielder."

"Don't be a smart alec. Miss I'm-so-nice is sounding like a bitch. We didn't murder anybody," Noah said. "Put that stuff away. I can't breathe."

"Okay, let me back that down a little. Attempted murder." Piper adjusted the top. "Seriously, who would we tell, and what should we say?" Piper was a pressure cooker that was on the verge of malfunction. "Shoot," she said as, again, her hand slipped and more polish ended up on her toe than her nail.

"I don't know." Noah brought a shaky hand to his forehead. "At least he's not dead."

"The whole thing makes me sick." Cooper's brow furrowed. "Literally, I'm going to vomit."

"Me, too. My insides are in knots." Piper pinched her eyes.

"What if Ned wakes up?" Cooper said. "He might not know our names, but it won't be too hard to figure out. Man, I don't want to ruin my chance to play in college, but I feel so bad." He jolted up and pointed at Noah, his face dark with resignation. "You know, Penn State will drop your scholarship faster than you can say, 'I'm sorry.'"

"Calm down, both of you." Noah leaned against the wall and crossed his arms. "We need to relax. Ethan said we should just keep quiet. Even if Ned comes out of the coma, there's a good chance he won't have any memory of the accident. He probably has PTSD, which according to Ethan, has a high likelihood of memory loss. Or maybe that won't happen. Maybe Ned will—"

"Die." Piper sniffed, letting the heaviness of the word sink. So Ethan had talked to Noah, but couldn't return her text. What was that about? "It's terrible. God, what's wrong with me? I hope that an old man dies." She glared at her brothers and bit her lip. Hold it together, girl. "Maybe we should confess." She grabbed a tissue from her nightstand and wiped it across her gummy toenails.

Noah took a deep, woeful breath, averted his gaze for a moment, and then met Piper's solemn watery stare. "I've thought about it. Hell, my mind races all night. I can't sleep, but it's too late. We can't undo it. Squealing will not make him better. We say nothing for now. You just focus on dance and school. Mom and Dad will freak out if Miss Perfect's grades drop. Coop, concentrate on the season. Stop the crazy praying all the time. We need to act normal. If Ned wakes up, we'll figure out what to do then."

Cooper hung his head. Nobody said a word for several minutes and then Cooper muttered, "Okay." And then louder and with more conviction, "Okay." He got up slowly, like an arthritic old man, and grabbed the Nerf ball. "I'm sure of one thing." He paused and squeezed the ball. "We're not losing another game this season, and that includes Concord. They're too big for their britches, as Dad would say. They got lucky in the scrimmage." Cooper ran his hand over his chest. "I'm ripped, right? Ever see a sixteen-year-old look this good?" He almost sounded like his old self.

Piper pulled out another tissue and blew her nose. "I can't think about this anymore. Can you guys scram? I've got homework to do."

Noah jumped up and grabbed the Nerf ball. "Let's go kick around."

Piper was glad to have her room to herself. The talk about Ned made their terrible predicament real. They were in over their heads—that was the only thing she was sure of. The moral lines of right and wrong had shifted and the landscape of what to do next was blurry. She swallowed and pressed her hand on her abdomen. When she thought about what had happened to Ned, she could hardly breathe. Part of her wanted to know who had pulled the trigger. Who was the most culpable? But they were all culpable—and maybe she was the most—because she had gone along with the guys' decision without protest.

She put on her pajamas, organized her study nook, and then wrote in her journal. When she was done writing, she placed Madame Rosemary's blue ribbon in the book's crease and then carefully hid it between her mattress and box spring. That Ethan had gotten in touch with Noah stung. Why hadn't he returned her texts? With her pillows piled against the headboard and one pillow resting on her thighs, she leaned back, nestled her laptop into the soft cushion, and clicked Google docs. French was due next Wednesday. And the Nazi Germany reading could wait. The only homework she had to tackle was Mr. Franks' writing prompt, which she pulled up next: *Describe a situation in which you helped someone or didn't and why?* Good God. Talk about irony. Mr. Franks would appreciate that she was thinking in literary terms. There was no way she could answer that question. Instead, she closed her laptop, adjusted her pillow, and lay down.

Her new pointe shoes were in the Gaynor Minden box atop her dresser. Now was as good of a time as any to sew her elastic straps and ribbons. She climbed out of bed and crossed the few steps to her bureau. Opening the box, she pulled back the tissue stuffing and ran her fingers over the shiny pink satin. She retrieved her mending kit from under her bed, found a needle, the pink thread, and a pack of matches and situated herself on the floor. After she attached the elastic and ribbons, she lit a match to burn the edges of the ribbons so that they wouldn't fray. The fringe smoked and curled, sealing the ribbon. She struck another match and watched the flame bloom; the glow mesmerized her. The tiny blaze vanished with a soft puff of air from her mouth. She lit another match, but instead of blowing it out, she held the burning stick close to the tender, white skin on the inside of her wrist. The heat tickled her arm and a little voice inside her head whispered, "Press. Press. Press." She pushed the small torch into her skin, making a red ring that bit into her flesh. She closed her eyes, and her mind cleared as she focused on the small, throbbing circle—and then she did it again. For the first time in four days, she felt okay, almost at peace. This was what she deserved—to burn, to suffer, to pay for her part in this nightmare.

It was clear. She should have stayed at the campfire. Fooling around with Ethan was a mistake. If she had not been with him, none of this would have happened. And whether Ned lived or died, leaving him was wrong. She knew that now.

And she had to make it right.

JOURNAL ENTRY
THURSDAY, SEPTEMBER 8

I tried. I really did. Maybe the universe is telling me to keep quiet. This morning, I lied and told Mom I had to leave early to meet Mr. Franks before school to discuss my research paper. She let me use the Pathfinder. I dropped her at the clinic at 6:45 AM and headed straight to the township building.

Now or never, I figured. Just spill it to Mismo. The parking lot was empty. I waited and waited. The sun got hotter and my nerves more fried by the minute. Where could he be this early in the morning? It's not like Millington Valley is crime ridden. I needed him to show up because my certainty of what to do was fading and I was afraid this moment of courage wouldn't last.
Then ping. Ping. Ping. Ping. The texts flew. Noah. Cooper. Noah. Cooper.

Pipe? Come get us.

Fuck, Piper. Where are you?

911.

We need a ride.

Can't be late for first period or Coach will dock us.

The Honda broke down on Covered Bridge Road and Noah and Cooper were stranded. (Dad had the truck in Lancaster County picking up lumber for some project).

I ignored them for a few minutes, willing Sheriff Mismo to pull into the parking lot. Then my phone rang and it was Mom.

End of story. I left.

And now I'm afraid. Things don't seem as black and white. I don't know what to do! I wish someone would decide for me. Then I could just react.

I did it again. The matches.

CHAPTER 15

"Who's that?"

Mom set her ragged paper napkin on her plate with purpose. Tossing her long braid over her shoulder, she went to the screen door.

The Rose family never broke with tradition. Every pre-game meal was a special occasion—pasta served with Dad's homemade meatballs and marinara sauce, garlic bread, salad, and chocolate milk. Piper wore a loose, long sleeve MVHS T-shirt, the cuffs covering her fresh burns. Tonight, the windows were open and the first hint of fall blew in with the long shadows of the setting sun. Tomorrow's game against Twin Valley would be an easy win. So should be the next eight games. Their first real challenge in the county would come in the Concord rematch.

If only beating Concord was their biggest worry.

From the kitchen table, Piper peered through the window over the sink. A car slowly crunched along the gravel driveway, its headlight bright and blinding in the dusk, dust ballooning in its path, and when it passed under the lamppost light, the police insignia was visible. Piper's pulse quickened, and she glanced at Noah, whose jaw tightened. She rubbed her index finger over the Band-aid on her wrist.

"What could bring Sheriff Mismo here?" Dad pushed back his chair and followed Mom, who had stepped onto the porch. As soon as their parents were out of earshot, Cooper set his fork down. "This is it. We're fucked," he mumbled.

"Stay calm," Noah said. Frozen in their seats, they watched Sheriff Mismo park next to the Honda as their parents crossed the yard to meet him in the driveway. Small talk was exchanged and then together the three adults walked toward the house.

"Get a hold of yourself," Noah said to Cooper. "You had to figure Mismo would want to talk to us. Everybody knows we had a party at the quarry and that's where Ned was found." Noah looked at Cooper and then at Piper. "Both of you keep your mouths shut."

"I will, but it's still freaking me out." Cooper sat on his hands, his face pale.

"Just act normal," Piper said, trying to camouflage the dry unease rising in her throat. She pointed and flexed her feet under the table.

Sheriff Mismo followed Mom and Dad into the house and the screen door slammed behind them. He was a former football player, and his big shoulders filled the entryway. With his deep tan, blue eyes, and closely cropped full head of hair, the sheriff was decent looking for an old guy. Piper had overheard a bunch of moms discussing his single status more than once.

"Sorry to interrupt your dinner. This will only take a few minutes." He nodded and took off his hat. "I'm hoping you guys can help me."

Mom motioned for the Sheriff to sit in her seat. "Can I get you a drink?"

"I'm fine. Thanks." Mismo eased into Mom's seat and placed his visor on the table. "Don't worry. I'm not here to bust anybody for partying. I'm just trying to piece together how Ned Walker got shot. We think the accident happened sometime Sunday or Monday." Mismo produced a small pad from his front pocket and flipped to a blank page. He motioned to Noah first. "Jacob Horn says you guys were at the quarry Saturday night."

Noah nodded. "Yes." He acknowledged Dad and then Mom. "It was my birthday. We had a little get together and then we were going to camp out."

Sheriff Mismo cocked his head to the side. "But you didn't stay over?" His voice held steady and his expression emotionless.

Piper waited a fraction of a second for Noah to say something and then snickered. "No, I ruined their night." She sipped her water and dared not to look at Noah. "I got sick. I made them bring me home." Point. Flex. Lie. She couldn't turn on her brothers. Not like this—in front of their parents. She needed time to sort out the situation. Her heart pounded with such intensity she feared Mismo would notice she was trembling.

"You mean from drinking?" Dad said.

"Sorry." Piper lowered her eyes and feigned embarrassment.

"She's a lightweight," Noah said. "Pretty much nixed our plans." Good. Noah took the bait and was running with it. Coach would verify he saw them leave and he was also at the picnic the next day and commented on Piper's supposed hangover. A believable story. And sort of true.

"Little Ryan said he was tired and hiked back to the cars to sleep. And Coach O'Connell met you guys out there around 2 AM. Did you notice any hunters or hikers? Any cars you didn't recognize?"

"No, but if I'm honest, I was a little—" Noah stopped himself. "It's just that it was late and I was wiped out. Coach will tell you."

"There wasn't anybody out there. We were the last to leave." Piper held her breath as the air in the room changed, growing thicker. Did Little Ryan know the bundle Cooper lugged was more than a sleeping bag? Had he figured it out and was he covering for them? Finally, Sheriff Mismo flipped a page and turned to Cooper.

"How about you? What time did you leave?"

A bead of sweat had formed on Cooper's lip and he swallowed. "Same as them. We all decided it was a bust. We figured it best to get Piper home after she got sick again." He glanced at Mom apologetically. "You guys were in Philly, so it didn't matter that we got home late. Me, Jacob, Ethan, Noah, and Piper, we all went home together. That's what we did."

Mom plucked the spaghetti bowl from the middle of the table and scooped out the rest onto Cooper's plate. "Geez," she said under her breath.

Mismo chuckled. "Rough night, Piper?"

"I don't party. I only went because it was Noah's birthday." She licked her lips and took a drink of water. Point. Flex. Her shoulders tightened. "It's not really my thing." Did Sheriff Mismo know she was at the township building this morning? Had he put two and two together?

2

23

"Did any of you see Ned?"

Noah sipped his water. "I don't remember even passing another car on the drive home." He looked Sheriff Mismo square in the eye and Piper awed at her brother's straight-faced lie.

"Well, I was hoping one of you might have noticed something. We're at a dead end. Ned Walker took a turn for the worse last night." Mismo tucked his notepad in his front pocket. "That'll be all." Before he shook hands with Dad and Mom and left, he retrieved three business cards and placed one in front of each of the kids. "Call or text me if you think of anything else."

"More meatballs." Cooper reached across Piper and nabbed the last piece of garlic bread, almost knocking over the Mason jar filled with yellow, pink and lavender roses.

"I think you meant to say, 'Excuse me.'" Piper gently pinched his bicep, rearranged the jar, and then tucked Sheriff Mismo's card into her pocket.

"Settle down, you two." Dad twirled his fork, spinning a mound of spaghetti. "God, this whole thing with Ned Walker is just awful." He ate a forkful and then wiped his mouth with the napkin tucked around the neckline of his Philadelphia Eagles T-shirt. "Before we came inside, Sheriff Mismo was telling us how Ned's elderly sister is distraught."

"I have to believe whoever shot him didn't realize it," Mom said. "Pass your plate, Cooper." She dumped some salad on it. "I'm glad you canceled the hunting trip. It's unbelievable that someone would leave him there. Are you sure you guys didn't see anyone?"

Piper didn't say a word, stirring the noodles on her plate. Did her parents suspect anything? Was she, together with Cooper and Noah, trying too hard to act ordinary? Her heart was about to jump through her mouth.

"Did Coach ever come into the clinic to get his leg checked?" Noah asked, desperate to steer the discussion away from Ned Walker.

"He was in Tuesday."

"What's going on?" Cooper ripped the garlic bread with his teeth, the butter dripping onto his chin. "Is everything okay?"

"Normally, I would never discuss a patient."

"We know, HIPPA," Noah said. "But it's Coach. Just tell us what's up."

"Keep this between us, but he has a blood clot on his shin. That's what's causing the tenderness." Mom drank the last of her chocolate milk.

"He never wears shin guards at practice." Cooper wiped his face. "Someone nailed his leg, I bet."

"Could have. I started him on heparin to break up the clot."

"How old is Coach?" Piper said.

"He's a few years younger than us." Dad pulled the marinara-stained napkin from his neck and crumpled it.

"Forty-one or two," Mom said. "It's probably nothing, but Doc Horn looked at the ultrasound and we both agreed that Coach should see a specialist," Mom said. "Just in case."

If their mother was encouraging Coach to seek more medical treatment, something was wrong even if she was pretending it wasn't. Piper's universe was disintegrating. First Ned. Now Coach. Mismo. They were in too deep. The hidden lesions on her wrist tingled. With her hands under the table, she pressed her thumbnail into the Band-Aid, digging until she felt the sharp pinch of her skin open. "I hope nothing is wrong with Coach," she said and smiled, while silently praying. Help. Please make things right and I will never do anything bad again.

JOURNAL ENTRY
FRIDAY, SEPTEMBER 9

Every hour gets worse. Sheriff Mismo scares me. I was ready to confess yesterday morning. But I've lost my nerve. Mismo stopped by the farm in the middle of dinner and it made the whole thing too real. He had all sorts of questions about the quarry party. Part of me thinks he's on to us. Noah stayed pretty cool, but Cooper was about to shit his pants. We vowed to stay silent about Ned. But I am having major, make-me-sick second thoughts. This is terrible. Act normal, I keep telling myself. The solution will make itself known. Noah says I had better keep my mouth shut. That we just need to wait. That everything will be okay. What the hell is he thinking?

Writing about this is freaking me out.

P.S. Ethan has still not returned my texts. What a jerk! He acts like we are not in the biggest freaking emergency of our lives. I never should have kissed him. Now, he's ignoring me? Go freaking figure. Sometimes he can be such an idiot Maybe going to dance tomorrow will make me feel better! God, I hope so.

CHAPTER 16

Things hadn't been the same between Brittany and Piper since the American Ballet Summer Intensive audition in New York City five months ago. Piper wished she could slip into a time loop and go back to the day their friendship had shifted and do something different—somehow make it better. Their parents had agreed they could take the Bieber Bus to the city unchaperoned as long as they stuck together. For weeks, they plotted, planned, and practiced.

The hallway outside the audition studio was jammed with ballerinas. Long legs, perfect points, tight buns, hairspray—dreams. Piper found an empty corner and established a triage area, arranging their bags to mark their territory. They warmed up, stretching, spotting turns in the glass window, retouching makeup, smoothing buns, quiet in their familiar togetherness. They pinned their numbers to the front of their leotards: Piper was eleven and Brittany was fifty-seven.

The plan was that after the tryout they'd go to SoHo to have dinner and shop.

The lights blinked three times.

"Attention, dancers, please report to the third floor," a pretentious male voice announced. "The audition will begin promptly in ten minutes. Proceed to the studio and line up in numerical order."

"Good luck." Piper hugged Brittany. "This is it!"

They climbed the steps single file. When Piper entered the studio, the rest of the world fell away. She didn't watch the other dancers or pay too much attention to the three judges and even forgot Brittany was there. First, they did barre work. Then in smaller groups, six girls at a time, they worked turn combinations in the center of the floor and later, leaps across the studio. She found herself in the zone, the place she entered when her movements connected with the music and to a deep part of her soul.

Three hours later, the audition ended.

Before leaving, each dancer had to approach the judges' table, and there she was handed a folded piece of paper. This was unexpected. They had assumed it would take a week or two to find out if they'd made it, and that the notice would come by email. But Piper knew she had nailed it.

Inside the brochure there were two boxes:

€ *Congratulations! You have been accepted in the American Ballet Theatre Summer Intensive, Level _____.*
€ *Sorry, you have not been accepted.*

A red check was scored through *Congratulations.* Piper's heart soared and she turned around and gave Brittany a little nod, then retreated to the hallway to wait. More than one girl broke into sobs as she stepped into the corridor.

Brittany didn't utter a word—the rejection was etched in her face. She gave Piper a weak smile and swallowed hard and then vanished into the restroom.

In hindsight, Piper should have followed her. She should have wrapped her arms around her friend and let her cry. Instead, Piper waited in the hallway, busying herself by repacking her dance bag, filled with a terrible mix of emotions. Happy. Sad. Excited. Guilty. When Brittany finally emerged thirty minutes later, her eyes were red and her cheeks blotchy. Piper pretended not to notice, deciding the best course of action was avoidance.

That was the beginning of the big chill. The rest of the day in NYC was strained. They attempted small talk, but ended up catching an earlier bus than planned. The ride home was quiet. Brittany leaned against the window, faking sleep. There were quick goodbyes at the depot.

And then Brittany stopped texting. Now she rarely spoke to Piper in class. If Piper's mom knew the true situation, she'd argue Brittany was jealous and she wasn't a genuine friend if she couldn't be happy for Piper. Maybe that was sort of true, but Piper knew how much dance meant to Brittany, how much she wanted to be accepted into the intensive, how much they had fantasized about rooming together in New York. Piper knew what was wrong. Her confidante was heartbroken, and Piper's success made it hurt more.

She wished she had Brittany now. Maybe, just maybe, she'd be able to tell her what had happened, and Brittany would help her figure out how to find her way out of this quagmire.

"How's school?" Piper had said when she found Brittany alone in the dressing room before pointe class. "Is your schedule tough this year?"

"It's fine." Brittany turned to fiddle with the locker. The muscles in her back were ripped and defined as if stretched to their maximum capacity, with not an ounce of fat.

"Your leaps were great last class."

"Thanks." Brittany's voice was noncommittal.

"Hey." Piper touched Brittany's arm. "Are you okay?"

Brittany flinched. "Fine."

"It's just that—I'm sorry for everything."

"What?" Brittany eyes were cold, hard, and flinty. "You're sorry you're better than me? That you do everything, right? That you're perfect? Beautiful? A superior dancer? Nicer? What exactly is it you're sorry about?" The words spewed from Brittany as if she were vomiting. Ugly. Disgusting. True words. Each one cutting Piper like a shard of jagged glass.

"No, I'm not better—"

The changing room door flew open, slamming against the wall. "Hey, hey, hey." Maya barged in with Allison on her heels. They saw Piper and Brittany and froze. The small muscles in Brittany's jaw jumped and her eyes filled with tears. Brittany turned back to her locker.

"I was just leaving," Piper said and pushed pass Maya and Allison.

Her friend was too hurt. Raw. Piper knew dance, like art, was subjective. And it pissed her off that the ABT couldn't see what a talented dancer Brittany was. If only she could make Brittany understand that Piper wasn't perfect. Far from it. *I am an accomplice to a crime,* Piper wanted to shout. *A total and complete fraud in dance and in life. A horrible person. And I need you right now.*

CHAPTER 17

Propped against the locker room's brick wall, Piper lounged on the cooler in the overhang's shade. She crossed her legs and zoned out, half-watching soccer practice. Flanked by two sets of rickety metal bleachers, the field was on the perimeter of the campus near the Heartbreak Hill drop-off. It was a freaky optical illusion, the way the pitch appeared to float in the space between the mountains. Generations of MVHS cross-country runners cursed their home course that included the steep dirt trail leading into the woods. The trees were dabbled with the first tinges of yellow and orange.

Sunglasses on his face and his blue and white umbrella overhead, Coach stormed the sideline. "Soccer is a game of nine-yard bursts." He thrust the umbrella to the left, his baggy Celtic jersey hanging loose. "Take it by line. Try it again."

Little Ryan dribbled and passed to Cooper who flew down the right side, made a move, and crossed the ball back to Little Ryan. The freshman nailed it into the goal. "That's how you attack the wings and score goals." Coached shouted, a gigantic smile on his face, his umbrella spinning. "That's how we're going to fucking beat Concord."

No adult was within earshot, not even Coach Marky. Thank God. A Sunday School "role model" Coach was not. Ryan and Cooper chest bumped and returned to their kick-off positions. Noah wearily jogged back to his sweeper spot in front of the goal. Piper didn't think he had slept for more than a couple consecutive hours since it happened. He wasn't too quick to the ball today, and he kept staring at the hills.

Time to get moving, she told herself. A semi–paralysis had settled into her psyche and her body; even the smallest, simplest tasks were monumental. Super A+, goodie two shoes, sweet Piper Rose was gone. Heaviness more formidable than anything she had ever known held her in a suffocating cocoon. She released the cooler's telescopic handle, tipped it up to engage the wheels, and dragged it toward the field, her bag knocking against her back.

The team ran through the give–and–go play several more times. After situating the cumbersome cooler on the lowest bench, Piper climbed to the top of the bleachers and settled into the corner against the chain link side. Rummaging through her book bag, she located the Purell and *Schindler's List.* Tomorrow there was a quiz on the first five chapters. She disinfected her hands and opened the book. *Read,* she warned herself, looking at the jumble of words. Turning the page, she couldn't remember a single notion of what she had just skimmed. She flipped to the beginning and started over. Again and again, her eyes zeroed in on certain words and phrases, blurring out the rest of the page: *good over evil, fatal human malice, ambiguity, abomination, damned.* God, she couldn't even get through the prologue. The blasted book was taunting her.

A warm breeze carried the scent of harvested hay and the drone of a distant mower hummed. From time to time, Piper glanced at the field and then forced herself back into the novel. The hollow clang of cleats against the bleachers jarred her from her pretend reading. Jacob bounded up the steps two at a time.

"Hey." He was red–faced and sweaty.

Piper closed *Schindler's List* and squinted up against the afternoon sun.

Pushing his curly, wet hair from his forehead, he revealed his scab from the chicken fight injury. "Sorry we haven't talked in since—you know—are you doing okay?"

Piper set the novel on the bleacher and motioned for him to sit. "I'm not operating at hundred percent." She took a deep breath. "Honestly, I'm not so good."

Jacob dropped next to her, close enough that she detected the scent of fresh grass and caked mud mingled with his perspiration. "Me either." They rested quietly together, watching the team take a water break.

Piper touched his hand and he turned to face her. "I'm not sure how to make things right. We really screwed up."

He whispered. "Ethan says to just lie low for a while."

"Ethan doesn't seem bothered by any of this. The rest of us are falling apart. Noah has insomnia. Cooper's praying like a monk. You know, we don't go to church. How long till my parents notice he's gone religious? They'll want to know why. And I'm—"

She touched the clear bandage on her wrist. "Let's just say I'm not handling things too well. It pisses me off Ethan is ignoring the whole situation like he has nothing to do with it."

"He's caught up with college and fitting into the new team."

"Stop defending him." Piper raised her eyebrows and gave Jacob a glassy stare. "At least he's talking to you."

"We might not need to worry about anything. Maybe Ned will—"

"That's the part I can't reconcile." Piper's eyes stung, blinking away the tears. "That we want a man to die? What does that say about us? Don't you feel responsible?"

"You went along with leaving him. It's just as much your fault."

Piper flinched. "I'm not the stupid asshole who fired a gun into the woods at night. What were you guys thinking?" She held his gaze and stared deep into his eyes. There were tiny golden flecks on his brown irises. "Who pulled the trigger?"

"Come on, we promised."

"It's one of my brothers, isn't it?"

"Stop. We vowed to be quiet about it. We're all at fault."

Piper shook her head. "Stupid, fucking guns. My parents never liked that your dad was always pushing the idea of you guys hunting together. Like that's the only way men can bond, by shooting helpless creatures. It's disgusting the way your dad hangs dead stuffed animals on your walls." Her voice was knotted with sarcasm and tears. "Now this. Happy fucking Second Amendment."

"I know. I've never been into it. My dad means well." Jacob extended his leg and reached for his toe to stretch his hamstring. "Forgive me for saying that about it being your fault, okay? It's not."

Piper swallowed the lump in her throat and held out her pinky. "It'll be fine. Friends forever?"

He hooked his little finger in hers, his eyes filled with hope. "Friends. Remember when we thought this was a secret handshake?"

"The Rose-Horn pump." She smiled at the memory. "It wasn't so secret after we taught it to our entire kindergarten class."

"You mean, after you blabbed it to Chloe Watchman." He stood up and took a deep breath, raking his hand through his sweaty hair. "Hey, do you want to be my Community Service Senior Project partner? I was thinking we could volunteer for the Visiting Angels."

"Sure," Piper said with little conviction. "I guess. I hadn't even thought about what to do yet. That sounds good."

There was a flash of surprise on Jacob's face, and then he started down the steps. Halfway to the ground, he turned around. The sun blinded him for an instant, and he raised his hand over his brow like a visor. "There's something else, too. I know it's the last thing any of us want to do." He spoke fast and rubbed his hands down the front of his shorts. "But would you go to Homecoming with me?"

Coach blew his whistle.

Then she surprised herself and said, "Sure, I'll go."

"We can still have a good time. Try to, at least. It's our senior year." Jacob smiled, his face flooded with relief. His expression pained Piper. Relieved. Earnest.

Why couldn't she feel about Jacob the way she did about Ethan? He was sweet and kind and he loved her, but there wasn't a spark. He was like her third brother. It was funny how she'd never thought of Ethan like a sibling.

"You better get back." She pointed. "It looks like Coach is about to go ballistic."

That night, when she couldn't sleep, she pulled on a hoodie and slipped into her flip-flops and sneaked out of the house. She pulled a handful of lettuce from Dad's patio herb bed and tore the leaves into small pieces. Down by the pond, she scattered the leafy bits onto the still water's edge. Ernie slipped from her nest and glided across the pond followed closely by Bert. They nibbled and stared at Piper as if to thank her.

Then Piper made her way over to the rose garden, which was a large rectangle set about fifty yards from the house. For every Mother's Day, special event, or accomplishment, her father planted a symbolic new rose. There was the light peach floribunda Anne Harkness for Noah's first call up to the Eastern Regional Team; Cooper's fuchsia English Blaze to celebrate making varsity as a freshman; Piper's tall, elegant white Maiden Blush bush to mark her Rock School acceptance; Mom and Dad's twentieth anniversary pink Rosa Peace rose. She walked along the pebbled path, her fingers brushing the top of the open flowers and coming away moist with dew.

She wished there was a way to eradicate the images of Ned—every detail of that night was branded in her memory, and her mind couldn't settle on anything else, except the possibility that he would die and it would be over. Which was dumb, because the same question would still be there like a billboard: Who shot him? They hadn't even talked about that, but, of course, the boys knew, didn't they? That they didn't trust Piper to keep her mouth shut hurt. It was like Noah, Cooper, Ethan, and Jacob had become one person, the person who shot a vagrant in the woods. And by default, because she was there, she was one of them, not a guy, not a soccer player, but still one of them. That was why she agreed to be silent. She thought she was protecting them, that she was a member of their team.

She hadn't really considered Ned Walker.

He was someone you'd say was nobody, but he was a human being, and he was suffering, and all they had cared about was not getting caught. They were more concerned about a winning season, Piper's dance, their soccer scholarships, and what people would think. It was more important that they stuck together and escaped the quarry.

What did that say about them?

Ned had a life, too, whether or not they thought it was a good one. He had a sister. Piper felt she might faint with fear and disgust and remorse. None of which solved the real problem: What should they do now?

Their parents would flat out not believe what they'd done. That their kids had left a man for dead was absurd. She sank onto the wet grass and plucked a blush pink Veríssimo flower head—Grandmom Rose's rose. Pulling one petal at a time, she silently chanted: *Let him live. Hope he dies.* The last petal ended with letting him live. She threw the naked stem on the ground and clasped her hands together. With the moonlight crowning the flowers of her family, she made a deal with herself. If Ned lived, she would tell the truth. Screw the boys and this asphyxiating secret. Do the right thing, that's what her parents had taught her. That's what Mom would expect her to do, right?

She returned to her bedroom, kicked off her dew-covered flip-flops, and plopped on her bed. Then she texted Ethan. Screw him especially. He shared as much blame as any of them. If he hadn't asked her to go for a walk, none of this would have happened. And now he had the nerve to snub her? Jerk.

You're right. We can never be. She texted. *We can never hurt Jacob like that.*

Immediately, Ethan replied.

Good.

His curt response stung. Jerk. She slipped her hand between her mattress and box spring and located a pack of matches. She scratched a match against the thin sandpapery strip and watched it glow in her dark room. Then she pressed the fiery tip into the soft naked skin inside her forearm. With her eyes closed, she felt her blood coursing in and out of the tiny welt, and the gentle thump, thump of her heartbeat. She had a plan to make things right. She opened her eyes and surveyed her room; in her mind it was a mess. Everything needed to be rearranged and reorganized. Her closet. Her bureau and half-built bookshelf. Shoes needed to be scrubbed. Windows washed. Woodwork polished. It was time to get to work.

In truth, there wasn't a speck of dirt or one item out of place.

JOURNAL ENTRY
THURSDAY, SEPTEMBER 15

I've been scanning the newspaper for more stuff about Ned. There's nothing. Going to Homecoming with Jacob. I hope that drives Ethan crazy.

No more to say.

Life sucks, except that Ernie laid three eggs.

CHAPTER 18

Piper didn't intend to eavesdrop, but the voices carried. Sipping ginger ale to soothe her upset stomach, she sat behind the locker room. Her Nazi Germany test was tomorrow, and the *Schindler's List* Spark Notes lay unopened on her lap.

"The season is off to a good start and I want nothing to tarnish our run." Piper recognized Mrs. Horn's syrupy, sweet articulation. How could Jacob be part of this woman? "I'm concerned." Mrs. Horn's voice dropped to a conspiratorial level.

"Except for the Concord scrimmage, we've won every game." The annoyance in Coach's voice was almost undetectable. "What're you so worried you?"

Mrs. Horn's voice grew even quieter, and Piper strained to listen. "You know how rumors get started. One thing leads to another and then it's a mess. I thought, perhaps, if you knew what was being said you could—" she paused. "Well, maybe you could monitor your behavior a bit."

With great care not to make any noise, Piper closed her book and leaned toward the voices.

"I don't know how this shit works. What are you saying?"

"There's chatter about the extra time you spend with the Roses. People say you're playing favorites. That you're only interested in helping Cooper and Noah get scholarships."

"The Rose boys are the best players on the team. They deserve every look and offer they've gotten. And what would anybody know about the conversations I'm having with college coaches? Lots of other players are getting looks. But those are private conversations I'm having with the kids and their parents. Like I did with you and Ethan."

"You haven't talked to us about Jacob."

"That's right." Coach softened. "I'm sorry, but there haven't been any colleges interested in Jacob."

"I know he's not at Ethan's level or the Roses', but I had hoped, perhaps, a smaller school might pursue him." The uncertainty in Mrs. Horn's voice made Piper wince.

"It's still early in the season. A lot will depend on how deep of a run we make in the district playoffs and what happens at States. Hell, if we win the whole thing, I believe I'll squeeze out a scholarship for every player."

"That's good to know. I'll spread the word."

Piper peeked around the edge of the brick wall and saw Coach's back and Mrs. Horn facing him. Coach moved to show the conversation was over. Mrs. Horn touched his arm, and he stopped.

"Yes?" he said.

"There's something else, too." Mrs. Horn avoided looking Coach in his eyes. "This is awkward to say, but there's chatter—"

Coach shook his head slightly. "What other prattle could there possibly be?"

"Perhaps you shouldn't be seen alone with Piper Rose. Like the other day when you dropped her at the clinic. Had somebody else seen that, it might have been interpreted differently."

"What the hell are you trying to say here?"

"I just I thought you should know the chitchat. It'd be terrible for something to get blown out of proportion. You know how the valley likes a good scandal."

"Gossip is called gossip because it's usually not the truth. It'd be best if you passed that message to Millington Valley. And tell them to sign their damn names to any letters they write."

Mrs. Horn laughed and clutched her arms across her chest. "It's just—"

"My mother always told me not to worry about gossip, but to pay close attention to the person delivering it."

Piper couldn't see Coach's expression, but she noticed how his body stiffened. He nodded a dismissal and went into the locker room, the door slapping behind him. Mrs. Horn flattened the front of her blue and peach Lilly Pulitzer tank dress, looked around, and then hurried to her silver BMW. Gosh, that woman was awful. Sometimes it was hard to believe Jacob was related to her, but it explained a lot about Ethan.

With the conversation over, Piper slid behind the wall. She slumped against the brick, wrapping her arms around her chest, forcing down a sick feeling. Her knees felt weak and her throat was thick. God. This was too much. Now people thought she was screwing around with Coach?

*

Still the September evenings grew cooler, and the soccer team ripped through the county games, winning by staggering margins.

They hammered Kutztown 5–1.

Annihilated Twin Valley 4–0.

And beat tougher Exeter 2–1.

The anticipation of the Concord rematch—the game that would set them up for a run in the district playoffs—was intense. The Millington County Eagle ran player profiles in the days leading up to the game.

Everything appeared to be perfect.

Cooper passed his driver's license test and continued his clandestine Bible reading and praying. It was seeping into his life as he began to quote religious passages to his family, his friends, and once, in practice.

Noah received his formal Penn State scholarship paperwork and publicly committed to play soccer for the Nittany Lions, posting #psu2022 with his picture on Instagram. It got 739 likes. His profile was the lead article on the sports page the day of the Millington-Concord game. Noah slept little, and dark circles formed under his eyes.

Ethan was MIA. Piper watched his Twitter and his Instagram, but he wasn't posting, and Jacob wasn't sharing any communication they might be having.

Jacob organized their senior project volunteering with Visiting Angels and startled Piper by manipulating things so that he was partnered with Wanda Walker, Ned's sister. Piper would go with him next week, though she didn't understand why he wanted to know Wanda. She wasn't sure she'd be able to look the woman in the eye without dissolving into a conscience-stricken mess.

To everyone around her, Piper appeared to be having a fabulous senior year. Homecoming was fast approaching, and to Piper's surprise, her mother had cut work and taken her on a special shopping trip to the King of Prussia Mall to find a dress. Her parents endorsed her decision not to dance every day after school in Philly, and they were delighted that she was supporting Noah and Cooper as the soccer team manager. Still, Piper trained non-stop at her local studio on the days she wasn't at the Rock School. She bargained with an unseen force to make Ned Walker better. Maybe helping Wanda would put motes of goodness into the air. Everything she was doing felt like delaying something inevitable, though she hadn't decided what that would be.

She kept her distance from Coach so that the good people of Millington Valley wouldn't get the wrong idea.

Even though she was trying to do everything right, she couldn't stop washing her hands, cleaning her room, and pressing hot match tips to her wrist.

JOURNAL ENTRY
SUNDAY, SEPTEMBER 18

My life is fucking wretched. Like my life and Noah's, and Cooper's, and Jacob's and Ethan's lives are ruined forever. I am so torn up inside. Literally, I'm sick. Noah can't sleep. Cooper's reading the Bible all the time. I NEED to clean my closet tonight, then wash the soles of my shoes, and reorganize my drawers. Everything is a mess.

Mrs. Horn is a gossipy bitch. Ethan is incommunicado. The Nazi Germany class is tough. I can't wait to get back to dance tomorrow. The fight with Brittany seems like nothing. I must make things better with her. And I've got to stay focused on the Tisch audition. I am trying to act normal. But I keep burning myself, which is NOT fucking normal at all. It's the only thing that gives me any relief. Honestly, I am about to blow.

If anybody's listening, please help.

CHAPTER 19

Wanda Walker opened her porch door and was momentarily surprised that Jacob was not alone. The huge blue Millington Valley sweatshirt Wanda wore dwarfed her tiny frame. Her white buttoned-down shirt peeked through the V-neck and her tan polyester pants were creased into perfect seams. Her gray hair was short and curly, teased into a perfectly sprayed helmet.

"I brought my friend. This is Piper." Jacob stepped across the threshold into Wanda's cozy, warm living room, and plopped on the sofa, dropping his book bag on the floor, totally at ease. A small fire crackled in the fireplace. "She's a whiz at setting up phones and stuff."

Wanda's green eyes twinkled and a mischievous grin spread across her face. "I am happy to meet your girlfriend. I recognize her from the soccer game." Wanda extended her little birdlike hand to Piper. "You sit at the scoreboard table."

"She's not my girlfriend," Jacob said, looking at Piper as if he wanted her to disagree, and when she didn't, he added, "Piper can help me set up your iPad and iPhone."

"Nice to meet you, Mrs. Walker." The air was too warm, almost suffocating. Piper's throat tightened and she quickly unbuttoned her coat. She couldn't believe she had agreed this would be a good senior service project.

"Please call me Wanda." She laughed and the tiniest blush colored her cheeks. "I've never been a Mrs."

"I like your hoodie," Piper said.

"Oh, this? Jacob got me it to show team spirit. I've worn it three days in a row since the cold front blew in. I hope fall isn't over yet." She gave herself a hug, rubbing her hands on her upper arms. "It's comfy." Pointing to the coffee table, she nodded. "All the computer gizmos are over there. I'm afraid to open the box. Excuse me a second. I'll be right back." She scurried down the hallway toward the powder room.

The brand-new electronic devices, the packaging still intact, were on the coffee table next to a tray of freshly baked cookies and Toasty Buns sticky cakes, along with a silver teakettle. Jacob motioned for Piper to sit. He picked up the kettle, pouring the steaming water over a teabag into a delicate teacup. After a few moments, he handed it to Piper.

"I don't know if I can stay here." Piper lifted the teacup, her hand shaking. "You're drinking tea?"

"It's cool. You'll see." Jacob rolled his eyes at the china saucer. "I'm full of surprises."

"Jacob and I always have tea for our meetings. I believe this is our fourth get together." Wanda leaned against the doorframe with a notepad in her hand. Her smile was brighter, her lips now painted a cheerful peach. The fire popped and crackled in the background.

Piper set her cup on the table and picked up an iPhone box. "Guess we better get started."

Wanda handed Jacob her tablet. "The Best Buy sales girl wrote down my cell phone number and email address so I wouldn't forget them. I got nervous because she was talking too fast. 'Swipe this. Input here.'"

Piper opened the box and powered on the device. They spent the next two hours teaching Wanda the ins and outs of a cell phone and Piper slowly relaxed. She set up Wanda's password, then showed her how to save their contact information, download apps (Instant Heart Rate, EyeReader, and Facebook), and schedule an event in the calendar (Jacob's next "meeting"). The last trick was walking Wanda through how to send and receive a text. Wanda filled her scratch pad with notes, arrows, and stick drawings. They ate the sweets and drank two pots of tea. Though Piper smiled, the heaviness wouldn't leave her. It was impossible to relax knowing what they had done to Ned. And what they had not done.

"One of the most important features of your phone is its ability to take pictures. Tap here." Jacob opened the camera icon. "Smile, Piper." He pressed the camera button. "See. The picture pops up right away."

Wanda chortled. "Oh, I love it. Let me try it!"

He handed the phone to Wanda.

"I want a picture of the two of you to remember this day. Wanda Walker a techie." She motioned for Jacob to sit next to Piper on the sofa. "Now squish together." Wanda pressed the phone against her cheek as if were a mechanical camera. "I can't see anything."

"Hold the phone away from your face." Piper wriggled under the weight of Jacob's arm.

"Frame the scene," Jacob said.

"Got it!" Wanda beamed. "I love this iThingy. Now, my picture goes in the sky, right?"

"Yes," Jacob laughed. "Your photographs are stored in your iCloud. If you ever lose your phone, you still have your pictures."

Her face radiated. "It's magic."

"We'll save the iPad for next time," Jacob said.

"Yes, yes." Wanda clapped. "You'll come back again, too, Piper?"

"I'd love to" she lied. What she really wanted to do was jump out of her skin she was so uncomfortable.

"We can order pizza from Four Sisters'." Wanda embraced Piper and then Jacob. "My head might explode, but I haven't had this much fun in a long time."

She straightened up and pulled down the sleeves of her bulky sweatshirt. "Since my brother has been in the hospital—well, I haven't felt like myself."

Piper and Jacob both froze at the mention of Ned. They waited for Wanda to continue, and as Piper slung Jacob's book bag over her shoulder, she noticed a framed photograph on the windowsill behind the couch. It was Ned as a young man. He wore a military uniform and a grave expression. Words slipped out of Piper's mouth before she could think if it was the right thing to do.

"I'm so sorry about your brother. It's horrible. Everybody's been talking about it." Her voice hitched and her heart beat a little faster. "Do you have any idea what happened?"

"I don't know, dear." Tears welled in Wanda's eyes as she snapped out of her reverie. "Nobody knows. Sheriff Mismo is out of theories. But maybe this is part of a larger plan." She sighed and slipped both hands into the hoodie's large front pocket. "Ned is very sick. He has Parkinson's from that Agent Orange in Vietnam. It was getting harder and harder to make him come home at night to sleep. I worried all the time. Maybe—well, maybe God figures it's time for Ned to go so that he won't suffer more."

Jacob flashed a knowing look at Piper and she flinched.

"His tremors were getting worse, and I would have had to put him in a nursing home soon." Wanda hugged herself again. "That would have sucked the life, the little joy he had, right out of him. He was an outdoorsman. Before the war, he fished and hunted all the time. He'd bring home fresh trout and I'd fry it up in butter." She seemed to drift into a long-ago memory. "Still, it chills me to think that he suffered. That he was by himself until that hunter found him. It was my duty to take care of him, and I feel like I failed him."

She shook her head and wiped the corners of her eyes. "Enough of this talk. You young people don't need to hear this."

Jacob reached for the doorknob. "Today was fun. You're coming to the game, right?"

"You bet. I'll be there with bells on—and my hoodie."

Piper stepped into the chilly evening, feeling lighter. Ned had been sick and that gave her some solace. Maybe the accident was part of a divine plan, and they were only pawns. Maybe. She wasn't sure she believed in any of that stuff. But maybe she should try.

"That was sort of weird in there, wasn't it?" Jacob pressed his key fob, and his truck's headlights flashed and horn beeped. "It helps me to be around Wanda and do things for her. The sorrow goes away for a bit. Does it make you feel a little better knowing Ned was, I mean is sick? That he's going to die no matter what?" Across the street, the fire company had changed the lettering in its illuminated sign to read: Beat Concord! Go Lynx! MVHS proud!

"Seeing Wanda . . . being in her house makes the nightmare pretty freaking real. But, yes, I'd be lying if I said it doesn't ease my mind knowing Ned was sick." For a moment, hope rose in Piper's chest. She saw her future. Maybe she needed to rethink her promises. Maybe it was best if Ned died. Maybe she would come back to see Wanda. Maybe.

Jacob motioned toward the kiosk. "Think we can win?"

"I do." Piper zipped her coat. "We need to."

Jacob exhaled, and his white, warm breath evaporated in the cold, and they climbed into his truck.

CHAPTER 20

"Pleeease stop texting." Piper held up her palm. "Pennsylvania is insane for issuing you a driver's license."

"I'm fine." Cooper handed her his phone and then clenched the steering wheel. "Better?"

"Much." Piper scrolled through the messages. "Noah texted. Coach wants to meet at Four Sisters' Pizza at 5. Says he's buying." She set Cooper's cell in the cup holder and it dinged again.

Dad's working in the garden. Says he's not cooking tonight. Mom's still at the clinic. Tell Piper to come too.

They arrived at Four Sisters' at 5:07 pm. Coach tapped his wristwatch as they approached the table. "You can't be late and dumb and get ahead in this world." He glared and then he threw his head back in a belly laugh, which made him cough.

"Sorry, sir." Cooper grabbed the chair next to Coach. "It's just that—"

"Save your excuses. We've got work to do." Coach tapped the clipboard on the table in front of him.

Piper sat across from Noah next to Coach. The roasting garlic smelled scrumptious, and she imagined the sugary burn of a real Coke. Four Sisters had a wood-fired stove, and their blistered sourdough crust made their pie famous throughout the valley and beyond. Noah flushed when he saw the drama club president, Mia Diaz, was their server. She wore her thick, wavy hair in two low pigtails and an apron around her tiny waist. Mia placed a pitcher of ice water on the table. "What can I get you?" she said as she retrieved her notepad from her pocket.

Coach ordered two pizzas, a carafe of Coke, and a beer. Mia leaned over to place three straws on the table and one long pigtail fell over her shoulder. It was then that Noah's neck turned a splotchy red.

Coach pulled the Camel pack from his shirt pocket.

"You know you can't smoke in here," Piper said as she noticed Noah watching Mia walk away.

"Quite a delight, eh?" Coach said. "Looking for a little Latin love?"

"Need a little drama in your life?" Cooper made air quotes around the word drama.

"Shut up." Noah took a big gulp from his cup, the dark circles under his eyes obvious in the restaurant's fluorescent light.

"She seems sweet." Piper flicked her napkin across her lap. "She certainly can sing." Noah shifted in his chair and the red deepened on his neck and fanned up his cheeks. Without saying a word, he poured two more cups and handed one to Cooper and the other to Piper.

"Ah, leave lover boy alone." Coach deposited the unlit smoke into the small yellow and white packet. "My guess is he's trying out for the play faster than you can say jack rabbit. He'll win a Tony, I'm sure."

Cooper laughed and snorted. Water spurted from his nose and he reached for a napkin. "You were checking her out at the quarry party, right?"

"Shut up, all of you," Noah said under his breath.

Ten minutes later, Mia returned, set a tray holder in the middle of the table, and then placed the piping hot pizza on top of it. "Here's the pepperoni. The meat-lovers should be about five minutes."

"Sounds good," Coach said and winked at Noah.

"Anything else I can get you?" Mia said.

"What's the musical going to be this year?" Noah said with a little too much alacrity.

"Mr. Franks picked *Bye Bye Birdie*. It's about a rock star in the 1950s who gets drafted." Mia fiddled with her apron pocket. "Like Elvis did. You know who Elvis is, right?"

"Sure, he was a famous boxer, right?" Noah blushed again.

"The music is great." Coach swigged his beer. "Jenny and I saw it in New York years ago."

"Noah wants to try out for the play," Cooper chimed in.

Noah kicked Cooper under the table and gave him a death stare.

"Really?" Mia said. "I think you'd be an impressive addition to the cast."

Piper bit her tongue to keep from laughing. Coach held back a grin too. Only Cooper allowed himself a full I-got-you-now smile, his eyes ablaze.

"He's been talking about wanting to get involved in the drama club," Piper added. Maybe this was just what Noah needed. A girl.

Mia blushed and blurted. "We could use more guys. I can text you with the audition dates if you'd like. It's really fun. At drama club we've talked about how to get people involved. What do you think?"

Noah took a breath. "That'd be cool."

They exchanged numbers. Good, Piper thought.

"Enjoy your pizza." A broad smile spread across Mia's face, then she turned and bounced back to the kitchen.

"I'm going to kill you guys," Noah said.

"You got her number, didn't you?" Coach said. "Hell, I believe we're all going to be going to the theater."

"Noah Rose—star of the soccer field and Millington Valley Stage," Piper said. "This might be the best meal of my life. You don't look too upset."

Noah smirked. "Guess not."

She cut the pizza along the pre-divided slices and took a piece. The hot-from-the-oven mozzarella cheese stretched and snapped and she caught it, twirling it around her finger. Everything felt nearly normal. Almost okay. It was oddly comforting to see Noah acting like a regular guy.

Coach pushed his plate away to make room for his clipboard. Piper finished her slice and excused herself to go to the restroom. In the mirror, she saw the bandage on her wrist and realized she had forgotten about it. She hadn't burned herself in three days—since she'd met Wanda Walker. She ran the tap until the water steamed, and then she ran through her hand-washing ritual—twice.

In the hallway outside the restroom, she inspected the community bulletin board. There was a small poster with a picture of a Lynx attacking a Tiger with a soccer ball and the game date. It read: *Millington vs Concord, Saturday! Let's teach the Tigers that the Lynx don't lose!* She snapped a picture of the poster with her cell to send a group text to the team. Then she made her way back to the table. Coach had fallen into his go-for-the-jugular send-a-message-to-the-league speech.

"About ready?" Piper asked Cooper. "I've got a bunch of homework and don't you have a chemistry test?"

"We're done." Coach pushed back from the table and grabbed the check. "I'll meet you guys outside." The door jingled and in walked Mrs. Horn, bee-lining to the takeout counter.

"I'll get the car." Cooper rolled his eyes and tiptoed out of the pizzeria, making goofy hand gestures behind Mrs. Horn's back.

Mrs. Horn turned around and scanned the café, her gaze landing on their table. She waved. "Hello, hello!" She walked toward them, the pizza box resting on her hip.

Coach pushed back in his chair, poised to make a quick getaway.

"Having a special pre-game strategy?" Mrs. Horn eyed the empty plates, pausing a second too long on Coach's beer bottle. "Jacob's in the car. Should I get him?"

"We were just leaving." Coach put two leftover pieces of pizza in a to-go box and handed it to Piper. "Take these for your parents."

"Your mom's working late again," Mrs. Horn said. "I suppose she doesn't have much time to cook for you guys."

Piper bristled. She was too well trained to say something rude, but she could narrow her eyes.

"We eat just fine," said Noah. "As you know our dad is the cook."

Mrs. Horn tensed, and Piper wanted to hug Noah on the spot.

Cooper was already in the Honda, with the AC blowing, and Meek Mill playing when Noah and Piper made it out of Four Sisters'. Piper waved at Jacob who was sitting in the driver's seat of his mother's BMW. That's the car he'd take to Homecoming. Piper slid into the front seat just as Sheriff Mismo turned the corner of the strip mall at the State Farm office. He gestured at them to stop and jogged toward their car. Piper bristled. Good god, was he coming for them?

"Big game coming up." Sheriff Mismo lingered beside Cooper's open window and nodded to Piper and then to Noah in the backseat. "Think you can beat Concord?"

"Plan to," Cooper said.

"I've been meaning to stop out at the farm again."

"Anything important?" Noah said.

"Not really. Just wondering if you guys know what involuntary manslaughter is?"

The three siblings didn't say a word, but Piper's heart jumped and she hoped her shock didn't show. Cooper turned down the radio.

Mismo leaned down and placed his big tan hands on the open window. "I didn't think so. So I'll explain. Sometimes it's called criminally negligent homicide. It's a crime in which the victim's death is unintended, but someone is responsible for it, nevertheless. Usually, a smart lawyer can argue for the defendant and not too much will happen if it was an unintended accident." He made air quotes when he said *unintended accident.* Piper's stomach lurched.

"But if the party—or parties—left the scene of such an accident, well, you've got yourself a real mess. And here's an interesting fact. It'd be the same charge for somebody who knew what happened to Ned Walker, if that person didn't tell me."

Cooper tapped the bass beat on the steering wheel and met Mismo square in the eye. With a confidence Piper didn't know he possessed, Cooper said, "Sheriff, we sure would tell you something if we knew something to tell."

Piper's mind reeled, hunting for something to add. Jacob was watching them from across the parking lot, and even at this distance Piper saw his face was ashen. Noah stared out the window, the sunlight catching in his chin hair, ignoring Mismo, which Piper thought wasn't a good move. The Four Sisters' door swung open, and Coach strolled out, Mrs. Horn at his heels.

"Hey, Tony," Coach called. "Giving my guys a pep talk?"

Sheriff Mismo straightened up and knocked on the door. "Something to think about, okay?"

"Sure thing," Cooper said. "See you, Coach," he called over Mismo's shoulder, shifting into reverse and backing up.

They couldn't get out of there fast enough. Piper felt scorched and cold at the same time. Cooper said, "Just–do–not–say–one–word." As if she could have spoken at all.

CHAPTER 21

The cicadas sang their incessant soft chant. Normally, Piper loved the first hint of dried leaves and the nippy dewiness in the autumn night air. *Good sleeping weather,* Mom was famous for saying. In the dusk, Dad wore his miner's hat, the light ablaze, and was hunched over a row of bush beans. Every once in a while his head bobbed over the top of the rose hedge. A frost would hit soon and he was in full harvest mode. The canning would be next. He lined their basement staircase shelves filled with colorful glass containers of stewed red tomatoes, yellow peppers, and pickled string beans.

Noah and Cooper played a fast game of soccer wall ball against the barn. One of them would shoot and then the other one had to one-touch it back to the wall. Again. And Again. As if they could pound the guilt out of their bodies and into the hundred-year-old limestone, and Piper understood this. They were hot and sweaty despite the nippy air.

Piper was on pins and needles as she studied on the porch, flipping through the *Schindler's List* Spark Notes in the dim lantern light. The test was tomorrow, but she couldn't concentrate. Every time she saw Sheriff Mismo, she became more convinced that he had put two and two together—that he knew they had something to do with Ned. My goodness, he practically handcuffed them in the parking lot.

Involuntary manslaughter.

She paged back to the beginning of her notes again. Then she gave up and tossed the book on the floor. She stood, then slid into a straddle and folded forward until her stomach pressed against the porch planks.

Turning her cheek to rest on the rough surface, she closed her eyes. Please, please heal Ned. Make him better. She needed Ned to be okay, to wake up, but not to remember anything.

A do-over, that was what she needed, a clean slate.

They were good kids; they knew better. They had even decided that if they'd found Ned they would have gotten him out of the quarry. Did that count for anything? They would never, ever run from responsibility again. Right? She could remember everything that happened. What she couldn't reconcile was why she didn't insist they go for help immediately. Hindsight was twenty-twenty. This was a mess they couldn't clean up.

She uncurled from the straddle and sat, her back against the chaise lounge. Running her index finger over the fresh tender match-tip blisters on the inside of her forearm, she closed her eyes again. Make this all go away. Help me end this. Then it hit her—what she should do. She went to the kitchen and retrieved the pizza box.

"I'm going to run this over to Mom," she called to her brothers and father as she crossed the yard to the driveway.

Dad popped up, his head beam shining, and said, "Tell my sweetie not to work too late."

She opened the car door and set the box on the passenger's seat. A rocketing soccer ball whacked the front side of the car as she swerved out of the driveway. Noah caught the rebound. He gave her a weak smile and then drop-kicked the ball back to Cooper.

She stopped at the Quick-Pick and bought a bottle of water and a Snickers bar to round out her mom's meal. Then before heading to town, she shot out route 663 toward the Manatawny Creek. At the red covered bridge, she pulled over, rolled down the window, and let her eyes adjust to the darkness. The moonlight shimmered on the stream and the water babbled and gurgled in the quiet. Their lives had been smooth and unblemished before Labor Day. Her heart thudded as if it were to burst through her ears. She knew. Knew in her core that any excuse they made was not okay. There was no way to justify leaving a man like they did Ned, even if they thought he was dead; one of them had shot him, and none of them had thought about him.

Manslaughter. Wasn't that just another word for murder?

Criminally negligent.

Leaving the scene.

Piper had to make it right. Do the decent thing. Her stomach clenched. She would tell Mom—tonight. Maybe her mother would be proud of her for being honest. In reality, Piper knew she would be crushed—disappointed beyond her wildest failures, and this squeezed Piper's heart. Dr. Amy Rose worked hard and was sometimes so busy it felt like neglect, but deep down Piper knew it was because her mother loved them and was trying to give them a good life. Then she thought about her brothers, and Jacob, and Ethan. If she told because she needed to, she would break her vow to them. Was it too late to correct their mistake? Would they go to jail? It would surely be the end of scholarships. Of Tisch. But that was the chance she was going to have to take. Because living like this was going to kill her. Swallowing hard, she took a deep breath. Mom would know what to do. She would be upset, but she would protect them, somehow make it all okay. Tonight, Piper would tell her mom. Better yet, right now. She'd go straight to her office, give her the pizza, and confess.

A large illuminated sign ruled over the Rose-Horn Medical Center parking lot. Piper remembered the day it had been installed, the day when Dr. Horn and her mother had officially opened their practice. Being the only girl out of the doctors' children, Piper was the kid they chose to cut the ribbon. The black and white newspaper clipping was in her scrapbook. Noah was on one side and Jacob on the other. Cooper squatted at her feet and Ethan stood behind her. Big smiles. Sloppy hair. Giant scissors.

She wiped her sweaty palms on her shirt and grabbed the pizza box, water, and candy pack. The State Farm storefront was dark and there weren't any cars parked in the glow of the H&R Block window. Her mother's vehicle would be in the back alley.

The office was locked. Piper found the kids' office key copy on her ring and opened the door. The lobby was dim and the examination hallway was dark. She placed the food on the receptionist's desk and started toward her mom's office at the back of the building, turning on her phone's flashlight.

As she turned the corner, she walked into a faint curtain of cigarette smoke. The florescent light from her mother's office cascaded into the empty corridor and she heard her mother speaking, probably on the phone with a patient. But the fumes—there was only one person she knew who smoked.

"I guess the clotting medicine isn't working too well," Coach said. "Your buddy, Doc Mayer, called me today."

"I spoke with him, too." Her mom spoke in her calm doctor's tone.

"And what'd he tell you?" A chair screeched across the floor. "He's holding back with me, eh?"

"It's not that. He wants to review the results of the other tests. Maybe order a few more."

"I've got five clots." Coach laughed and coughed at the same time. "One on my lung, Doc Amy. It's got me a bit fucking worried."

Nobody said anything for what felt like an eternity.

"Be straight with me, eh? Why the hell would I have these clots? I was afraid I was going to break the ultrasound machine. The technician, pretty redhead, got quiet real fast."

Piper strained to listen, placing her ear and hand against the wall. She thought she heard Coach inhale. Smoke swirled in the fallen light outside her mother's office door.

"Certain diseases mess with the body's ability to clot." There was a rustle of papers. "You're right, it's not normal."

"They've run a million tests. I don't need this shit right now. Just when things are going great—the season, Jenny's promotion, I landed two new battery customers. Hell, we're going to beat Concord—some crap like this pops up. Be straight with me, Amy."

"The body is a funny thing."

"But it's not nothing, eh?"

"Right." There was a pause. "By Wednesday, Doc Mayer will have the rest of the lab work back." She paused. "It's most likely something. I'm sorry, Chris."

"Well, fuck me."

Piper turned and tiptoed back to the receptionist's area. She jotted a quick note on the pizza box for her mom and then left as quickly as she had come.

Now was not the time to talk.

She went home and snuck up to her bedroom unnoticed.

It was all too much. Piper yanked the sheet, pulling it to her chin. Sleep. If she could fall asleep and forget everything for a few hours, maybe things would be fine. She had every intention of telling her mom. But overhearing about Coach's situation had shattered her bravery. Thank God this would be the last September she lived in this bedroom. Come New York, prison, or high water, she was getting out of this valley. The place was suffocating her. She opened her eyes. The tree branch from outside her room made a claw–like shadow on her wall. She went to the window and kneeled. The moon was full and small in the sky. The tender lesions on the inside of her wrist pulsed as she dug her fingernail into the small circular burns.

Stop. Make it stop. Ned. Coach. Mrs. Horn's rumors. Ethan. Everything.

JOURNAL ENTRY
SATURDAY, SEPTEMBER 23

Something is wrong with Coach. Like a serious, really vile sort of disease. Not a cold, but something more. I was going to tell Mom about Ned, but I chickened out when I overheard her talking with Coach. I wonder how long his diagnosis will be a secret.

Secrets. Secrets. Secrets. UGGGGGH!

I am forcing myself to go to Homecoming. I've got to pretend everything is "okay" until I can sort out this mess. It's like I am having a constant out-of-body experience—I'm watching this girl who wants to do the right thing, but who can't. I want to shake her!!!

I know I have to tell the truth. Otherwise, I'm going to crack. The big question is HOW?!?! I'm paralyzed.

Tisch is next week. I need to get my head straight.

Sorry, I can't write anymore.

CHAPTER 22

Five days later, after four self-directed, physically crushing dance sessions and zero words uttered to anybody about Ned, Piper was on the sideline after the Hamburg game, collecting stray water bottles and arranging the guys' duffle bags. Nothing had changed. Her stomach was an acidic jungle and her wrist had become an oozing mess. She had taken to wearing long sleeves all the time.

The team was sprawled on the grass in a sloppy ring around Coach on the far side of the soccer field near the pole vault pit—a spot no parent would accidentally wander near. His shadow stretched twenty feet behind him. He wore his dark sunglasses and faced the setting sun. An injured umbrella lay at his feet. Coach Marky was next to him, his arms crossed.

"3-0 is decent," Coach paused, "but we haven't had any actual competition. Those overgrown farm boys couldn't kick snow off a rope." He gestured at the Hamburg West bus idling in the parking lot across the campus.

Pulling the cooler, Piper made her way over to the group. The lounging guys, their faces still red and their jerseys wet with sweat, listened to Coach with their full attention. She tossed a fresh water bottle to Jacob, who was sitting slightly apart from the team. He smiled half-heartedly as she weaved through the guys.

"Send a message. Let the league know we are here to win—that there is a team as good—no, there's a team better than Concord. The Millington Valley fucking Lynx." Coach jabbed his clipboard. "Show no mercy. I want you pumped. Concord is going down. It's time for the mighty Lynx to crush those pansy Tigers."

Cooper snorted and laughed. "Coach, I love you!"

"For an old guy, you're kind of cool," Little Ryan said.

"Who you calling old?" Coach's expression was halfway between a smile and a dare, giving them his movie star stare.

The late afternoon was still, the air gentle and warm around the edges. Piper handed out the last of the water, saving a bottle for herself, and then she sat behind the players. The grass was dry and prickly. She ran her hand over a patch of clover and pinched off a white flower and then jerked back. There were dirty bugs and toxic pesticides, and she had left her hand sanitizer in the locker room. No go.

"We have a team member with a big day coming up, too." Coach nodded at her. "Make sure you wish Piper well. Next Friday, she's going to New York for her college dance audition." Everyone turned around. Embarrassed, Piper waved. There were murmurings of good luck and break a leg. She wiped her palms along her shorts.

Coach waited till it grew quiet, and then he raised his sunglasses and looked around the group. "There's something I've got to tell you."

A shiver passed through Piper and she forgot about the grime on her hands.

"You might have noticed a gimp in my walk." Coach motioned to Coach Marky who nodded encouragingly. "Turns out I have a blood clot on my shin. I have several, actually." Coach glanced at the goal and then refocused his attention on the team. "These clots, well, they're all over my body. Doc Rose and Doc Horn sent me for a million tests. And then I had to go see a couple specialists." He swallowed hard. "It turns out—"

A hawk squawked and flew overhead toward the mountain ridge. Everyone gazed skyward, including Coach. The bird was a deep brown bullet against a brilliant blue sky. Coach shifted, jamming his hands into the front pockets of his perfect white sweatpants. "The thing is, I have cancer." He spit out the words, looking half-surprised as if he couldn't believe what he'd said. "Small cell lung cancer."

Everyone was silent and still, the only sound the rev and rumble of the Hamburg West bus as it shifted into reverse and backed up. Across the field, parents and siblings scattered into their cars in the distance. Mr. Franks cranked the concession stand awning.

"It's in my spine, too," he said softly. "Tomorrow I start chemo in Philly. Coach Marky will run practice. I'll be back for the game Thursday and practice on Friday. And, of course, I'll be at the Concord game next Saturday." He squared his shoulders. "Don't look so scared."

Jacob stood, brushing the grass clipping from his shorts. "What can we do, Coach?"

Noah rose, too. "Yeah, what?"

"There is something you can do. Beat Concord." Coach pointed at Noah. "And you, my friend, need to try out for that damn play."

There were a few chuckles from the team.

"Screw cancer," Cooper chimed in. "And fuck Concord."

"Better watch your mouth or you're going to get me fired," Coach said and picked up his umbrella.

Noah tossed the car keys to Cooper as they walked toward the car. It wasn't until they were in the Honda, had descended the hill, and turned onto Main Street that Piper said anything.

"Should I Google small cell lung cancer?" She swiveled around to Noah in the back seat.

"No, it'll freak us out." Noah stared out the window. "WedMD will have him in the grave. Mom will tell us what's going on."

"He sure didn't give us any warning." Cooper slowed to the stop at Lake Road. "The part about it being in his spine doesn't sound too good. If feels like a punishment. Like we deserve this because of what—"

"Shut up," Noah said. "Coach's cancer has nothing to do with us."

"No, it doesn't," Piper said. They drove in silence for a mile or two. Now was as good of time as any to warn them she was going to confess. "Hey, I've been thinking about what Sheriff Mismo said when we saw him at Four Sisters." She forced her voice to stay calm, but her heart thumped. "I think he suspects and I think the longer we wait to tell him, or if he finds proof, the worse it will be. We come clean now, and I think Sheriff Mismo would work with us."

"No way. We're not saying anything. I could lose my scholarship. And Ethan could, too. Cooper is about to get an offer."

"But you're not sleeping," Piper said. "I'm not either. That's not normal. You can't tell me the whole Ned thing has nothing to do with it. Guys, it's never going to go away. It will always have happened."

"Shut up about it. We just have to beat Concord, then everything will be fine." Noah tapped the window. "Bury Concord. We have no choice."

"You're right," Cooper said. "We're going to war. For Coach. We have to do it for Coach."

"How does beating Concord have anything to do with Ned? It's not like you'll suddenly be forgiven. Your thinking is distorted. You're completely illogical," Piper said.

"Goddamnit, Piper!" Noah hit the seat. "Just keep your damn mouth shut. If we win, everything is going to be all right."

"You're nuts. Plus, Millington hasn't beat Concord in twenty years. Concord has a one hundred sixty-six game winning streak."

"Were you even at the scrimmage?" Cooper stepped on the gas. "We outplayed them."

"But they still won."

"We're better than them," Noah said. "Have some fucking faith."

"Okay, beat Concord," she said. "Then what?"

"Wait and see. Let us have our rematch. Don't force me to force you to keep your mouth shut."

"And how would you do that?" Piper turned around to face him.

"Let's just say . . ." Noah's eyes narrowed. "That you might want to keep a close eye on Ernie's eggs."

"You're an asshole, but I totally cannot believe you are that evil." Piper faced forward, her heart throbbing. That asshole better not go near their nest.

"Don't test me," Noah muttered, his voice less confident than his words.

"Don't say stupid shit like that, Noah," Cooper said. "Everybody needs to calm down. Let's play and then we'll figure it out. Homecoming is this weekend. Let's try to be nice to each other."

"Good God, you've gone soft with all that Bible reading," Noah said.

CHAPTER 23

"Mom's flight is delayed." Dad hung up the phone. "I'm to take lots of pictures on the porch, in front of the stone wall—"

"We know the routine." Cooper ran his hand through his wet hair. "Can you help me with this?" He tugged the loose tie at his neck. His shirt was untucked and the cuffs frayed on his wrinkled khakis.

"Where are the new pants Mom bought you?" Piper prepped at the kitchen table, applying a clear topcoat of nail polish. "She laid everything out for you before she left for the conference." She didn't want to go to Homecoming, but until she figured out what to do, she had to act normal. Noah incensed her with his threat to harm Ernie's eggs. Maybe he was a psychopath. That would explain a lot. She was sick of trying to be his friend, forever attempting to gain his acceptance. She was right and he was wrong.

"Can't find them," Cooper said.

"Check the hall closet." Piper blew on her nails.

They heard Noah on the staircase before they saw him. He came into the kitchen and nobody said a word. He wore a blue suit, a crisp white button-down shirt, and a pink tie—every piece of clothing carefully ironed. And most surprising of all, he'd shaved off his trademark Billy goat tuft.

"Well?" Noah lifted his palms.

Piper flashed a quick thumb's up.

"So handsome." Dad snapped a picture with his iPhone. "I hope the plane has Wi-Fi. Mom won't believe it unless she sees it." He texted the picture.

Cooper feigned a cough. "And I hope Mia's not allergic to Don Juan's cologne."

"What do you think?" Noah looked at Piper. *He wants to be friends again?*

"Maybe keep the windows open on your drive over." She smiled, all fake. "Try to blow off a little."

Noah flicked a piece of lint from his pant leg. "It's that bad?"

"You're fine," Dad said. "Go pick up Mia and hurry back. The Horns will be here to take pictures soon. Coach and Jennifer are stopping by too."

Cooper broke into song. "Mia and Noah sitting in a tree, K I S S I—"

Noah lunged at Cooper, wrapped his arm around his brother's head, and dug his knuckles into Cooper's scalp. "You say one stupid thing to Mia and I'll pound you."

"Stop with the noogies," Dad said. "Be civilized tonight. It's your last Homecoming together. Next year Noah and Piper will be at college." He pinched his eyes like he might cry. "Hold on a second, Noah." Dad went to the refrigerator and returned with a fresh cut, carefully wrapped bouquet from the rose garden. "For Mia."

Noah released Cooper and said, "Thanks." Then he slapped Cooper upside his head. "You're just jealous because Little Ryan's your date. Maybe next year you can take a real girl."

Cooper straightened up and tugged at the front of his shirt.

"Is Ryan coming for pictures?" Dad asked.

"He's not my date."

"Right. Of course," Dad said.

"Be back in a few minutes." Noah took the flower bundle and as he passed Piper he whispered, "I'm sorry. Truce?"

Piper twisted the nail polish cap. *Here's goes nothing.* It was rotten, but she would go to the dance and pretend to enjoy it—just to buy some time. In the foyer, she made one last check in the mirror. It didn't feel real. She'd dreamed about a night like this with Ethan, but that could never be and it would be best if she stopped thinking about him. Nevertheless, part of her hoped Mrs. Horn would send a photo of her and Jacob to Ethan.

Piper slowly twirled, the hem of her dress lifting. When they'd spotted it at Nordstrom's, she knew it was the one immediately. The fabric was a deep burgundy. The half sleeves rested off her shoulders. Her mother's string of pearls lay over her collarbone and she wore the matching stud earrings. The gown's top was fitted and tapered in to her waist and then flared way out at the hip in layers, falling an inch above the knee. Her hair was twisted into a bun and she'd pulled out wisps to frame her face. She moved to within an inch of her reflection. Her eyelashes were thick with black mascara and her lids glimmered with a silvery dusting, which made her irises appear almost cyan blue. She rubbed her lips together, blending in the pink gloss. The flesh-colored Band Aid taped across the soft skin of her inner wrist was almost invisible. To get through the night, she promised herself, she wouldn't think about Ned.

"They're here," Cooper shouted from the kitchen. Piper went to the dining-room window. Jacob's red truck led the caravan, followed by Dr. and Mrs. Horn's BMW, and then Mom's Pathfinder—the "good" car Noah had spent all afternoon washing and vacuuming. A couple seconds later, Coach's red Jeep turned onto the lane.

Piper, Cooper, and Dad headed to the porch. "How are you getting to the dance?" Piper asked Cooper.

"One of you guys."

"You're not going with us," Piper said. "And you're delusional if you think Noah is going to let you in the Pathfinder with him and Mia."

"Stop fussing. I'll give you a ride." Dad lifted his camera to his eye and took a shot of Noah opening the car door for Mia. "He's being such a gentleman. Mom would be proud."

"He's a dork," Cooper said.

Piper elbowed him. "Be nice." Still, it was good to hear her brothers throw barbs at each other like old times. Like they weren't hiding a deep, destructive secret.

Cooper stuffed his hands in his front pockets. "Let's party."

Piper watched Jacob check his rearview mirror, reach across the center console of his truck to grab something, and open the door. She descended the front steps to meet him and he smiled. "This is for you," he said and opened the clear plastic container to reveal a huge burgundy mum surrounded by sprigs of baby's breath. It matched her dress perfectly. He slipped it over her wrist, covering her bandage. "Hurt yourself?"

"Just some mosquito bites."

"These little flowers came with it. I think you're supposed to give them to me."

"It's called a boutonniere." Piper laughed and removed the small matching stem of mums from the container. She pinned it to his label, catching a whiff of their herby fragrance.

"You look—" Jacob stuttered, "—beautiful."

"Thanks. You don't look half bad either," Piper said, and she meant it. He wore a navy-blue blazer similar to Noah's, a starched white shirt, a burgundy tie, khakis, and bright white Converses. His curls were tamed and his face cleanly shaven. Sort of handsome.

"Picture, picture," Mrs. Horn said, barreling in. "Jacob, Piper, look here."

Snap. Click. Turn. Pose.

Noah introduced Mia to everyone. Coach and Jennifer remained in back, watching, smiling. Dad circled like a National Geographic photographer, having spotted a pack of endangered African cheetahs.

"Something smells around here." Cooper pinched his nose and stepped next to Mia for a group shot. "Farmer Fischer must have spread the pig shit."

With incredible stealth, Noah enveloped his hand around Cooper's bicep and squeezed. "I don't smell anything." He tightened his grip. "Really, Cooper, what smells?"

"Nothing. I must have an olfactory malfunction."

"Damn right you do."

They crammed together on the front steps for the last shot. The sun was setting and they had to squint a little, though the enormous oak trees that lined the lane blocked most of the blinding rays. The gentle breeze held a hint of sheared hay. It was the most normal Piper had felt in weeks. And it was good. This was what senior year was supposed to be like.

"Say cheese," Dad said.

And they did.

Click.

It was then that Piper and Coach locked eyes, and she saw his gaze was sad. Piper smiled and noticed Mrs. Horn watching. Great. She'd probably read something ridiculous into an innocent glance.

"Maybe you should try out, too," Mia said.

"For what?" Piper said, snapping out of her reverie.

"Bye Bye Birdie." Mia tucked her long black hair behind her ear. "You'd be great." Then she nudged Jacob. "We need more guys, too."

"I'll do it if Cooper does it," Jacob said.

"Sounds like good team bonding to me," Coach said and turned to Mia. "I told you I'd make an announcement at practice and I will this week. I'll get you guys."

"That would be fabulous." Mia clapped.

"Hey, I don't want too much competition," Noah said as he reached for Mia's hand.

They said their goodbyes and scattered into the cars. Coach and Jennifer told Dad they would drop Cooper at school and then come back and wait for Mom. They wanted to see the other players walk in with their dates. On the drive to the school, Piper and Jacob were quiet. Not awkwardly, but in the way of two friends who were used to each other's company, who had grown up together, who didn't need words. They followed Coach's red Jeep. Cooper was in the back seat, gesturing with animation. Every few minutes Piper checked the side mirror and saw Noah and Mia behind them in the Pathfinder.

The student council had lined the school driveway with hundreds of mums. Cornstalks were tied to the canopy poles. A huge sign made from brown poster paper bridged the transom over the front double doors. MVHS Homecoming, it read. On the doors themselves, hand-painted messages said, *Beat Concord! Catch a Tiger!* Jacob parked the truck and told Piper to hold on. He jumped out of the vehicle and ran around to open the door.

Inside, the hallway was dim, and music blared from the open gymnasium doors. Kids milled in groups by the trophy case, while others congregated at the concession stand. The guys were almost unrecognizable in suits or sports coats. The girls wore every type of dress and it was obvious they had spent the afternoon doing their hair and makeup.

They made their way to the ticket table and the first thing Piper noticed was a placard; the sign read: *Donations for Army Veteran Ned Walker's medical treatment.* An empty pretzel container stood next to it. Her heart sank, and she exchanged a knowing look with Jacob who dug into his wallet and dropped in two tens. Piper retrieved the twenty-dollar bill she kept in her phone case for emergencies and added it.

"Come on, let's check out the gym." Jacob walked toward the music and Mia and Noah. "Don't think about that tonight. Promise?"

"Okay," Piper said.

They paused at the entrance and watched the chaos inside. Cooper and Little Ryan were already in the middle of a mosh pit in front that DJ's had set up. They were thrashing and bumping. Sweat mixed with the musty, peppery perfume of the mums. They danced every fast song; when a slow ballad was played, Piper went to the bathroom or to get a drink. She didn't want to give Jacob the wrong idea, but he looked cute. At one point, Piper caught herself laughing, and it was such an unfamiliar and surprising action that she dug her fingernail into the Band Aid until the scab beneath split. Despicable.

"Time for the big announcement," the DJ said, and cut the music. The crowd quieted and parted toward the sides of the room. "Let everyone in the hall know I'm about to announce the court." Parents filled into the gym.

Piper watched the horde of people spotting Mom and Dad, the Horns, and Jennifer and Coach.

The DJ announced the court and then called Noah Rose as Homecoming King. Piper jumped to her feet. "Go Noah! Go Noah!" Cooper and Little Ryan joined her, hooting and hollering.

Noah went to the front of the gym, blushing, clearly mortified. He kept his gaze on Mia, who waved and smiled. Cooper and Ryan rammed through the throngs of people to stand with Piper.

"He's going to be impossible." Jacob wiped the sweat from his forehead. "We'll have to address him as King Noah."

"I'm not calling him anything but asshole." Cooper exploded in laughter.

"And our Homecoming queen is . . ." The DJ paused. "Drum roll, please." People stamped their feet and pounded the wooden bleachers.

"Piper Rose!"

Shocked, Piper walked to the front of the gym and slid next to Noah. Boy, this was weird—brother and sister—king and queen. Two fakes. A rhinestone tiara was placed on her head, and someone gave her a bouquet of red roses. The cameras flashed and Piper's stomach reeled. Noah motioned for Mia to come forward. Piper knew he thought it would be icky to dance with his sister and the feeling was mutual. Like puppets, side-by-side with their dates, they swayed in the center of the gymnasium impersonating ordinary kids.

*

The moon was bright, making the white cinderblocks of the fairground buildings glow against the blackness. On the gravel path, Piper found her high heels to be treacherous walking shoes. The din from the school parking lot across the street was abuzz as everyone schemed about where to go next.

"We thought it would be cool." Jacob stopped and plopped on a bench. "Pump you up for the Tisch audition."

"Whose idea was it?" Piper sat down, setting her wilted Homecoming bouquet in the space between them.

"Mine. And I talked Noah into helping me." Jacob plucked a stem from the bunch. "You haven't been yourself since—you know. I figured being Homecoming Queen would be good bump going into your audition. And well, Noah, just popular Noah . . . that's why he won."

In that moment, something shifted in Piper and she saw Jacob differently. He had orchestrated the win to make her feel better. And her psycho, self-centered brother was involved, too. Maybe she was being too hard on Noah. The stress was getting to all of them. And wow. Jacob looked good in a suit. She tapped a loose fist against her heart and then pointed at him. He smiled, his brown eyes soft and glowing. She set the roses by her feet and slid closer. "That was nice. Thank you."

He twirled the drooping stem between his hands and then handed it to her. "Anything for you."

She brought the flower to her nose and inhaled. "Maybe."

"What?"

"Maybe." She stared into his eyes, searching for a feeling, a spark. There was a tiny ember—something warm and bright. "Maybe we could . . ."

"Don't say something you might not mean. Please be sure first." He evened the front of his pant legs, and then he touched her wrist, his fingers brushing the Band-Aid. "I don't want to be your consolation prize."

She was quiet. Then she took a deep breath and shifted away from him. "I'm sorry. The excitement of the night is getting the best of me. I'm not thinking straight."

"That's what I imagined." His face was crestfallen.

But Piper wasn't sure.

Maybe there was something there.

CHAPTER 24

The newspaper was crumpled in Piper's dance bag. She had read it and reread. It was more in depth and much more incriminating that the one she had pasted in her journal. She knew it was coming. On their last Visiting Angels meeting, Wanda offhandedly mentioned that the Millington Eagle was going to interview her about her brother's unsolved shooting. Those few words were enough to ground Piper in reality. Who was she kidding? Hanging out with Wanda didn't erase her liability. Sometimes it made her feel worse. Last visit, Wanda's doting reached a new level. She made them fancy crust-less chicken curry sandwiches, brewed organic tea, and even took them on an impromptu antique trip to Stoudt's Black Angus where Wanda bought them each "a little treasure"—a set of 2000 Topps Premier League Player cards for Jacob and a 1927 vintage art deco print of a dancing girl for Piper. Wanda's kindnesses made Piper feel like a fraud. An imposter.

"This isn't the kind of town we live in. We care about each other. We take care of one another," Sheriff Mismo was quoted in the article. "This total disregard for another human being, well, this doesn't belong in our valley." It continued, saying Ned Walker was clinging to life, and that there had been a break in the case, and that Sheriff Mismo expected to make an arrest in the next few weeks. That he was determined to put the person responsible for this tragedy behind bars. The knot in Piper's stomach tightened. Did somebody know something? She wanted to untangle this gnarled ball of mistakes on her terms, but she sensed time was running out.

"He's bluffing," Noah said when they were finally out of their parents' earshot, in the privacy of the old Honda. "Nobody knows anything. Think about it, Piper. He's hoping to scare somebody into talking."

"Maybe we should tell Mismo what happened," Cooper said. "Maybe he'd go easier on us—"

"We made a vow. A promise. Now, because you're a little scared, you're going to forget about all that?" Noah's voice had a steely edge. "I can't believe you'd throw a teammate under the bus. Win as a team. Lose as a team. Remember that?"

"You're taking the whole team thing a little far. And what are you saying? Was it Jacob?" Piper said with disbelief. Jacob hated guns. He would be the last person Piper believed to be the shooter. A flashback of Jacob, blood–smeared and frantic, popped into her head. No. No. It couldn't be.

"I'm not saying that," Noah said.

Cooper whispered something under his breath.

"What?" Piper said.

"Jacob shot Ned."

"Shut the fuck up." Noah reached forward and nailed Cooper's shoulder. "We're all wrong. We all, equally, screwed up. Hell, you're the one who said we should bury Ned. So, yes, I think the team analogy works. We're only as strong as our weakest link. Piper, you and Jacob are kinks in this chain."

"If I could go back, I'd do things differently," Cooper flinched under Noah's grip. "And what if Little Ryan figured it out? He might have said something to Mismo. Whatever happened to honesty is the best policy? If we tell them the truth, maybe they'll understand that it was an accident."

"Relax. It's all going to work out."

"How?" Piper hit the dashboard. "How is this going to work out?"

"First, stay calm. Ethan says there's no way they can trace it back to us."

"Ethan? He's not even here." Piper exploded. "Plus, what the hell does he know? I am sick of us listening to Ethan. And what? How are we supposed to live the rest of our lives with this guilt hanging on our shoulders?"

"I agree with Piper. I'm not sure how much longer I can take it," Cooper said, and pulled off the side of the road.

"We're stuck." Noah sighed and leaned back, closing his eyes. "Could you really turn in Jacob?"

"It was only you and me with him. It would be our word against his. We could say that we went back to the car and when we returned Jacob had shot Ned. We had nothing to do with it."

"But that's a lie. You can't frame Jacob." Piper's voice caught.

"Damn Mom and Dad's whitewater rafting trip," Cooper said. "If we'd just gone back to the quarry and found him."

Noah hit the window. "Shit. Shit. Shit."

"So you agree? That this isn't working?" Piper turned around and glared at her brother.

Noah sighed. "Fuck no. But I don't know how to make it right. Like Dad says, 'Sometimes a problem needs time to sort itself out.' Let's wait."

"Brilliant plan," Cooper said. "Brilliant fucking strategy." He pulled onto the road, the tires spitting as he slammed on the gas pedal.

They rode the rest of the way to school in silence.

That afternoon, when her mother dropped her off on Broad Street in front of the Rock School, Piper motioned that she was going to Two Beans Coffee Shop and then slid behind the corner and hid. When she was certain her mother had driven away, she crossed the street to the bus stop and waited for the bus to take her north to Temple University. Ethan wasn't too hard to find. She had Googled the campus map to locate the soccer fields. The old Piper never would have skipped dance— especially the last training session before the Tisch audition, but the girl she used to be was long gone. This was the first step in taking control of the situation.

In the stadium stands, she watched the team practice unbeknownst to Ethan. She didn't want to feel anything for Ethan, but a physical itch flared in her chest, irksome and hot—a vexing bonfire compared to the tiny ember she'd felt with Jacob the other night.

"Hey," Piper said, and stepped out from underneath the stadium as the Temple team passed on their way to the locker room. Ethan was at the back of the gaggle. For a split second, he didn't recognize her.

"It's me," she said stupidly.

"What are you doing here?"

"My studio is just down the street. I thought I'd say hi."

He stepped into the shadows of the stands. "Really, why are you here?"

She couldn't stop herself. In a flood of tears, she told Ethan about the newspaper article, clumsily pulling it from her backpack and shoving it into his chest, and that she knew Jacob was the shooter, and that Jacob didn't know she knew. That Cooper and Noah were fighting. That his mother thought Coach was having an affair with her. That Coach was probably dying. That her feelings were hurt, that he didn't return her texts. That he seemed like he didn't even care what happened to them at home. That she was here with him when she should be practicing for the last time before her Tisch audition tomorrow. And she almost told him about how she couldn't tolerate it when something was out of line, or when she thought her hands were dirty, or how she kept a pack of matches under her bed and how the mosquito bites under the bandages were tiny, pulsing, sore third-degree burns.

Tears ran down her face and her cheeks burned. "I can't pretend that we aren't responsible for Ned." She held her head high and squared her shoulders. "I won't." She snuffled, and her body shook, but she stood strong. "My brothers might hate me. Maybe you will, too. But I'm done. The only way this will end is if we make it right. Can you honestly tell me you can live the rest of your life knowing what we did?"

"You're right." Ethan pulled her into his arms and hugged her. "We need to do something." He nuzzled her head.

"Just nail your audition tomorrow and I'll come home Saturday after my game. I've got to be back Sunday morning, but I want to be there for the Concord rematch, too. We'll meet with the guys and figure out what to do."

Piper wiped her face. "Promise?"

CHAPTER 25

Later that night Piper sat at their kitchen table, with her parents, Noah, and Cooper sharing a Four Sisters' takeout dinner of hoagies and potato chips—it wasn't quite a pre-soccer game meal. Nevertheless, Piper was touched they had gathered to eat together before her big day in New York. Dad gave a quick good luck speech and they clicked Solo cups. Then the conversation turned to Coach.

Dumping potato chips onto Cooper's paper plate, Mom said, "Right now he's jacked up on steroids and antihistamines. It's usually a couple days after the actual chemo treatment that a person feels crummy."

"Coach seemed fine." Cooper cut his hoagie into two pieces. "He wasn't any different from any other day."

"Still swearing up a storm," Noah said. "And he ran all our drills."

"How long till he's back to one hundred percent better?" Piper asked.

Mom's gaze met Piper's for a split second, and then she glanced away, reaching for the two-liter Coke bottle. "I need to make them some food." She topped off her Solo cup. "We'll invite them over for Sunday dinner and send a casserole home for the week."

"Our chicken noodle soup would be good." Dad crunched on a handful of chips. "They could heat it up in a jiffy. Next week he has chemo every day."

"That's a better idea." Mom flicked her braids over her shoulders.

"What do you think?" Noah said.

"About what?" Mom said.

"Piper asked how bad it is. Coach's cancer?" It was at this moment, a car turned down their lane, its headlights shining into the kitchen. Dread gushed through Piper, and she had a disorienting flash of déjà vu. She knew it was Sheriff Mismo. She went to the screen door and sure enough, his squad car neared the house. Busted. The cool night air touched her skin and she crossed her arms, rubbing the goose bumps that suddenly popped up. He had figured it out. They were done. They had a plan to make it right after Tisch. Not tonight.

Cooper stepped beside her. "Shit. This will not be good," he said under his breath. His face blanched.

"Who's there?" Dad and Mom said at the same time.

"It's Sheriff Mismo," Cooper said, his voice husky.

Piper and Cooper watched Sheriff Mismo park the cruiser and walk toward the house.

Mismo paused at the bottom step and met Piper's gaze. "Are your parents home?"

"Yes," Piper said through the screen in one quick breath. She opened the door, her heart ramming inside her chest. Noah set down his sandwich and froze like a man anticipating a bullet to the brain. The color drained from Cooper's face.

"Hello, Tony," Dad said and extended his hand. "Funny seeing you twice in one month. Rumors are going to start."

Mismo took off his hat and shook Dad's hand. "I'm here to chat with you about an incident that happened earlier this evening."

"Sure." Dad indicated to the chair by his right. "Have a seat."

At the sound of earlier this evening, Piper let herself breathe. Mismo wasn't here about Ned. But what?

Mismo leveled his gaze on Cooper. "Have you told your parents?"

"No, sir, I haven't."

Dad swatted his hand toward Noah and Piper. "Don't you guys have homework?"

Piper was never so happy to be told to get lost. She grabbed her book bag and quickly retreated to her room. A minute later, she heard Noah's thud on the staircase, his door open and close, and then the heavy base of his rap music.

Cooper. Cooper. What could he have done?

She locked her door and then collected her Arch Genie from underneath her bed, slipped her foot into it, set her stopwatch for five minutes, and stretched her right foot. The alarm sounded and she switched feet. As she lay on her bed, the physical panic dissipated, which was good, because she needed to focus. That meant clearing her conscious. Waiting until Ethan got home wouldn't help her with tomorrow's audition. She couldn't do her best with this secret weighing her down. Noah would kill her and Ethan wouldn't be happy about it, but on the drive to New York she would talk to her Mom and tell her what happened. She needed a clear head before she stepped on the Tisch stage.

CHAPTER 26

Her mother appeared not to have slept the entire night. Her eyes were bloodshot and her hair was pulled into one tight plait. They had risen at 5:30 am to a steady, hard rain.

"With the roads so slick, there must be an accident up ahead. Someone was probably texting, hydroplaned, and crashed." Mom adjusted the rearview mirror. "I just can't believe your brother. How many times have we talked to you about drugs?"

"Pot's not a real drug." Piper checked the time on her cell phone, willing the traffic to move. They'd been stuck on the New Jersey turnpike for two hours. "It's legal is some states." She understood Cooper's need to calm his nerves. Cars zoomed by on the other side of the highway.

"Yes, it's a drug—a gateway drug. Even if it were legal in Pennsylvania, Cooper is still under age."

"It's not like he's shooting heroin."

"Really, Piper?" Her mother gripped the steering wheel, her fingers pressing in the soft leather. "I don't need you making light of this, too. It's serious. I wish Sheriff Mismo and Coach hadn't agreed to let Cooper's four game suspension start after the Concord match. How is he going to learn? Plus, he's corrupting under-classmen. Terrible."

Mom wasn't talking about anything other than Cooper's marijuana bust. Several times Piper tried to broach the subject only to be cut off. Coach had discovered Cooper and Little Ryan after practice in the fairgrounds hidden on the amphitheater steps, stoking a joint, a half-full zip-lock bag on the cement floor between them. Cooper pleaded with Coach to keep the episode secret, but Coach called Sheriff Mismo and negotiated a four-game suspension that would start after the Concord rematch, along with twenty-five hours of community service, as restitution. There would be no formal charges. But if Cooper got caught again, all bets were off. If Mom was freaking out about a little doobie, there was no way she could handle the news that her kids were almost-murderers. Ethan and Noah were right.

For now—silence.

"Cooper has a lot of nerve being mad at Coach. He's the one who was stupid enough to smoke pot, and doubly stupid enough to get caught." Mom hit the steering wheel. "Damn it! Move."

Piper checked the time again. The cars in front were at a dead standstill, the rain pelting their roofs and bouncing skyward. "We're not going to make it, are we?" She bit her lip, trying not to cry. Now this. She had worked too hard and too long to miss this audition. They couldn't be late. She needed enough time to warm up.

"Google an alternate route," her mom said.

"My check-in time is in twenty minutes." Piper's hands were clammy and her stomach roiled. They had made it to the mouth of the Holland Tunnel, the toll booth just ahead. The day was a disaster. Piper hoped the light blue ribbon Madame Sylvie had given her, tucked inside her leotard, would give her luck. She needed it.

"You'll have to go in by yourself. I'll drop you at the front of the building and then find a parking spot. I might be a couple minutes late for the parents' tour, but that's okay." She put her hand on Piper's thigh. "Relax. You deserve this. You're going to do great." A horn blared and her mother stepped on the gas. They got through the tunnel in a flash, pulling into a flurry of wet Wall Street traffic.

Thirty minutes later, after a frantic registration check-in, and a quick change in the dressing room, Piper stretched on a bench in the hallway, listening for her number: 237. Her phone sat face-up next to her. Bending forward, she told herself: Do not look at the other dancers. Stay focused. You made it. Everything is okay. Her phone vibrated. It was probably her mother, reporting on the parking situation. She reached for her cell. Number Unknown. The anonymous message read:

Take some advice . . .

Piper froze. Then a second text popped up.

Secrets are safer.

Piper's heart hurtled and her fingers fumbled as she typed. *Who is this?*

The reply was immediate: *A friend. Good luck today.*

And then a moment later: *Remember: secrets are safer, P.*

"237, you're on deck," a woman shouted. "Let's go!"

With jittery hands, Piper shoved her phone into her dance bag, rammed it under the bench, and inhaled. Calm down. Do not think about that text right now. Focus.

"237, come this way." The woman motioned to Piper. Despite her racing heart and wobbly legs, Piper clasped her clammy palms together and followed the woman down the corridor.

At stage right, slightly behind the heavy velour curtain, Piper bounced from foot to foot and slid her finger underneath the Band Aid on her wrist. Jabbing the crusty wound with her fingernail, she picked the scab, ripping it away from her skin. A graduate student with a clipboard in hand motioned Piper to move onto the stage as an invisible voice called, "Next," from the dark empty theater.

Piper stepped onto the stage and into the halo of the spotlight. She walked to the center and slid into fifth position.

"Your name?"

"Piper Rose." Her heart pounded.

"Your high school and applicant number?"

"Millington Valley High School. Number 237." She took a deep breath and closed her eyes, sinking into the moment, collecting her energy and intention.

"You'll perform your solo and then exit stage left. Decisions will be sent in the next month."

Tchaikovsky's *Song of the Swans* filled the auditorium.

Piper opened her eyes and smiled her best smile. And then froze.

The music continued.

"Cut," the anonymous voice said. "Let's try again. Music."

For the second time, Tchaikovsky reverberated, thundering over and around her, but all she could do was hold fifth position and smile. Her mind shouted:

Move.

Turn.

Lift.

Dance.

Piper couldn't stir. It was like a movie reel looped on repeat, whipping through her brain. Ned convulsing. His blood spilling out of his gut. Cooper and Jacob on their knees, their hands fouled in red. Their shirts soiled and stained. She squeezed her eyes shut. Secrets are safer.

The music stopped again. "Miss Piper Rose?" the voice said. "Do you have an audition piece prepared?"

Her throat tightened and she felt dizzy. Her hands trembled and she stuttered, "I'm . . . I—"

"Miss?"

The room closed in on her. Ned's green eyes. His dank breath hot on her cheek. A pain shot through her chest and then her body went numb, but still she couldn't begin her routine. Then she felt a gentle hand on her back, pushing her. "Right this way," a kind voice said. The grad student guided her to the opposite side of the stage. It was as if she watched herself exit the drama. She was somewhere else, not a part of this world, this day, this audition. She had slipped away and wasn't sure how to find her way back. The raw burns on her wrist thumped.

The grad student located her mother. Piper refused to speak. It wasn't until they were back in the car, heading toward Pennsylvania that she wept. She wept for the night at the quarry, for Ned, for the audition she just bombed, for everything that might have been, and for everything she couldn't tell her mother. The miles passed. Mountains. Double-yellow lines. More tears. Mom knew not to pry.

Piper blew her nose and wiped her eyes, and she calmed down enough to check her phone. She looked at the unidentified text again. A friend? Her brother was a certifiable dick. Then she scrolled through Twitter, SnapChat, and Instagram. Nothing registered. The blur of smiling faces meant nothing. It was all fake. She checked the MVHS student portal.

Her grade for her *Schindler's List* essay was posted: C. Her first ever. She was average.

There was nothing special about Piper Rose. Nothing at all. Her eyes teared as they pulled onto Rt 663, and then rain fell again, as if the valley wept with her.

**JOURNAL ENTRY
SUNDAY, OCTOBER 1**

I fucked up Tisch and I deserved it. Goodnight. I want to sleep for a year.

CHAPTER 27

The next morning Piper woke with a stuffy nose, puffy eyes, and two fresh match-tip burns on her wrist. She rolled onto her side and pulled her covers over her head. Yesterday was a dream—something that happened long ago to someone else—a nightmare, really. She wouldn't think about it for now. For twenty-four hours she would allow herself a reprieve and then come clean. She had to do it; otherwise she would lose her mind. But first there was a game to play.

Tonight was redemption time: Millington Valley versus Concord, take two. Kick-off was at seven o'clock, under the lights on George Field in Reading. Despite Piper's unstable state of mind, she was looking forward to the game. To beat Concord would be monumental. For Noah. Cooper. Jacob. Coach. Deep in her bones, she sensed they could do it, and that somehow the win would turn things in the right direction. Their path would become clearer.

There was a hard knocking on her door.

Noah pushed the door open gently. "Can I come in?"

"I guess it doesn't matter what I say." Piper rolled over to face him.

He plopped on the side of the bed. "Mom said you had a rough day yesterday."

"You didn't help matters." Piper yawned.

"What?"

"That nasty text. Don't play dumb."

"I don't know what you're talking about."

Piper yanked her phone from the charger. "That's not from you?"

"No, I swear on Grandmom Rose's life." Noah's face paled. "It wasn't me."

"Then who was it from?"

"I don't know, but it wasn't me, I promise. I'm not that much of a dick."

"I don't believe you."

He looked away for a second. "Mom said it was bad."

"That would be an understatement. I choked. Completely crashed and burned. Totally freaked. And don't say anything that's going to piss me off."

"Who, me?" He squeezed her foot through the blanket. "Actually, it's reassuring to see you screw up once in a while. I can't depend on Cooper to be a constant diversion for me." He chuckled despite his tired, bloodshot eyes. "Though he does a pretty good job."

"That's comforting."

"Talk about a fuck up. After tonight, he can't play for two weeks. Coach isn't even going to let him practice. That's just what he needs: time to sit around and think. He's about to crack as it is."

"What's that stupid thing Dad's says? You reap what you sow?" Immediately, she wanted to take the words back. They'd flung some nasty seeds. Smoking a joint was the least of them.

"Something like that." Noah shifted and crossed his legs. "I want to crush Concord. It's weird, but I have this hunch that if we win, things will get better."

"I think you're making excuses, putting off something you don't want to do. It's always, wait until this or wait until that. At some point, we just have to do something." Piper kicked off the blanket. "You don't look like you slept much last night."

"It's there all the time—"

Piper scooted up and leaned against the headboard. "As soon as I close my eyes, I see Ned. I smell his breath. I feel his blood. Sometimes I feel I'm losing it. I freaked out at the audition. It was like the universe wouldn't let me dance."

"Look, let's get through the game. Crush those mothers. Ethan's coming home and we have to figure out what to do." Noah stood and leaned against the wall, quiet for a moment. "This cancer stuff with

Coach stinks. There hasn't been time to nail Mom down. Did she say anything to you on the drive yesterday?"

"No. We were late, then lost. On the way home, I was a basket case."

"That's why I came in here—to say I'm sorry. I know how much you wanted Tisch. It sucks."

She twirled a piece of hair around her index finger. Noah's uncharacteristic kindness was a surprise. Maybe he hadn't sent the text. But then who? "Thanks. Let's not think about it today. Let's Beat Concord and worry later."

"Breakfast is calling." Noah went to the door. "Put on your happy face. You will not believe this, but I got the part of the mayor in *Bye Bye Birdie*. We'll all in it: Cooper, Jacob, and Little Ryan."

"Wow, you must be in love."

"Maybe."

The stands were packed at George Field by 6:30. Huge stadium lights cast a silvery white aurora in the early evening, and the breeze was cool enough for a jacket or sweatshirt. Millington Valley's pep band occupied the first few rows of the bleachers. The student section filled in the stands behind them, creating a sea of royal blue and white. The crowd churned as the MV troupe played *Louie Louie* followed by *Shout!* Mr. Franks held court on the lowest bleacher, conducting the musicians, his hands flying with confidence and determination. The MV cheerleaders bounced and jumped. One girl ran and flew into a series of ten handsprings, eliciting a rabid roar from the crowd.

There was a clear demarcation between the MV fans and the Concord supporters at the midfield line as the primary colors of the supporters turned from blue to red. The Concord cheerleaders, their ruby skirts swinging, shouted and flipped with equal enthusiasm, but Concord didn't have a band, so for a spell—that magical-anything-can-happen-time before the first kick—it felt like Millington Valley had the advantage.

The funnel cake truck parked by the concession stand wafted the scent of fried dough and cinnamon. Little kids, dressed in both blue and red, ran around the space behind the chain-link fence near the soccer field, trying to catch the attention of their favorite players.

Piper had the best seat in the house. On the far side of the field, facing the bleachers, she occupied one of the two official chairs designated for Millington Valley at the score table. Principal Unger was next to her. On the other side of the principal was Tom Rago, the sports reporter for the *Millington Eagle*. Their Concord counterparts hunkered at the other end of the table. The adults made small talk. Her parents, the Horns, Wanda Walker and Mia were seated directly across the field at the fifty-yard line. Ethan had shown up like he promised, and with his former MVHS star status in check, he had an honorary spot on the MV bench.

The guys were jacked up on the bus ride through the valley and into Reading. Even Coach was hysterically confident. He'd plugged his iPhone into Little Ryan's speakers and blared that old Queen song *We Will Rock You* throughout the bus. Standing up, he danced and gyrated, whipping the team into a frenzy. Coach Marky was subdued in his regular seat, watching the road, ignoring the antics of his boss. When they had hit the George Field parking lot, the guys exploded out of the bus, chest pumping and thrashing, prepped to slam the field.

Now, though, they had settled. Coach and Coach Marky were equally composed, directing the boys with serious commands, running them through the pre-game routine, ignoring the commotion of the stadium, focusing on one thing—victory.

It began.

The National Anthem. The American flag flapping gently in the night.

A full moon.

The starting lineup. Noah. Cooper. Little Ryan. Jacob.

A coin toss.

Bright faces.

Kick-off.

At half, 0-0.

Sweat.

A slide tackle.

Doc Horn cursing the ref.

Direct kick.

Grass stains. White shorts.

Turn and go.

More sweat.

Some Blood.

Mud.

The ball in the back of the net.

1–0, Concord.

A long throw in.

Take it byline.

The roar of the crowd.

An elbow in the back.

Injury time.

A prayer.

The thump and thud of a hundred broken hearts.

Losers. Again.

A silent bus ride home.

Piper was still waiting in the car an hour after they arrived at Millington Valley High School. No one had emerged from the locker room. It was almost eleven o'clock. She texted her mom.

Still here.

A quick reply came back: *Take your time. They're disappointed. It might be a while.*

She didn't want to see her brothers, anyway. Just one more shitty piece of life—losing to Concord again. She turned off the car and got out. Pausing at the locker room door, she pressed her ear against it, but couldn't hear much. She sent a group text to Noah and Cooper. They had all agreed to meet after the game to discuss the Ned situation. At this rate, it would be dawn before they rendezvoused. Where was Ethan anyway? It would have been nice to steal a few minutes with him alone— to reassure him she hadn't gone completely batty.

She texted Noah and Cooper. *Going for a walk. Text me when you're done.* She rounded the front of the school. The main parking lot was eerie, the overhead lights dropping puddles of light on the empty black asphalt. She passed under the bus canopy, crossed the road into the fairgrounds, and climbed the split-rail fence, and hopped over to the other side. The main thoroughfare dipped and sloped downward as she wandered deeper into the fairgrounds. The gravel path was lined with trees and a lamppost every twenty yards, most of them with burned out bulbs.

When they were in middle school, they used to dare each other to run through the fairgrounds alone. In those days they already knew about Ned, the village vagrant. Fear that they might encounter him was thrilling.

Now he was the central focus of their lives.

There was a bench next to the amphitheater, and Piper lay down on it. She reached her hands overhead, her coat sleeves pulling up. Her left wrist was covered with a bandage. She lifted her right leg into the air and pulled it to her chest, stretching her hamstring. It was a bright night, and the trees cast shadows. A gentle breeze blew, and Piper inhaled the cool, damp autumn air.

A wave of exhaustion swept through her, and she closed her eyes. Yesterday had been a horrible day. And the night at the quarry had been the worst few hours of her existence. It was unbelievable that so much awful stuff could happen in such a compressed time period. Bad things came in threes. So, what was next? She had worked so hard and come so close to her dreams. It was all for naught. She wanted another chance, a do-over. Two do-overs. Why was it every time she was ready to do the right thing, she cracked?

And on top of all that, they had lost to Concord. Again.

She tried to clear her mind, breathing deeply, picturing blackness—a void in which none of this chaos existed. The welcome pull of sleep tugged at her consciousness, and she let herself fall toward it. She felt the tiny thump, thump of blood beating against the raw welts on her wrists.

There was a hand on her shoulder. "Piper?"

She jumped up.

"Sorry to startle you." Coach held an unlit cigarette between his lips. "You've given us a bit of a scare."

"Why? What's wrong?"

He tapped his watch. "It's two-thirty in the morning. Half the town is in a tizzy, looking for you."

"Oh my God, I must have fallen asleep."

"Noah and Cooper took off in the car to find you. Your parents are frantic. Come on, I'll drive you home."

Piper rubbed her eyes and pulled out her phone. Sure enough, there were a bunch of texts. Mom. Dad. Noah. Cooper. Jacob. Even Ethan. Their strategic, secret planning meeting was not happening tonight.

Sorry, I fell asleep in the fairgrounds. Coach will bring me home. Next time, don't keep me waiting so long. ;-) she typed and sent.

They walked toward the school. Piper wrapped her arms around her stomach as the air had turned colder. "Sorry about the loss," she said, kicking the stones in the walkway. "We played hard. It seemed even."

"Concord got lucky tonight. It sucks. Your brothers are pretty down about it. I am, too. Honestly, it's not been one of my better weeks."

"It's been a few bad days. I guess you heard I bombed my audition."

"Yup." He tapped the unlit cigarette against his forearm and then slipped it back into his mouth. "Trying to quit. Figure it's not too good to smoke when you have lung cancer."

Piper chuckled. "Sorry. I know it's not something to joke about." As they crested the hill, Piper froze.

"What's going on?" she said.

"I told you, everybody was hunting for Piper Rose. When Noah couldn't find you and you didn't respond to his texts, he called 911."

In the school parking lot there were two police cruisers, their sirens silently flashing, an ambulance, a fire truck and a dozen cars. A group of people milled around Sheriff Mismo. He was talking, but he was too far away for Piper to hear what he said. Still, she knew he was giving instructions about her. And this is what broke her. In the darkness, shielded by the Arts and Crafts building, Piper's knees buckled and she fell to the ground, her knees digging into small sharp stones. She sucked in air and exhaled in a rattling gust.

"Piper, it's okay." Coach's hand rested on her back. "Calm down. Nothing's happened. You're fine."

She pressed her knuckles into her eyes, trying to make the tears stop.

Coach lifted her up and pulled her into his arms.

Piper heaved against his chest. "I'm sorry. It's been a terrible week. I wanted Tisch so much." She hiccupped and he patted her back. "And then the loss. And there's something else." She grasped Coach's arm. She smelled yesterday's smoke on his jacket. "Coach," she said, "I need to tell someone."

There was a cough and then a flashlight beam. Mrs. Horn turned the corner. For a moment, time slowed, and Coach and Piper froze like deer in headlights. Even in the dark, Piper saw Mrs. Horn's body language change. The woman's accusatory energy hissed through the night, stinging Piper. Coach felt it too and stepped aside.

"Piper! Piper!" Mrs. Horn jogged across the path, her heft jiggling. She gave Coach a death stare.

"She'd fallen asleep on a bench," Coach said.

"Are you okay, Piper?" Mrs. Horn stepped between Piper and Coach.

"I'm fine." Piper wiped her eyes and sniffed.

Mrs. Horn hooked her arm in Piper's. "Thank God I found you." She pulled Piper along, not looking back.

CHAPTER 28

It was after 3 am when Piper slipped into bed. The quiet thump of bass in Noah's music echoed. Wanda's ballet dancer print hung above her vanity mirror and Piper stared at it until her lids grew heavy. Her phone buzzed and she opened her eyes. Ethan's group text read:

Glad you're okay, P.

Then, *Guys, I've got to be back at Temple by 8 am. Read and then delete. You know what I'm saying. Keep quiet.*

There were three links to Philadelphia Inquirer stories about hit-and-run accidents. Piper clicked on each link, her anxiety increasing the more she read. What those people had done was too much like what they had done. Someone was injured and abandoned. It was a felony to do that. It made an accident a crime for sure. There would be no mercy.

Jail time. Fines. No college. No scholarships. No future. No getting out of the valley.

Okay, Noah texted. Followed by a *Confirmed* from Jacob. And fifteen minutes later, Cooper's *K* pinged.

P? Ethan texted.

How was it possible to love and hate someone at the same time? One second Ethan acted like he cared about her, the next moment he vanished. Right now, he wasn't too attractive, and though she despised him for dodging the reality of their situation yet again, she had to admit he was most likely correct. They had to hope their secret would die with Ned. Too much time had passed for them to speak up. Piper wished an alternative would magically appear. With deep hesitation, she sent the thumb's up emoji.

Now DELETE, Ethan replied.

Piper pressed the little X.

Would you like to delete this conversation? You can't undo this action.

No, she sure wasn't sure. But she'd made a promise, and she was out of options. She hit the Delete box.

Then she reached under her mattress and pulled out her journal and the matches. She opened her diary to the last page and reinserted Madame Rosemary's blue ribbon into the crease. Some luck it had brought her. Snapping shut the book, she traced the embossed letters on the front cover. To write a single sentence would be impossible.

The pack of matches had small printing at the bottom that read *Keep Away From Children*. Was that her? She felt like a helpless child. Opening the matchbook cover, she brought the tiny sticks to her nose and inhaled. Sulfur. She pulled off her Band-Aid and studied the red crusting scabs on her wrist. The letter she was making was taking shape. She ripped a match from the pack and struck it. A quick flame popped and crackled. She watched it burn, the flare turning from orange to a light peach ringed in blue. Then she tipped it toward her wrist and slowly, so that she didn't rush the sting, pressed it into her skin. She repeated the sequence three more times.

When she was done, she hid her journal and the matches back under her mattress and crept to the second-floor bathroom, flicked on the faucet, and retched in the toilet. Sleep didn't come until the dawn seeped through the sides of her window shades. Eight hours later, as she ate breakfast at the kitchen table, nibbling on a dry piece of toast, her mother made an announcement.

"Executive decision. No dance for the next two weeks." Mom stirred the chicken soup (her parents' this-will-make-anything-better recipe) on the stovetop. "You scared me to death last night. You're under too much stress. I know you're upset about Tisch, but you haven't been yourself lately, even before the audition."

"Mom's right," Dad said, dropping a handful of chopped parsley into the pot. "A brief break will be good for you. This isn't the end of the world. Let's regroup."

If only they knew, Piper thought and attempted to finish the toast.

*

The first two weeks of October, Piper didn't go to Philadelphia, didn't dance, didn't stretch, and didn't work on her arch. Instead, she wore sneakers every day, let her hair hang loose, and ate whatever she wanted. In the afternoons, she helped with the soccer team and nested in the cushy foam of the pole vault pit, pretending to do her homework or to read a book. Or sometimes, she'd sit on the pond bank and watch Bert and Ernie, forcing her mind to go blank, thinking only about the three cygnets that would be here soon. The less she did, the less she felt like doing. It took too much mental energy to keep her thoughts off Ned.

Her shame had sharpened into a clear, hard diamond that pierced every aspect of her life. The more she replayed what had happened in New York, the more she believed her failure at the Tisch audition was exactly what she deserved. Even if she hadn't intended to freeze—it had been as if she turned to ice or stone—her focus had been on her malfeasance and not on dancing. She wished they could talk about it—Noah, Cooper, Jacob, and Ethan. But an invisible, impenetrable veneer had formed around them; the subject was completely off limits. The longer they went without speaking, the thicker the barrier grew. It left Piper alone with her guilt and contrition and terrible ambivalence.

On her own, she considered what to do, over and over. She had taken a vow with the guys, but she had to tend to her own soul. She was starting to believe that there was a Right Thing To Do, and that it was bigger than friendship and love and promises. If she confessed, then she was sure to get in a lot of trouble, and it would mean admitting the guys' part in it. Cooper was a juvenile. And she might be referred to the juvenile justice system, too, because she was only seventeen. Noah, though, had turned eighteen the day after it happened. So looking back, would the law say he was the boy of that last day, or the man of the next? Certainly, his silence was something he kept now. Poor Jacob had pulled the trigger. He was still a minor until November, so maybe that would help. That left Ethan. He was nineteen—definitely an adult.

It did no good to think about all the ifs. There was only one question, clear as a bell: Should she tell the truth? She thought that if she didn't say anything, the secret would swallow her. Then, in the very next moment, she was convinced that she was blowing things out of proportion. She should keep her mouth shut. Whenever she was around Wanda Walker, Piper felt like she was going to rupture. But the visits were good for Jacob, plus she needed the service hours. For now, she would keep going, thinking of the meetings as her secret penance.

Piper rolled onto her side in the pole vault pit. Principal Unger was leaning against the bleachers. It was weird how when they were training, he would sometimes pop by practice for a few minutes unannounced and then leave, and it made it seem likely that he might show up again before the end of training. As a result, Coach had reduced his profanities. Coach Marky was always around.

Cooper was sidelined, spending each training session on the bench, forced to watch, but not permitted to take part, or to say a word. His partner in crime, Little Ryan, was banished to the visitors' bench to serve his punishment. From time to time, Coach stopped practice, instructing both the JV and the Varsity Teams to gather behind.

"Tell me what you see." Coach gestured toward Cooper and Little Ryan. "I see two dummies who have let their team down. Smoking a joint was more important to them than their teammates. They made a stupid decision. Life is about making good decisions."

Then Coach turned and faced his players. "Now does anybody else want to be an arsehole and join them?"

"No, Coach," the guys would mutter, and then practice resumed.

There was a time when Piper would have been outraged at Coach's bullying and preaching. Was it really that big a deal?

Hell yes, it was a big deal. Hell yes, Coach was right about decisions. What was unfair was that sometimes you only had an instant to decide what the right thing to do was. A few moments in the quarry with a man in mortal danger was not enough time. They hadn't even realized he was alive. The five of them hadn't added up to one mature person when they tried to figure out what to do. Not one of them had ever had to decide something this important before. But sometimes you have to be better than who you are; you have to grow up in a moment. This wasn't something their parents could have prepared them for. There wasn't a class at school they should have taken.

She thought of something her mother had told them months ago. She had read about a little boy who called an ambulance when his mother fell unconscious on the kitchen floor. That child saved his mother's life, her own mother said in wonder. But Piper thought the child's mother had probably practiced with him, had him punch in 9-1-1, taught him to say his address.

And Piper thought, if there had been cell service, everything would be different now.

Piper was a plotter and a planner. Her way of deciding took time. She was sure if she'd had time to think about the Ned situation—even an hour—her verdict would have been different. She would have made the right decision, because what she could see now was how obvious it was, what they should have done. When something bad happens and you can't fix it, you get help. You don't run away and pretend it didn't happen. You don't say: I'll come back later.

Piper was astonished that the Concord loss wasn't mentioned again after Monday's session. "Sometimes you eat the bear. And sometimes the bear eats you." Coach leaned on his umbrella at midfield as the players lounged on the ground during their first water break. "You played well. But the damn bear got us. And that's the way it is in life. You'll have your shotgun, your arrow, your camo, and the damn bear will still get you. It's not over yet. We'll see them again in the playoffs."

And that was that. Next time. There was always next time.

It was Friday before Piper noticed that Coach's limp was more pronounced and that he wasn't running during the drills. Two times he'd left the field and disappeared down the backside of Heartbreak Hill, only to return a few minutes later. The third time he vanished, Piper followed him. Screw the gossipers. She needed to find out if he was okay.

The dirt trail was steep and dotted with smooth rocks. Tree branches shaded it from the sun. She heard him before she saw him. He gagged and vomited, his arms propped on a tree, his head hung toward his chest.

"Coach," she yelled, stumbling toward him. A wild raspberry vine scraped her leg. "Are you okay?"

"Go away, Piper. I'm fine." He wiped his mouth with his forearm. "This is gross. Get out of here." He straightened up and brushed his lips with his fingers. "Please." His eyes watered, and his face was pale, his white T-shirt smeared with a yellow residue and streaks of red.

"Are you bleeding?" Piper's pulse increased. "You vomited blood." She pointed to his sleeve and gagged at the smell. Her heart raced, imagining the germs and disease that festered in the sickly splatter.

"No, I'm all right, and I don't want you to see this. It's private, Piper." Coach crossed his arms and glared like a fighter. "Turn yourself around and head up that hill."

"You have to go to the hospital." She pulled out her cell. "I'll call my mom. Or 9-1-1."

"Put your goddamn phone away." He took a deep breath as if summoning all of his strength and climbed the slope, stopping in front of her. "Piper—" He stared until she met his gaze. "I have Stage IV non-small cell lung cancer. It's metastasized and spread to my spine, my lymph nodes, and my liver. I'm not wasting one minute in a goddamn hospital bed. We're walking up that hill and we're going to play some soccer." His eyes blazed like wild fire.

"You have to get help!"

He grabbed her wrist, and she winced.

"No. I'm doing the chemo for Jenny. But that's it. I know how this thing works. I know how it ends. From now to then, it's my life and I get to be in charge of it."

"What about an operation? Can't they cut out the cancer?"

"It's too far gone." He let go of her arm.

"Are you sure there's nothing to be done?" Piper bit her lip, and tears welled in her eyes.

"Sure, there is. Play some good soccer. Have a beer. Watch my Celtic FC beat Manchester United." He chortled. "See your brothers perform in *Bye Bye Birdie.* Just live."

"You're dying, Coach?" Her voice wavered and that panicky sensation in her belly flickered. "You're giving up?"

"We're all dying. I'm just doing it faster." The color had returned to his cheeks. "I need to talk to your brothers, too. The whole team doesn't need to know every detail of my health. But you guys—" His voice caught. "Well, you're different." A deep sadness crossed his face. "Enough now. Let's get back to practice."

They trudged up the hill, Piper deliberately following Coach, so she could catch him if he fell. They crested the hill and there met Principal Unger and Coach Marky on the plateau drop-off.

"Everything okay here?" Principal Unger's eyes darted from Piper to Coach and back again.

Coach nodded and walked past him. "Fine. Just fine."

"Yes, everything's good." Piper nodded and followed Coach.

The field appeared smaller. The sun was not as bright or the grass as green.

Everything was not all right. The world had never sucked more.

CHAPTER 29

Piper ran toward the girls' locker room at the end of the hall. Once inside, she found a remote corner behind a row of lockers and sank onto the floor. She hugged her book bag, squeezing away the nasty, morbid feeling that coursed through her. Pressing her eyes with her knuckles, she tried not to cry. It was hard to think clearly. Coach was going to die, and it felt like it was their punishment, like Cooper believed—a balancing of the scales. Payment for what they'd done.

She hunkered there for a long time. Two hours later, when the field hockey team trickled in, Piper quietly gathered her bag and slipped out the rear gymnasium door. The sun was setting over the hill, and the sky was a smoky lavender tinged with tendrils of magenta and pink. She found the Honda and waited inside, listening to Meek Mill. She needed to talk. Her parents were out of the question. Noah and Cooper stonewalled her every time she opened her mouth. Ethan didn't want her to put anything in a text. That left Jacob.

Play rehearsal wouldn't end for another thirty minutes. Killing the ignition, she sneaked into the auditorium to watch and settled into the back row, hidden in the darkness. The teen chorus was practicing a song called "A Lot of Living To Do," and Cooper, Little Ryan, and Jacob were a part of it. They were having fun, singing, joking—dancing poorly.

The chorus took a quick break, and then Noah, as the mayor, ran his scene with Mia, the head of the teenyboppers, and Sam Reiter who played Birdie. Noah was better than Piper ever could have imagined, and she involuntarily smiled. She could tell by the way he looked to Mia for encouragement after each take that Mia meant a lot to him. He wanted to impress her, and this made Piper sort of less mad at her brother.

After about ten minutes, the ensemble trickled back into the auditorium. They sat in the front row or on the edge of the stage to watch Mia, Noah, and Sam finish their scene. Piper spotted Jacob seated at far stage left. He had his knees pulled up and his arms wrapped around his muscular legs. His hair fell over his forehead, making it hard to see his eyes. Mia squatted next to him. Leaning over, Mia brought her hand to Jacob's ear and whispered. A nip of possessiveness needled Piper. Jacob nodded and infinitesimally shifted as if he couldn't let another person get too close, his movements measured and hesitant. It was the self-condemnation. He was carrying it, too.

Piper shifted and stretched her legs over the seat in front of her. It would be fun to be a part of a play. Dance had always put her on the outside looking in. Now, she wished she hadn't put so much stock in dance. She had made it everything and then bombed her most important chance to make it count. Everything she'd worked so hard to achieve didn't seem important anymore.

When Mr. Franks called the actors to center stage for his wrap-up speech, Piper left. She waited in the shadow of the huge street lamp at the far edge of the school's parking lot, where Jacob always parked his truck. The cast members scattered onto the sidewalk, chatting and laughing like ordinary kids with typical problems. The crowd thinned as people went to their cars. Noah and Cooper got into Mia's VW Rabbit. Finally, Jacob and Mr. Franks exited. As Jacob strolled down the hill, his keys jingling, Piper stepped out of the darkness.

"Hey," she said.

Jacob dropped his fob.

Piper grabbed his arm as he stooped for his keys. "I know who it is. I know you shot Ned." Jabbing her finger into his chest, her voice trembled. "And I can't believe you're willing to keep it a secret."

"Who told you? Ethan?" He touched her wrist, which made her flinch.

"He knows, too?"

Jacob nodded.

"So, you're all keeping a secret from me? That's why he's set on not saying anything. He wants to protect you. If it was one of my brothers, he would feel differently. Or maybe it's because he's nineteen and wants to save his own hide."

"I thought that's what you wanted. For us not to say anything." He wrapped his fingers around her wrist, pressing the Band-Aid against her tiny burn wounds. "I'm ready to talk to Mismo. I told Ethan. This is eating me up. But Ethan says you're as guilty as any of us and that the only way to keep you safe is to keep quiet."

"Tell Ethan to screw himself. Your brother is the king of mixed messages." She wanted Jacob to protest, to object, to say that he trusted Ethan and Ethan's judgment completely. Her chest emptied. "All Ethan cares about is keeping himself out of trouble." Her voice caught. "Why can't he—"

"Why do you care so much about what Ethan thinks?" He tightened his grip on her wrist and the little burn scabs ripped loose. "Isn't what I think important?" He gazed deeply into her eyes. "I see the way you look at him, how your entire personality changes when he's around. Know this: he doesn't care about you the way I do. I will give it all up for you. If it means I have to carry this guilt the rest of my life, I will. Piper, I just want you to be okay." He released her hand.

It was as if Jacob had struck her. The air seeped out of Piper and with it her desire to fight. "Oh, Jacob." Her voice soft, her eyes wet. "Just tell me what happened."

And then he did. He explained how mad he was when she and Ethan disappeared at the quarry. How he raged inside. For the first time in his life, he understood how it felt to be so frustrated and angry that you wanted to destroy something. So they set up the beer cans and blasted them away. When the bushes rustled and he thought it was a deer, he aimed and fired. As he spoke, his tears fell. "I'm sorry. I never wanted to hurt Ned. I was just so angry. But that's no excuse."

A lump caught in Piper's throat and she couldn't stop her own tears. "It's my fault. I'm so sorry, Jacob." She curled him into her arms and they cried together. Finally, he pulled away and he put his finger to her mouth. "It's not your fault." He touched her cheek, wiping away a tear, and then pushed a strand of hair behind her ear. His gaze was full of resignation.

Without thinking, Piper leaned toward him and lifted her lips to his. He hesitated for a moment, and then his mouth opened and he kissed her. She felt his longing, like a gift. Piper knew she couldn't rat. She had to protect him. Her brothers. And even Ethan.

Piper left the Honda keys under the floor mat for her brothers and hopped in the truck with Jacob. They drove around the valley for a long time. He held her hand and while there wasn't a crazy electrical buzz between them, his hand on hers was steady and reassuring and felt good. He parked his truck by the pond and they watched Bert and Ernie glow on the sleek ebony surface.

"I can't wait for the cygnets," Piper said. "They'll be one good thing. A bit of beauty in this fucked up world, eh?"

"Man, Coach is rubbing off on you. You're swearing like an angry Scotsman."

Piper smirked. "Too bad my foul mouth isn't the only thing that's changed. I wish things could go back and I would reset my fucking moral compass. Just turn back the damn clock." She reached for the door handle.

Jacob brushed her arm. "Nothing will ever be the same. Even if we get through this—"

"I know. I hate myself and I can barely look at Noah. I am not sure I can forgive him. He's said and done things I never would have thought possible."

"Ethan, too. He was . . ." Jacob's voice caught. "Like my hero. It's sounds corny, but I looked up to him and thought he'd always do the right thing. You know, he was always sort of our leader.".

"It's painful that people—our brothers—are not turning out to be who we thought they were. Even if we can somehow fix this, things will never be the same."

*

The house was quiet and still, the hum of the refrigerator the only sound as Piper entered the kitchen. A tin-foiled covered plate was at her place setting. She ate a bit of chicken parm, dumped the rest in the trash and put the dirty dish in the washer. On the second-floor landing, she noticed that Cooper's door was ajar, the dim light of his bedside lamp falling into the hallway. Piper paused and watched her brother. He was on his knees, his hands clasped, his head bowed, leaning against his bed, praying.

"Hey," Piper whispered and opened the door. "Can I come in?"

Cooper jerked up. "Sure?" He raked his hand across his forehead, pushing his hair from his eyes. "What's up?"

Piper plopped on his bed. "Does it help? The praying?"

He tugged a loose thread from his bedspread, his fingers shaky. "What can I say? It makes me feel better." His face was full of apology. "Maybe I don't deserve it, but trying to talk to God gives me some comfort. Helps me to think straight. To sort out this fucking shit-crazy situation."

Piper smiled. "Maybe you shouldn't use curse words when you're chatting with the big man." Piper touched Cooper's hand. "But I guess it's good." They were quiet together for a moment then Piper rose and tiptoed out of his room careful not to disturb their parents down the hall.

It was a strange day. Coach was most likely dying. She had kissed Jacob. There was still no resolution about Ned. But for the first time in a long time, she felt like maybe she could carry on. Maybe she could hold this secret for the people she loved. Maybe this was just the way it would be. The new normal. Maybe.

Or maybe not.

She was waiting for the answer to drop from the sky. In the meantime, maybe Cooper's God would reply.

And maybe sometimes no decision was a decision.

CHAPTER 30

"My darling, it's good to see you again." Madame Sylvie cupped Piper's cheeks. "Your mother told me about your audition."

Piper swallowed the acid in her throat. "I'm sorry. I wanted to make you proud, to represent the studio properly."

"No sorry. This is part of being an artist. Things don't always go exactly the way we want, but this is when your true character shines, when your soul speaks. For if you find yourself compelled to continue when rejection hits, then you know dance is your calling—your passion—and must be your life." She smiled, her eyes warm and kind. "You're here today. That's what is important. Now it's time to get back to work." She kissed Piper's right cheek and then her left cheek.

Piper faced the empty classroom. It was a dull morning and the enormous windows were filled with pregnant gray rain clouds. Madame Sylvie walked to the stereo system, her long black chiffon skirt swaying. The music shot through the speakers from the rear of the room and Piper went to the barre. She placed her hand on the well-worn banister and ran her fingers over the smooth wood. She worked through her barre combinations. Her arms felt heavy and her legs were stiff. And when tipped forward, there was a small roll of skin that escaped over her waistband. She checked the mirror and sucked in her stomach. But lightness filled her chest and spread through her limbs the more she moved. It was good to be back in the studio. Fourteen days without dance was a long time.

Before class, she had stopped at Two Beans Coffee Shop and bought two Caramel Pumpkin Spice Lattes, one for herself and one for Brittany. She placed the warm travel cup in Brittany's locker with a homemade apology card. Enough was enough. The mess with Ned had put everything in perspective and she was not going to let hurt feelings impede their friendship.

Piper continued to practice as the other girls arrived for class. She ignored the whispers and looks of surprise. And she smiled brightly at Brittany when she entered and, in return, Brittany's expression softened, and Piper took that as a positive sign. Maybe her goodwill coffee worked. Baby steps.

The pianist didn't show. Madame Sylvie ran the first half of class as she always did, working them through barre exercises: releve plie, arabesque attitude, reaching rond dejambe, plie pulse to passé. Then she broke the girls into groups of two, placing Piper and Brittany as a pair and Maya and Allison together.

"Today, we do something a little different. With your partner, I want you to take the next fifteen minutes and choreograph sixty-four counts as a duet. Then you will dance for the group and we'll vote on the best piece." Madame Sylvie's eyes twinkled playfully.

Everybody froze. This was out of character for Madame Sylvie. The Rock Ballet School was a serious ballet conservatory. They didn't play games.

"Now go." Madame Sylvie waved her hand. Two-by-two, girls shuffled to the corners of the studio.

"I guess that means us," Piper said to Brittany. They found an open spot in the front of the room with a good mirror view.

"Thanks for the Joe," Brittany said. "So what do you want to do?"

"You're welcome." Piper pointed her right foot to the side and prepped to turn. "I'm a little rusty. Let's do something that showcases your leaps."

"Where have you been?"

"I needed a break. The Tisch audition didn't go so well." Piper did a triple pirouette, sweeping her foot behind her to pose in fifth position. "I really screwed up." She shrugged.

A momentary flicker of relief passed across Brittany's face. "What do you mean?"

"I bombed."

"Is NYU out?" Her voice lifted and Piper felt a flash of resentment. "So then, what? Goucher? Oklahoma?"

"I don't know. Probably. I'm trying not to think about the future. My whole life I've been planning every detail," Piper said. "Try not to look so happy."

"I'm not. I just can't imagine you messing up. You're always perfect."

Piper swallowed. "No, I'm not. Perfect is not the proper adjective to describe me. If you only knew." For a moment, Piper was tempted to tell Brittany everything. But that was not a prudent idea. Not yet. She had only accepted a coffee, which was not the same as an olive branch.

Brittany slicked back her hair and tightened her bun in the mirror. Then she lifted her arms into third position. Piper slid next to her and matched her pose. Side by side, their body types were so different: Piper was tall, lean, and long-limbed; Brittany was small, compact, muscular—but thinner than she had ever been.

"You look good." Piper switched to fifth position.

"Thanks," Brittany's eyes softened as they looked at each other in the mirror. "We better put something together." She motioned to Madame Sylvie stationed by the stereo. "She's about to get started."

They quickly made up their sixty-four-count routine, and when they performed in front of their classmates, the applause was electric. And, of course, they won. It was as if everybody was happy to see Brittany and Piper together again. Class ended in laughter and hugs.

"Maybe I am too hard sometimes," Madame Sylvie said as the girls left the studio for the locker room. "We will do this again."

In the changing room, Piper took off her sweaty leotard and tights, showered, then slipped into her Millington Valley sweatshirt and a pair of jeans. Class had been fun. It felt good to have Brittany talking to her again. Mom was going to let her drive home on the Schuylkill today and she wanted to be comfortable. Her phone buzzed with a text. Ethan.

At dance today? Want to drop by and get a bite to eat?

My God that guy was unpredictable. This is what she dreamed about—her and Ethan hanging out at Temple. But it didn't feel right. Hell, she had kissed Jacob yesterday and liked it.

Sorry. With Mom, she replied. *Maybe another time.*

K, he texted.

K meant it was definitely not okay. Well, screw him. Ethan said jump and she was supposed to say, "How high?" She peeled off the band-aid on her wrist and threw it in the trash. At the sink, she pushed up her sleeves and ran her hands under the hot water, rubbing soap between her fingers and over her tender burn wounds on the inside of her wrist.

"What happened?" Brittany asked.

Piper startled and covered her wrist.

"How did you do that?" Brittany pointed at Piper's arm.

"Just a cut from working in the rose garden with my dad."

Brittany reached for Piper's hand and turned it palm up. "That's not a cut."

In the harsh light of the dressing room, it was clear that tiny match tip burns branded Piper's wrist. The deep purplish-red burns bubbled with pinpricks of blood and pus in the shape of an N. Piper's face flushed with shame.

Brittany's eyes were kind and concerned. "Did somebody do that to you?"

"No." Piper pulled her hand away and dried it on her jeans. "It's fine. Just a few bug bites I scratched too hard. It's nothing." She grabbed her bags. "I've got to go." Dashing out of the dressing room, she didn't wait to continue the conversation.

She wasn't ready to talk.

Secrets *were* safer.

CHAPTER 31

It was hard to believe a person could change so much in three days. When Piper returned to soccer training on Wednesday, Coach was different.

Thinner.

Paler.

Angrier.

He coached from the bleachers, a lit cigarette in hand, bellowing plays, adjustments, and insults. After a few puffs, he'd throw the smoke on the ground and stamp it out with his cleat. Piper's Tupperware container was filling up fast.

"Tobacco is illegal on school property." Piper scooped up the butts, dipped them in a cup of water, and sheathed them in a piece of notepaper. "Principal Unger might stop by again. Or worse, Mrs. Horn. You could get in a lot of trouble. You know, you're supposed to be a role model." The corners of Piper's lips curled. "And you have cancer, you know."

"Can't get in deeper shit than I'm already in." Coach lit another stick, inhaled and focused his attention to the field. "Turn your beady little head back to the field, Coach Marky! Work them through on the set plays, eh? Maybe we could score on a fucking corner kick if you concentrated on the field more than on me. Maybe then we would finally put Concord in their place."

Piper cringed at each f-word. "Has anyone ever told you that you aren't too politically correct?"

"Fuck PC." He dropped another cigarette and dug his heel into the smoking butt.

Coach Marky was constantly watching Coach, then scanning the parking lot as if waiting for a calm, responsible adult to arrive and take over.

The players ran hard. Tackled harder. And gave more than they ever had before. An unseen electric, urgent energy hovered over everything. The spirit of something about to happen.

Coach coughed and spit. "This, sucks," he said under his breath and, with great effort, he walked toward mid-field and then over to the pole vault pit. He leaned on the huge cushion and motioned for the players to gather round. Piper grabbed the water bottle carriers and followed.

The afternoon sun was low, half-hidden by the mountain ridge, but it still threw a warm yellow dusting of light. The guys, red-faced, their clothing drenched in sweat, fell onto the grass at Coach's feet, looking expectant. Jacob sat a good distance away from the crowd. Cooper and Little Ryan were in the front row.

"Come here a second, Coach Marky." Coach patted the area next to him on the pit. "Man, I'm sorry. I don't mean to be screaming at you like that."

Marky plopped down and Coach sank deeper into the foam. "It's okay, Boss."

"I've not been quite myself lately." Then he studied his team, his eyes slowly moving from one player to another, memorizing their faces. "Remember that. When you know you've been an arsehole, don't be slow to apologize. Trust me, I've had practice." He gave a wry smile. "It's never too late to do the right thing. I'm pushing you, I know I am. This season means a lot to me." His brows drew together and he ran his hand over the top of his white sweat pants. "This might be my last."

"Come on, Coach," Cooper said. "Don't say that. You're going to beat this thing. Think about the Pharaoh on the shore of the Red Sea, watching it split in two. The odds were against Moses, but he parted the fucking sea."

"Yeah, yeah, Cooper." Coach rolled his eyes.

"I've got three more years," Little Ryan said. "Nobody else can be my coach." He glanced apologetically at Coach Marky who gave a slight nod.

"Maybe I will and maybe I won't. I'd like to believe life will keep on keeping on, but shit happens. Like this fucking cancer. There's a lot of nasty shit out there—shit so bad you can't even see it coming. It'll knock you right down. Lots of things will be out of your control. But not now. Not this season. You can control what you do on the field. You're good enough to write the ending to this story."

The guys were silent.

He rose from his seat and squared his shoulders. "Listen to me, eh? This is your moment. You've worked hard. You've sacrificed. It's time to make a run to the state championship. You lived in Concord's shadow too long. Make Millington Valley proud. Show this town that we know how to win. You fight for what you want. So if I yell more than usual, it's because I know you can do this, and I know that if you don't try your hardest, it will be one of your life's greatest regrets." He gestured to Noah and then Jacob. "Up."

Noah slid beside Coach, and Jacob stepped to the other side.

"You voted these two men as your captains." Coach placed one hand on Noah's shoulder and the other on Jacob's. "They've been outstanding leaders. But I'm asking them and I'm asking all of you to step it up even more, to leave it all on the field."

There were murmurs of yes and we will. The guys rose and shuffled across the pitch, Coach Marky leading the pack. In the distance, Piper spotted Principal Unger, his arms crossed, leaning against the brick wall of the school next to the empty concession stand and her pulse quickened. As the players approached him, they said a quick hello and then headed to the locker room. Coach Marky waited with Principal Unger as Piper and Coach neared.

"How's it going?" Principal Unger extended his hand.

"Fine, sir." Coach shook his hand.

Piper went to the concession stand to put away the water bottles. She opened the door and stepped inside and wiped her clammy palms down her pants. She took her time, idling in the perfect spot to hear the rest of the conversation, hoping it had nothing to do with her.

"Mark reported that you've been having a bit of trouble. Not keeping up so good," Unger said.

"That so?" Coach's voice was laced with surprise.

"Well, Boss—" Marky stammered.

"I've discussed it with the school board and we think with the stress of your treatments it might be a good idea for you to step down, to let Mark run the show. You'd still consult and advise, but Mark would be on the field."

"I don't think much of your idea," Coach paused. "Sorry, Marky."

"Maybe consider it overnight. We want to do what's best for the team—for our boys. This is a big year for them. We've had reports you've been ill. And frankly, your temper's gotten the best of you at times."

He crossed his arms. "And who's giving you these reports?" He glared at Marky, who shriveled.

"Several people."

"I'll tell you what's best for the team. My team. Me. That's what's best. You can tell the goddamn school board to shove it. I'm not going anywhere until my arse is in the coffin." He hacked again and wiped his forearm across this mouth. "Which might be sooner rather than later."

"Think about it," Unger said. "Full pay. No change there."

Piper let the concession door slap shut. All heads turned toward her. "Coach, do you need anything else?"

"No, I'm fine." His face was hard and his eyes cold.

"Hi, Piper," Principal Unger said.

Coach Marky wouldn't make eye contact with Piper when she passed him. *Traitor,* she wanted to scream. *How dare you?* It was obvious that Coach Marky was still sore that he hadn't been named head coach three years ago. Wait till she told Noah and Cooper and Jacob. That was not how you treated a teammate.

JOURNAL ENTRY
MONDAY, OCTOBER 23

My life is over. Everything has gone to shit. It's been so long since I've written, I don't know where to start, and when I flip back through the pages and reread my entries from last year, I can't believe how naïve I was. I want to shake that girl, tell her to just enjoy, to be grateful. I want to make things right. I just don't know HOW. Sometimes I wake up at night and forget for a few minutes. I feel like my old self before I remember and then reality crashes in. In a nutshell:

The Bad:
We lost to Concord. Again. (This is the best of the bad. Who'd have thought?)
Bombed my Tisch audition—NYU is a bust even though we're trying to secure a second audition.
Mrs. Horn is spreading a nasty rumor about Coach and me. Like I would crush on an old guy? She's out of her freaking mind.
My love life is a total mess. Crazy mixed-up feelings about Ethan. And I kissed Jacob.
Coach is dying—This is really, really bad. But it gets worse.
I'm an almost murderer. Ned Walker is on life support. The guy might die. Or he might live and talk. The situation is a complete NO win.
Fighting with Noah and Ethan about what is the right thing to do about Ned. They're both assholes.
My grades are tanking.
The matches—I want to stop, but I can't. The burns take the pain away. I know I can't keep doing this. I'm losing it.

The Not-So-Bad
Homecoming Queen
Dance—Brittany is talking to me again
Baby swans coming soon
Cooper is being the least dickish

The Not-So-Sure

Visiting Angels—Wanda Walker

Jacob?

Till next time. I'll try to write more often.

CHAPTER 32

The fairground was dimly lit, and the night air brisk, the old oak trees' branches shaking in the gentle wind. Noah was atop the amphitheater stage, pacing and swatting a flashlight like a sword. Both the JV and varsity teams huddled below him, loosely grouped by class: the freshman together on the front row benches, the sophomores behind them, and the juniors and seniors on their feet flanking. Inconspicuously in the rear of the group, Piper sat with Mia, both girls bundled in sweatshirts. Since Homecoming, Mia and Noah had made their status official—they were in a relationship.

"I hate a snitch." Noah slammed the torch into his palm, making a slapping sound. "What happens with our team stays with us. It's nobody's business." Jacob sat on the edge of the platform with his back to Noah, his feet knocking against the hollow wood. He nodded in agreement.

"Coach is our coach. I don't know which one of you pussies doesn't like him. If you'd stop fucking up so much, maybe he wouldn't have to yell. If he didn't care, he wouldn't get crazy." Noah glared at his teammates. "Who's telling their mommy that Coach is mean to them?" He made a pouty face and rubbed his knuckles into his eyes. "He hurt my feelings. Waa, waa! Well, I've got two words for you: Grow up."

Piper watched Jacob. She was sure Mrs. Horn was the busybody feeding Principal Unger bullshit. But as she paid closer attention to the group, she noticed guys shifted from side to side uncomfortably. Maybe not everybody saw Coach as she did. Noah so fired up. It was as if his feelings about Ned had focused into an indignant laser pointed in Coach's defense, giving him purpose and a distraction.

"The chatter has to stop." The muscles in Noah's neck were tense and his voice quivered. "Worry about what you do on the field. Keep it between us. It's our job to win. We are a team and don't forget it. Through thick and thin. Good and bad. And Coach Marky can go screw himself if he thinks he's taking over." He thumped the flashlight against his thigh.

Jacob rose and crossed his arms, his feet planted wide like a fighter. He stared out into the sea of faces. "Yeah, it's our shit. Let's deal with it."

"That's right," somebody yelled, but Piper couldn't see who it was. Then the crowd broke into a chorus of "okays" and "yeah mans."

"Now, get out of here." Noah swung his arm wide. "Any tattletales about this meeting and I will deal with you one-on-one," he shouted at their backs as they scattered. The guys broke up and Noah bounded toward Mia and Piper. Cooper and Little Ryan fell in step beside him. Jacob wavered for a moment and then followed.

"You told them." Mia lifted rose on her toes and kissed Noah on the cheek. He draped his arm over her shoulder and the tension eased out of his body as he relaxed against her. He kissed the top of her head.

"Effing assholes," he said.

"You're right!" Little Ryan whacked Noah on the back. "Nobody's business but ours." He ran his hand across his lips as if closing a zipper. "I know how to keep a secret."

The group walked up the gravel path toward the road and the school parking lot where they'd left their cars. Little Ryan and Cooper broke into a jog and took off ahead.

"We'll catch up in a second." Noah and Mia detoured behind the Arts and Crafts building, leaving Piper and Jacob by themselves.

They walked in silence. Piper tried to think of something to say, but each time she opened her mouth, she reconsidered and stayed quiet. Jacob kept looking straight ahead, staring at his truck in the distance. Car doors slammed and mufflers roared as vehicles pulled out of the school lot.

Finally, Piper said: "Do you think Coach is that bad?"

Jacob shrugged his shoulder. "No, but I can't speak for my mom." He glanced at her knowingly and then shoved his hands in his sweatshirt pocket and quickened his step. As they approached the split–rail fence, Jacob stopped. "I've been wanting to talk to you."

"About what?"

"Don't play dumb, Piper." Jacob leaned on the railing. "The other night, that kiss. You leaned in and you kissed me."

"I'm sorry."

"It felt like you wanted to kiss." He shook his head and pushed his curly bangs from his forehead. "I know everything is messed up. Ned, Coach, your audition. That we're freaking out. We're going to get through this and then there'll be an after." He paused. "I want you in my after. Like in a real way." He let the words sink in. "You and Ethan need to get whatever it is between the two of you out of your system. I know it's not real." He paused and looked across the street and then back at her. "And then give me a chance."

She stared at him, dumbfounded.

He brought his fingers to his lips. "Shush, say nothing. Just think about it." He hopped the fence and jogged across the road without waiting for her.

I wish it were that easy, Piper thought as she watched him go.

Later that night, after her family had fallen asleep, Piper found her ratty sleeping bag tucked in her closet. She draped it around her shoulders and sneaked downstairs. With great care, she opened the door and stepped into the night, first heading to the pond to check on Bert and Ernie and then over to the garden. The crescent moon was tacked high in the night sky and her bare feet were wet with dew after a few steps. She pulled the sleeping bag tighter. The crickets and cicadas sang, their buzz a soothing noisy static. Piper paused and listened harder and heard the howl of a distant dog. Then she turned over the garden bucket and sat on it, letting her eyes adjust to the darkness. Before long she could make out the red of the tomatoes.

Jacob had given her an ultimatum, sort of. Maybe she deserved it. Why had she kissed him? She wasn't thinking with a clear head. No kidding. She was screwed up, guilt–ridden, and depressed. The list could go on and on. But she felt something for Jacob, and she couldn't tolerate the thought of hurting him. In her childhood memories, Jacob is always there. The sun is shining. They are happy. Buddies. They've run back from a stream, mud caked on their legs. Or they've been picking strawberries. Or playing soccer. He is her truest friend. That she didn't want him in the way he wanted her made her heart ache. But she couldn't deny something had shifted in how she thought about him. It was confusing. Maybe she was a shitty person. She physically longed for Ethan. At least she thought she did. If she closed her eyes, she could recall the smell of Ethan's neck, the electric touch of his kiss, the weight of his arms around her back—his forbidden heat.

But what was that? It was Jacob who made her smile. And if she was honest with herself, she had wanted to kiss Jacob. And part of her was curious to kiss him again.

If that night at the quarry had never happened, then everything would be fine. The catalyst igniting the chain reaction was Piper telling Ethan how she felt. If she had just kept her mouth shut, everything would be okay. She never would have left the bonfire with Ethan. Jacob wouldn't have gotten pissed and picked up the gun. Ned would be okay. The Tisch audition would have been a breeze. She'd have an NYU acceptance letter. They'd have beaten Concord (maybe). Her life, and Noah's and Cooper's lives, would be on track. She wouldn't be pressing molten match tips into her skin.

Ethan was the problem—he felt so right, but he was probably wrong.

Piper shifted, her bottom digging into the bucket's hard ridge. She crossed her ankles and doubled-wrapped the sleeping bag around her legs. Close enough to the garden, she reached out and touched the rosemary bush, massaging its pointy leaves between her thumb and fingers, releasing its pungent woodsy aroma. She twisted and picked a sprig.

They would go to jail; that was her greatest fear. If the truth came out, it would ruin them. But she was wrecked already. What was the difference? She gazed at the sky, the stars like holes in a black piece of construction paper, and knew she was screwed either way. Jacob had talked about after. After what? How did she get to after? She twirled the rosemary, tracing it over the inside of her wrist and then threw it into the garden as she stood. The sleeping bag puddled at her feet on the damp grass. There was plenty of evidence that summer hadn't been too long ago. But much had changed since the long hot vacation days and they felt like they existed in another life a long time ago—a time and place in which bad things didn't happen.

She took a deep breath.

A few short months ago, she had been sure of her life's trajectory: Dance, New York, and hopefully Ethan. Now she knew she had been foolish. There was no controlling who or what might get thrown into her path. The shit, as Coach would say. She rubbed the wounds on her wrist. The night air was sharp with the hint of wet dirt. A car engine rumbled in the distance. And then the rhythmic *wou wou* whistle of a swan answered in return. It was time to get to bed. Shivering in the yard would not make the morning come any faster. Plus, they had a game to play tomorrow.

A light flicked on from the third-floor window. For a moment, she stared at Noah's silhouette, then he raised his hand and waved ever so slightly, as if Piper alone in the backyard in the middle of the night was the most ordinary thing in their newly extraordinary lives.

CHAPTER 33

"Out!" the ref screamed and thrust his red card skyward. The rain fell in sheets.

"You can't card me! I'm not a player." Dr. Horn stabbed his wife's pink and yellow umbrella into the ground and the spokes buckled. "Can't you see that was all ball? Which game are you reffing?" He dramatically gestured to the empty field behind him. "Certainly not this one!"

"I said, out!" The ref repeated, his gaze stony, his feet planted squarely, and his arm held high like the Statue of Liberty.

Mrs. Horn quickly sidestepped her husband. "I'm so sorry," she mouthed to the official and then scolded her husband. "Calm down."

"He's certifiably blind," Dr. Horn said, albeit decibels quieter.

Coach rose from the bench and walked over to the commotion, each step an effort. The ref turned toward him. "You've got one minute to get this guy out of here or I'll stop this game."

Coach put his arm around Dr. Horn's shoulder and whispered in his ear. Dr. Horn shrugged, flicking off Coach's arm. "What do you know?" he said loud enough for the crowd to hear. Mrs. Horn reached for her husband's hand and gestured toward the car.

"That's right. Out of here." The ref crossed his arms and with the whistle in his mouth, watched the Horns get into their car and depart before restarting the match. Dr. Horn's ejections were becoming a regular part of each game.

It was a muddy, wet contest. Clad in a poncho, Piper sat on one end of the bench and Coach on the other. He was too spent to pace the sideline. He held his blue and white umbrella as the rain dripped off its edges. From his sweatsuit pocket, he yanked a handkerchief and coughed, and then called down the bench to Piper. "Those boys would be lucky to hit a crow's arse with a banjo, eh?"

She smirked and huddled under her drenched wrap.

Forty-five minutes later, the players fanned in a loop around Coach. Their uniforms sodden, their faces red, and their hair plastered to their heads, they were waiting to enter the warm, dry bus.

Cooper stepped forward to push open the doors.

Coach lifted his hand. "You'll enjoy this fine weather until you hear what I've got to say. To win by only one goal against Kutztown is pitiful."

Piper crossed her arms. The poncho wasn't giving her much cover and she'd stupidly worn shorts. Her legs were wet and cold and her sneakers soaked. The parking lot was dotted with thin pink earthworms, and the bus exhaust fumes mixed with the damp smell of raw dirt.

"You're all charged with the worse-played soccer game in the history of futbol." He gestured to Cooper. "You should take to your knees and thank the Lord you won. That was one sloppy victory."

It was true. Millington Valley should have crushed Kutztown. On paper, they were a much better team. But the Kutztown boys were big and pumped to play Millington Valley. It seemed like every team was saving their best for Millington Valley—playing them was like their championship game. This had to be what Concord came up against all the time.

Coach coughed again, this time deeper and more violently. He stopped mid-thought and banged on the bus doors. They swung open. Before ascending into the bus, he said, "All of you need to do some serious soul-searching." He climbed inside and leaning heavily on the grab bar, turned around. "I don't want to hear a word on the ride. None of that Meek Mill music either."

"I guess that means we're leaving." Noah half laughed and grabbed his waterlogged bag. The guys rustled around for their gear and entered the bus. Noah waited for Jacob and patted him on the back as they climbed inside. Jacob nodded at Piper as he slid by, a moment of understanding bouncing between them.

Coach was perched in the first seat behind the bus driver, Mr. Robinson. He was silent and didn't make eye contact with anyone as they passed. Piper slid into the seat across from him. He didn't look at her either. Too bad Coach Marky wasn't here. He might have softened the mood, but Piper figured he'd been too afraid of Coach's wrath in the wake of the school board's suggestion that he take over as head coach. Marky had been just a little too eager to agree, and this infuriated Coach.

It was a twenty-minute drive from Millington to Kutztown, but on the slick, curvy roads, the quiet journey took almost an hour. Piper felt Jacob's gaze on her shoulders. She still wasn't sure about their kiss. Maybe ignoring that it ever happened was best. Only Coach's barking cough broke the silence from time to time. Guys slumped in their seats, ear buds in their ears, their eyes closed. Piper peeled back of the Band-Aid on the back of her wrist. A gooey outline surrounded the moistened, crusting sores. She popped off the scab and blood oozed. Squeezing her hand sanitizer, she let it burn before she scraped off every bit of gummy Band-Aid adhesive. When she was done, she stared out the window. Raindrops splattered against the dark glass. She knew the way his dad had acted would embarrass Jacob.

It was full night by the time they arrived at the school. Coach told Mr. Robinson to hold the door. He turned around to face the team, his hands on the seat in front of him. "If I didn't care so much, I wouldn't get pissed. You were sloppy and slow to react. That's not how you are going to win a State Championship."

He paused and wiped his brow.

"You're a better team than what I saw on the pitch today. You need to leave it all on the field. Play every game like it's your last one. Practice as if you'll never get to practice again." Coach was quiet as he met Piper's gaze. Then he slowly made eye contact with each player, pausing on Cooper and then Noah, until the silence was almost unbearable. Guys squirmed and checked their phones, fiddled with their bags, anything to break the force of Coach's stare. Mr. Robinson killed the ignition and the only sound was the slap of rain against the bus.

He cleared his throat. "I will not sugarcoat this for you. The truth is—" He coughed again, this time deeper and longer, his cheeks turning red. "This is my last season."

The bus was still, the air thick.

Piper studied Coach in profile. The light was dim, but she noticed that his skin was ashy and his cheekbones more pronounced than they'd been a few days ago. His hair seemed grayer and his clothing hung loose. He gripped the seat in front of him, clearly needing it for support.

"Go for the jugular under all circumstances. No mercy, men. Walk off the pitch unbowed. I want you to win the whole thing. For the seniors, that was the last time you'll ever play Kutztown. You need to make every minute count." He thrust his hands into his pockets. "There's no such thing as a do-over. You can't know this yet, but now—right now, today—you're making the memories that will sustain you later in life, the stuff that is going to keep you going when shit hits the fan. You'll remember the laughs, the jokes, the wins, the damn Meek Mill music on the bus, and your teammates. You'll remember what it felt like to give your all—to be young and strong—and fearless." Coach coughed and pinched his eyes. "I'm going off, eh?" He slapped the seat and smiled for the first time all day. "Get the hell out of here. Tomorrow is a new day. We'll begin again."

But in the morning, as Piper was grabbing a granola bar before bolting out the door for school, she heard the news in her father's hushed baritone: Coach no longer had a job.

CHAPTER 34

Piper slumped in the hard plastic chair and waited outside Principal Unger's office. On her wrist was a fresh scab and she nervously picked at it until blood seeped from under the crust. The word all over school was about Coach's dismissal. The team was enraged and indignant, and the players had started a petition to have Coach reinstated. It was unbelievable.

Mrs. Weidner, the office receptionist, was so short that, from Piper's vantage point, only her hair clip poked above the counter. Mrs. Weidner's desk was decorated with press-on jack-o'-lanterns, skeletons, and witches. Her head was tilted toward her computer screen, and it was impossible for Piper to get any read from her on why she had been called to the office, but this didn't stop her heart from galloping.

The phone rang and after a second of low chatter Mrs. Weidner pointed to Unger's closed door. "Piper, you can go in now."

"Thanks." Piper slung her book bag over her shoulder and smiled, trying not to let her nervousness show. When she opened the door and spotted Sheriff Mismo, her heart clapped against the inside of her chest like a hundred thundering horses.

"Have a seat," Unger said. His face was smooth and friendly.

This was it. They were busted. No more time to think about what to do, how to make things right. Mismo had figured out that one of them had shot Ned, and he was here to rip the truth from her. Piper's mind raced, running through possible reprieves, delaying tactics, outright lies.

As much as she wanted the guilt to be lifted, her body shifted into sheer panic and protection mode.

Piper hooked her book bag on the armchair and took the seat directly in front of Unger's desk. Mrs. Weidner had decorated his office, too. A huge pumpkin with a painted face perched on his filing cabinet.

She slipped her hands under her legs and looked at Sheriff Mismo.

Unger hesitated as if weighing his words before he spoke. "We—" he paused again. "We need your help. You might have heard that Coach O'Connell has been asked to step down."

"Yes." Her heart slowed by a fraction.

"It's a shame that he is sick, but too many parents have complained." He tapped his pen on the desk. "Something had to be done."

"Right now?" She brazenly met his eye, surprised at the indignation in her own voice speaking to the principal. "We're heading into playoffs. The timing is not so good."

"I know. But an accusation was made that I can't ignore. In fact, I could lose my job if it's not addressed."

"Is it because he curses a lot?" Piper shifted. "He can be politically incorrect."

"No, that's not it." Unger titled his head and paused. "It's more than that. Quite a bit more, I'm afraid. You can trust us and tell us anything."

"He smokes on school property occasionally. I guess you can't allow that. Maybe give him a warning or a fine?"

Unger picked up a file and glanced at Sheriff Mismo.

"Piper," Mismo started. "This is a safe place. You can say anything. Has Coach O'Connell ever made you feel uncomfortable?" Maybe this wasn't about Ned.

Piper tilted her head. "Me? No."

Unger shuffled the papers in the file and met her gaze. "Has he ever acted inappropriately?"

"No, nothing like that has ever happened. Coach is a gentleman."

"You've been seen together. Alone." He paused and closed the file. "To some people, it doesn't seem normal for a middle-aged man and a teenage girl to hang out. As the principal of this school, it's my duty to protect its students and investigate any complaints."

"You know, Mr. Unger, I'm the soccer team manager. That puts Coach and me in proximity of each other." Piper didn't hide her sarcasm. "Where are my parents? Are you even allowed to talk to me about this sort of thing without my mom or dad here?" She reached for her phone.

"Hold on."

"I hate this town. Everybody is so close-minded. Of course, Christopher O'Connell can't be just a coach, a friend, someone who cares about us. He's practically a member of my family! No, there's something sinister going on. Somebody saw something they wanted to see." Her voice shook, and she gritted her teeth so as not to cry. "Who would say such a thing about Coach? About me?" She bit her lip and sucked down a sob that threatened to erupt. "You must give Coach back his job. Tell the stupid school board you talked to me and none of it is true. This will kill him."

"Now, calm down," Sheriff Mimso said. "Your parents are on their way."

"Piper, it's the law," Principal Unger said. "If a school employee or medical professional suspects any type of child abuse, it has to be reported to Child Protective Services. And then an investigation must be completed. It's a Pennsylvania state law."

"A medical professional?" Piper tripped over the word. For a long moment she said nothing. It was Mrs. Horn—that nosy, gossipy witch. She couldn't believe she had birthed Ethan and Jacob. Piper's jaw tightened. It all clicked. Of course. Piper was sure Mrs. Horn had put Dr. Horn up to it. But why? What had Piper ever done to her? "This is ridiculous." Piper reached for her phone. "Coach and I are the ones being abused—here, in your office. So you get those child protective people over here, so Coach can get back on the field. And I'm calling my mom."

The next morning as her family ate breakfast around the kitchen table, Piper watched her mother phone her partner, Dr. Frank Horn, and tell him she wouldn't be in for the rest of the week.

"What's this about?" Dr. Horn's voice echoed through the Rose kitchen. Mom's cell was on speakerphone and the whole family congregated around the table listening.

"I think you have a pretty good idea." Mom squinted as if Frank Horn sat across from her and she was giving him the evil eye.

"Give me a hint, Amy."

"I'm too pissed to speak. I consider you not only my partner but also my friend. So I can't imagine what would possess you to go to Unger and not me if you suspected Piper was in danger."

The line grew quiet.

Then the hollow echo of Frank Horn's voice reverberated through the Rose kitchen and Amy Rose hung up on her partner. The vein in her mother's neck twitched and she inhaled deeply, setting her hands on the table. She exchanged a knowing look with Dad and then her gaze bounced from Noah to Cooper and finally settled on Piper. "Standing up for Coach is the right thing to do." Her mother swallowed as if her words caught in her throat. "You amaze me. Your grades. Dance." She placed her hand atop Piper's. "I want to go on record." Again, she looked at Noah and Cooper, then at Piper. "You've been a supportive sister putting up with all this soccer for so many years. Still, you've excelled at your sport in the shadows of our family. I'm sorry if sometimes it seems like I am too busy. Know your father and I are proud of you." She paused. "You really are perfect."

Getting Coach reinstated wasn't so easy. Child Protective Services couldn't meet with Piper until the following Wednesday. In the meantime, Coach Marky took over the team. Millington Valley won 4–0 against Hempfield and Coach Marky seemed to believe it was because of his coaching. Piper, Noah, and Cooper visited Coach at his townhouse almost every day that week, only missing Saturday because of the game. Sunday night, Jennifer met them in the parking lot. Piper held a warm Tupperware container of chicken noodle soup to deliver.

"He'll be so happy to see you guys, but he's not doing so good." Her lips were pinched. "His energy is zapped, and he's been throwing up. Slept little last night. It's hard for him to get around."

It was good, she warned them, because what they saw was worse than they had imagined. Coach lay on the sofa, shrunken and buried under several blankets. The TV was turned to the Fox soccer channel. The sound was a soft hum.

"Marky can't coach for shit," Noah said. "We need you back on the pitch."

Coach perked up. "You're the leader. Command the field." He pushed himself upright and called to Jenny. "Please bring me a clipboard and pen." He mapped two plays that he wanted Noah to have Marky run through. Piper tried not to stare at his birdlike wrist and the way his hands trembled.

"I sure would like to see you play again."

"Hell, you'll see us play tons more games," Cooper said, and his voice cracked. "And Bye Bye Birdie is this weekend."

"That's right, mate." Coach coughed and his entire body shuddered. "They'll have to pack me in my coffin and nail it shut to stop me from seeing your stage debut." He laughed, but nobody else did.

The Roses jumped into action. Piper knew she had cleared Coach's name, and therefore the biggest obstacle was how to physically manage him on the field. It turned out that their dad had always wanted a four-wheeler to zip around his farm. A golf cart would work too. He cut a quick deal with Arrowhead Golf course and bought one of their used carts. Mom didn't go back to the clinic right away.

The next Monday afternoon, Dad and Mom delivered the golf cart to the Millington Valley High School athletic fields. Jennifer and Coach waited in the parking lot until Piper emerged from the locker room. Piper helped Coach into the cart and placed a blue Millington Valley blanket over his knees. She felt protective, like she was the wall between him and the rest of the valley. When Mom handed Coach a thermos of chicken broth, he said. "I would never hurt Piper. Amy, you've got to know that."

"We know, Chris. I know. Now go coach our boys."

CHAPTER 35

Noah sent a group text, commanding everybody to find a Halloween costume and to meet at the main entrance of the Millington Valley General Hospital at 3 pm. Coach was in the ER. At three in the morning, he had woken unable to breathe, and Jennifer had rushed him to the hospital. The doctors drained fluid from his lungs, and he was now stabilized.

The Rose kids were dressed as ballerinas. Noah and Cooper packed themselves into Piper's stretchy-est costumes. Noah wore a purple leotard tutu over his white compression shorts. Cooper dressed in pink. They both donned flowered hairpieces. Piper put on her Sugar Plum Fairy getup from last year's *Nutcracker* production.

"On the steps," Mom called, her camera in her hand. "This is a once in a lifetime photo op."

Cooper did a clumsy arabesque. Noah curtsied. Piper stood on the top step, placed her hand on Noah's head for balance, and grabbed her left insole, lifting her leg so that it touched her ear.

"Freeze!" Mom laughed.

Despite her brothers' jokes and jostling, Piper sensed an underlying nervousness in both of them. Cooper drove with great care, obeying the speed limit, checking and double-checking both ways before pulling out at a stop sign. Nobody spoke too much, each of them studying the mountains in the distance and the bright yellow and orange leaves like autumn cotton candy. They picked up Mia. She slid into the back seat next to Noah, wearing a curly red wig and an apron with a blue polka-dotted shirt underneath—her Little Orphan Annie costume from last year's musical.

"You look cute," Noah whispered. Mia snuggled next to him.

The entire team waited at the main kiosk. Jacob wore an FC Barcelona uniform with the number ten on it—Messi's jersey. Their Instagram feeds would blow up with all the selfies they were taking. Piper dodged the camera and found Jacob, pulling him aside, too pissed to worry about what their kiss might mean. "Do your parents know you're here? They will not like that you're supporting the town pedophile."

"Knock it off, Piper." Jacob's cheeks turned pink. "I feel bad enough already."

"It's ridiculous. Your mom acts like she's in middle school. What does she have against Coach? Against me?" She poked him in the chest. "She's out of control. And your dad is her puppy." Angry tears built in her eyes. "It's just disgusting. I had to give a report to CPS. Isn't it bad enough he has cancer to deal with? You don't believe that garbage about Coach, do you?"

Jacob studied the ground and then muttered, "No, and I'm sorry. But I don't think it matters what anybody does." He met her icy stare. "He's dying."

"So coach is expendable, like Ned? Save it," she said under her breath as she walked away.

Noah instructed the team to sit in the waiting room while he went to the reception area to find Coach's room. The guys jostled for chairs and were loud. Piper caught her reflection in the glass partition and didn't recognize herself for a moment. Her face was drawn and the tendons in her neck taut. She didn't match the beautiful costume that she wore. Throughout her years of dance, the Sugar Plum Fairy had been the role she had worked hard to earn. She had been ecstatic when Madame Sylvie had posted her name on the *Nutcracker* cast list. The part had been everything she'd dreamed. But now that time period and those ambitions seemed far away and unimportant.

"This way." Noah pointed, and the guys followed him down a hallway labeled R Building. "Be quiet," he said as Mia fell into step beside him. He draped his arm over her small blue polka-dotted shoulder.

Piper hung back and motioned for Jacob. "Hey, I'm sorry. I know it's not your fault. I'm just so pissed. Everything is out-of-control right now and it's making me insane." She reflexively touched the Band-Aid on her wrist.

"I get it," he said. "I am sorry, too. No scholarship offers, and that's eating at my mom and she needles my dad. She can't accept that I'm not as good as Ethan." He tugged at his shirtsleeve. "It doesn't bother me. Ethan's always been better than me." A note of self pity crept into his voice and their eyes met, Jacob holding Piper's gaze, daring her to contradict him. When she didn't blink or look away, he said, "I'm used to people preferring Ethan over me."

Piper shrugged. "Boy, you get an Ethan dig in whenever you can. Come on. We have bigger things to worry about."

"You know it's true."

She ignored his comment and walked toward the greeter's table. "Can you tell me what room Ned Walker is in?"

The friendly looking receptionist entered Ned's name into her computer. "C233. Here's a map of the hospital." She handed Piper a glossy tri-fold pamphlet.

"We're taking a quick detour."

"That's not a good idea." Jacob peered around. "We shouldn't be seen near him. What if somebody gets suspicious?"

"No one will see us." Piper waited and watched the team until they turned the corner and then she tugged Jacob toward the C building. As they passed the gift shop, she spotted a small, hand-painted pumpkin in the display window. "Hold on a sec." She slipped into the store and paid the $4.99 posted on the tag. They moved through the hospital's maze of corridors until they found the hallway that led to C. It was quiet, and the nurse's station was vacant. Piper checked the placard outside of each room, finding 233 the last chamber before the emergency exit stairwell. She closed her eyes and took a calming breath. Seeing Ned, she was convinced, would clarify what they should do. The air was heavy with the smells of disinfectant and latex. Jacob's arm tensed, and she unhooked her hand.

"Is someone there?" a shaky female voice called from Ned's room. "Come in. Please, come in."

"Shit," Jacob whispered. "Wanda's here."

"You are not turning back." Piper stepped over the threshold and pretended their visit was intentional. "We brought this for you." She held up the jack-o'-lantern. Wanda was relaxing in a recliner at the foot of Ned Walker's hospital bed, a blanket over her lap, and bundled in her MVHS hoodie.

"Oh, thank you!" Wanda's face lit up. "Put it right there." She pointed to the windowsill. "Ned will see it first thing when he wakes up. You look just like a princess. A beautiful fairy."

"It's my Swan Lake costume." Piper studied the room and saw that there weren't any cards or flowers, just a pile of Agatha Christie mysteries and half-full glass of iced tea on the small table next to the recliner. She noticed Wanda had her new iPhone.

"We're headed to see Coach O, but we hoped you'd be here," Jacob said. His voice was jumpy and he rocked from side to side. Piper had the urge to grab his arm to steady him, but that would only draw attention to his nervousness.

"You're our first visitors." Wanda patted her teased curls. "If you don't count Sheriff Mismo. He's been here twice, but I don't think I can consider him. He's investigating." She stretched each syllable and then nodded toward Ned.

"How is he doing?" Piper followed Wanda's gaze, landing on Ned. His long brown hair, streaked with heavy strands of gray, was combed and tucked behind his ears. His face was freshly shaven and his fingernails trimmed and neat. But he was smaller than Piper remembered, not the hulking fur-covered beast who slammed on their car hood. Thin and frail, his bony arms rested atop the light blue blanket pulled across his chest. A heart rate monitor was clipped onto the index finger of his right hand and it chirped at a regular interval. An IV drip was attached to his left forearm. Under this paper-thin skin, pools of purplish black blood congealed, making it appear as if he had been stained with shoe polish. Piper wanted to touch him, to make sure he was breathing; she wanted him to live, to be okay. He wasn't the scary, crazy monster of their childhood terrors. No. He was a sick old man.

"He's been in and out of ICU, but he's been in his own room for a day now. I think it's a good sign." Wanda pushed the lap throw off her legs and stood. "How did you know I'd be here? I'm so touched that you came."

"We took a gamble," Piper said. "And I'm glad to see you because you haven't responded to my texts." Piper noticed Jacob couldn't tear his eyes from Ned, and his rocking became more pronounced.

"That phone dinged a couple times. I can't remember what to do when that happens."

"Can you come to the school play this weekend? Jacob's in it. *Bye Bye Birdie.*"

"Oh, I'd love to." Wanda clasped her hands together and smiled and her movements jolted Jacob out of his swaying trance.

"That's right, I'm making my debut," he said.

"Perfect. I'll text you. You've got to check your messages." Piper picked up Wanda's iPhone and swiped. "Like this—"

"Piper!"

Piper and Jacob spun around. Noah was in the doorway.

"What are you doing?"

"Nothing. We were just about to leave."

Noah walked into the room, the tulle from his ballet skirt swaying from side to side.

Wanda chuckled and drew her hand to cover her mouth. "I've never seen a boy in a tutu." Then recognition crossed her face. "Oh, you're Piper's brother, aren't you?"

"Yes, I'm Noah." He extended his hand. "Sorry to pull these two away from you, but we only have a small window of time to visit our coach." He put one hand on Jacob's shoulder and one on Piper's shoulder and applied pressure. "Have a nice day." He turned them toward the door.

"Please come back again," Wanda called.

In the hallway, Noah pushed open the emergency exit door and closed it with a hard pull. "What the hell were you two doing in there?"

"Nothing. I only wanted to see if Ned was okay," Piper said.

Noah stared at her. "Are you fucking nuts?"

CHAPTER 36

The auditorium was dimly lit, the stage curtains closed. The Bye Bye Birdie overture played over the din of conversation. At the back of the theatre in Row U, Piper was sandwiched between Dad and Mom, with four rose bouquets from their garden on her lap—one each for Cooper, Noah, Mia, and Jacob. Piper leaned across Mom and smiled at Jennifer, handing both of them programs.

"I never thought I'd see this." Piper tapped Noah's picture.

"This is going in my scrapbook." Mom tucked the flyer into her purse.

In the aisle, as close as he could get to Jennifer, Coach was parked in a wheelchair. He'd rallied and been discharged from the hospital the day after their Halloween visit. This week, he had attended every practice and grunted orders from the golf cart. The playoffs started next week, which breathed new life into Coach. There was talk of another treatment at an immune therapy clinic, and the prospect gave everybody hope.

The seat next to Dad was empty. Wanda had left a voice mail (and texted), saying that she had been called to the hospital, and she was sorry to miss Jacob's show, but her brother had taken a turn for the worse. The Horns were in the first row, front and center. Mrs. Horn twisted around, caught Piper's eye, glanced at Coach, and twisted back around sharply. A bestial growl raged in Piper's throat, and she wanted to leap over the seats and throttle Mrs. Horn, choking her with the huge, preppy aqua blue beads she wore. Little Ryan interrupted her murderous fantasy.

"Hey, Coach." Little Ryan said. "Think we can do it?" He was, of course, referencing the upcoming Concord rematch. It was top of every soccer player's mind, and they could almost speak telepathically.

"Yes, mate, yes. We're going to kick some Tiger arse." He laughed and coughed when the house lights blinked three times. "To your seat now. We've got a fine cultural display before us."

The show was wonderful. Piper noticed that Jennifer and Coach whispered to each other, pointing to their soccer players whenever one came onstage. Smiles. A laugh. Then Coach reached for Jennifer's hand when the lead sang, *Put On A Happy Face*, and he seemed content, normal—as if he wasn't in pain. The finale brought the audience to its feet.

"Woohoo!" Piper shouted through cupped hands when the chorus appeared during the curtain call. Using Jennifer as a crutch, Coach stood, clapping and hollering.

The hallway was jammed with people. Jennifer navigated Coach's wheelchair away from the crowd, and Piper and her parents followed. Noah, Cooper, and Mia came out together, their post-show glows radiating.

"Wonderful! You were fabulous, mate!" Coach patted Noah's arm. "You were too," he said to Cooper. "But you, Mia, you stole the show."

Mom and Dad raved and Piper handed each of them the flowers, proud of her brothers for trying something new. For the first time since the Ned accident, they were carefree and radiant. They wore the sort of glow Piper would have expected after a soccer victory.

"We're going to celebrate! It's Toasty Buns for ice cream. Our treat," Coach said.

"Sounds like a plan to me." Dad took Mom's elbow and kissed her cheek.

Piper had the urge to pirouette and leap through the crowd. Then her gaze landed on the Horns. They huddled around Jacob who was just as jacked as the other actors. He spotted Piper and smiled hopefully. She pointed the last bouquet at him. "For you," she mouthed into the deafening crowd. Normally, the Horns would have joined them in an after-party excursion like the one they were about to take to Toasty Buns. But lines had been drawn and the Roses stood on the side with

Coach and Jennifer. Only Jacob traveled back and forth. Piper made her way through the horde and congratulated Jacob on his performance, explaining why Wanda couldn't make it. She said a quick goodbye, turned around, and smacked into Mia who, flowers in hand, had crept up behind her.

"Noah and Cooper were great," Mia said. "And Jacob, too."

"I know. Who'd have thought?" Piper smiled.

Mia's gaze darted over Piper's shoulder and she stepped closer. "I wanted to talk to you without Noah around. He gets weird anytime somebody mentions Ned Walker."

"Yeah?"

"It's about the party at the quarry. Sheriff Mismo's been asking more questions. He stopped by my house again two days ago and wanted to know if the guys, specifically Noah, Cooper, Jacob, and Ethan, had any guns with them that night. You know, for hunting."

Piper's heart raced. "Well, that's easy enough to answer."

"Right. I told him no."

"Nothing but the truth." Piper scrutinized Mia for a moment. Did she know something? The hunting trip had been a secret. Not even Little Ryan knew they had hidden the guns in the woods. Piper had to stop second-guessing herself. But was Mia trying to warn them? To protect Noah? Had she sent the anonymous text? "Well, we better get back. The gang's waiting for us and I think they're hungry."

Toasty Buns was packed with after-show celebrants. They waited a few minutes until they could get two tables together. Dad made room for Coach's wheelchair at the head.

"I'll have a double chocolate sundae," Mia said. "It's an ice cream sort of weekend. My parents are coming to tomorrow night's show and they will want to come here afterwards too."

Noah touched Mia's nose. "And give me a banana split."

"Good God," Cooper said and plopped into a chair. "Save it for when you're alone."

"Ah, young love." Coach grinned, his eyes sparkling, and handed out the menus. "Get whatever you want."

"Well, then I'll take a root beer float and a chocolate chip, vanilla ice cream cookie sandwich." Cooper closed his menu. "And a sticky bun."

"You'll have diabetes before we leave." Coach coughed.

The mood was festive as they joked and ate, their voices rising above the café's cheerful din. Noah rehashed every scene. It was like they were almost happy. Piper decided she would go back to visit Ned again, and this gave her some peace and allowed her to enjoy the evening more. Maybe she would read to him. Or bring music to play. She wanted him to get better, and when he recovered, she would talk to him, and explain what had happened. She would ask for forgiveness and lay her fate at his mercy. And accept whatever he thought she deserved. If he wanted to press charges, then so be it. She wouldn't let the exchange with Mia bother her. It probably meant nothing.

The place was swarming with people; it took some time before Piper noticed Sheriff Mismo seated at the counter. Goosebumps popped out on her neck. He was talking with Mr. Dierdorf, the owner, a hot cup of coffee in his hand. Noah turned around and saw him and then Cooper noticed, too. Piper detected a shift in Noah's tone of voice and how Cooper's back stiffened.

"I'm going to check out the muffins," she said, not daring to make eye contact with Noah or Cooper. She made her way through the busy space and squeezed in near the display case. Pretending to study the baked goods, she strained to hear Mismo's conversation.

"Just came from there," Mismo said.

"It's such a tragedy," Mr. Dierdorf said. "And to think nobody knows who shot him."

"I wish I had more of a lead." Mismo placed a travel lid on his coffee cup. "His sister is taking it hard. Apparently when his blood pressure crashed, there wasn't much they could do. Damn shame." It was as if someone poured cold water on Piper. Like that, the contentment of a few moments ago vanished.

She didn't have to ask of whom they spoke.

Ned Walker was dead.

She turned around and locked eyes with Noah, telling him without speaking a word what had happened. Dead men can't talk and this should have eased Piper's mind, but the blame whispered in her ear with soft, steady, and unceasing taunts. You are a murderer.

CHAPTER 37

Piper fled Toasty Buns, giving her mother and dad a quick peck, hugging Coach and Jennifer, saying she was meeting a friend. As if she had one. She sprinted down Main Street and hopped the chain-link fence into the fairgrounds, the truth chasing her like a pack of wolves. The full moon cast a pearly light on the empty fields and buildings.

A car rumbled on Main Street, and she whipped around only to find her shadow and the thump of her heartbeat. She walked deeper into the fairgrounds, past the amphitheater, until she reached the livestock building. Under a naked oak tree, she lay down on a bench, pulling her legs to her chest. Her phone buzzed. Wanda had mastered how to text. The group message to her and Jacob read:

I am sorry I missed the play, but I had to sit with my brother tonight. My heart is broken. He died at 8:02 PM. I will send the funeral arrangements. It would mean the world to me if the two of you attended.

Cry, she told herself, but no tears fell. Numbness slithered through her body and she rolled up her jacket sleeve. The bulbous, tiny scabs were a deep purple. With the edge of her thumbnail, she lifted the dry crusty blood until it stung, and then she picked off the scab and pressed the sharp edge of her fingernail into the lesion. She had been ready to make things right, to visit Ned, to help nurse him back to health. And when he woke up, to tell him what had happened. But it was too late for absolution, if there had ever been a chance.

The fragile man she had seen at the hospital hadn't been the freaky beast she and her brothers had made him out to be. He had been a human being, a sick war veteran, probably suffering from PTSD—another living soul. She closed her eyes and took a couple deep breaths. *Please show me the way.*

"Hey, Piper?"

She jerked up. Jacob was there.

"What are you doing here?" she said.

"Out walking. Enjoying this fine, clear evening."

"Bullshit."

"You're right. We stopped at Toasty Buns for a post-show, celebratory ice cream. My parents didn't go in when they saw Coach's Jeep. But I wanted some—"

"Mint chocolate chip."

"You know me too well. When I stopped to say 'hi' to your crew and saw Noah, I knew the shit had hit the metaphorical fan. He was ghastly pale and Cooper was sitting on his hands like he was afraid they were going to give him away. Mismo had just come over and told them about Ned." He tapped his phone. "Then I got Wanda's text."

"And you rushed to find the damsel in distress?" She gestured for him to sit.

"Sort of." He toed the gravel, making a divot. "What do we do now?"

"I have no idea." Piper unrolled her jacket cuff to reveal her wrist. There was a deep sadness pulling at Jacob's cheeks and around his eyes.

"I'm scared, Piper," he said, his voice catching, "I killed somebody. I can't keep pretending it didn't happen. You can't imagine what it feels like."

Piper couldn't speak. Instead, she turned up her sleeve to reveal her wounded wrist. He studied her arm, confused. "What's—"

"The guilt is eating me, too."

"What happened?" Jacob's face was pained as he lightly traced his fingers over Piper's raw welts.

"These secrets aren't good. The whole thing is making me sick. I can't stand it so I—"

"You did this? Did you cut yourself?"

"Burned." Piper bit her lip and her eyes welled. "I'm terrified, too. The only time I feel a little relief is when I—" She half laughed, choking down a sob. "When I hurt myself. Sick, right? Somehow, we have to fix this."

"Promise me you won't do this again." He touched her arm.

"I can't. I'm losing it. You're right. It's worse now that he's dead. It's so final." Speaking the words aloud, she couldn't contain her panic and horror. "It's all my fault. If I'd insisted that we carry Ned out of the quarry, or found him the next day, I think he'd be alive. I know it." Her tears burned hot tracks across her cheeks. "I wasn't thinking. Everybody believes Piper is perfect, that I never do anything wrong. That I never make mistakes." A sob racked her chest. "I do. I screw up a lot. I've got flaws. Lots of them."

"Stop it. This total mess is my fault. I shot the guy." He took a deep breath. "I had no business with that gun in my hands, especially when I was pissed."

The gentle breeze blew Piper's hair against her neck. The moonlight sprinkled a silvery glitter on the pathways. Jacob wiped the tears from her face and then he leaned toward her, and she jerked away.

"No," she whispered. "I can't. We can't. I can't think straight right now. It's not the best idea to be kissing my best friend."

"Okay. But, Piper, maybe someday there'll be an us?"

"I don't know. How can I know?"

A far-off train whistled. Jacob said, "The only thing I know for certain is that I can't live with this secret any longer. I think we should tell Coach. He will know what to do."

"You're right. Our parents would freak. Mismo—he scares me. Coach will tell us how to handle this."

"But I won't say anything to Noah, Cooper, or Ethan."

She held out her pinky, and he linked his finger in hers. "Promise."

"Deal," he said and smiled weakly. "Let's go. I'll drive you home."

They drove through the valley, the mountains black against the deep blue night. In the driveway they parked by the pond and made a plan for tomorrow.

"I'll get out here," Piper said. As Jacob backed down the lane, Piper walked to the edge of the water. She snapped a stalk of duckweed, tore it in two, and threw it. Bert drifted across the velvety surface while Ernie stayed perched on her nest.

"Take some over to Ernie," Piper said. The regal bird nudged the floating vegetation. "Secrets aren't safer, are they?" she said, and Bert's elegant neck straightened and his deep black eyes focused on her. Right, he seemed to say.

The house was dark and quiet when she entered. Her eyes were swollen and her throat was scratchy, but she felt lighter, knowing they were going to talk to Coach. She took the throw blanket from the sofa in the family room and wrapped it around her shoulders. She hoped there wasn't an invisible germ festering in her itchy throat, ready to mutate and make her sick. An empty wine bottle with three pink roses nested on the table—her father always picked her mother a small bouquet for their date nights. She wondered if she would ever find someone to love like her parents loved each other. One minute she thought it could be Ethan. The next Jacob. She plucked a petal and rubbed it between her fingers. The frost would come soon, and the roses would die for the year.

Still chilly, she pulled the throw tighter. Maybe things could be okay. Coach would help them. She went to the sink and ran the faucet until the water warmed. Then she squirted a pea-size dollop of lemon dish soap into her palm. She lathered the suds into a white froth, which she tenderly washed over her hands and against the inside of her sore wrist, and counted to twenty.

Finally, she climbed the steps two at a time. When she saw the light from Cooper's room tumbling into the hallway, she quietly inched into his space. He had fallen asleep with the light on. She knelt beside her brother, watching the rise and fall of his chest, and wished she could read his dreams.

She was pretty sure she didn't believe in God, but if praying helped Cooper to deal with this fiasco, okay. He was still a boy, and he had done nothing wrong except follow along out of loyalty. What had all this done to him? He had always looked up to the rest of them, and they had taught him he did not have to be responsible for his actions.

She closed her eyes, slipped her hand atop Cooper's, and rested her head on the bed. The tangy scent of soap was still on her fingers.

CHAPTER 38

Noah knocked on Piper's bedroom door. "Time to go."

Piper opened her eyes. The light crept through the sliver of space between the shade and the window frame. Her throat burned, and it was hard to swallow. Damp strands of hair stuck to her neck. She noticed a sandpaper-like rash on her forearm. *No. No. I can't be sick today.*

Noah jiggled the doorknob and unlocked the antique latch. "What's wrong?"

Piper nuzzled into her pillow and, with her throat on fire, murmured, "Can't go." She pushed up onto her elbow and immediately slumped back onto her side.

"Need a bucket?" Noah picked up the living room throw and laid it atop Piper's comforter. "Mom and Dad already left." He plopped down next to her legs. "Should I call Mom? Get her to bring home some meds?"

"Yes." She nestled her face into her pillow. "And tell Jacob I can't meet him today."

"Do you two have a date or something?"

"Just tell him."

He squeezed her calf through the covers. "Last night, it was like the whacked-out scene from Unsolved Mysteries when Mismo told us about Ned. I feel shitty he died."

Piper moaned.

"I know, but if I'm honest, I'm relieved, too. With him gone—well, we don't have to worry. Our secret dies with him."

"Maybe you'll sleep better now," Piper mumbled.

"Feel better." He patted her leg and left.

Piper made the trip to the second-floor bathroom, wrapping the throw around her shoulders. In the mirror, she inspected her throat. It was deep, sore red and covered with patches of white puss. She snapped a quick photo and sent it to Jacob.

Current situation. I can barely stand up. Will text later about when we can go see Coach. Sorry.

Piper's strep throat turned her weekend into a febrile blur. She woke from time to time to sip a lukewarm tea and to take her pills, but her sleep was filled with hallucinations of Sheriff Mismo, the night at the quarry, and Ned in the hospital. She vaguely remembered Noah and Cooper coming into her room to tell her Coach was back in the hospital.

By Monday morning, the antibiotics were working. In the bathroom, she gargled with salt water. Then she showered and brushed her teeth for the first time in three days. She spent the afternoon lying in bed, watching *Vampire Diaries* on Netflix, then ate half a bowl of chicken noodle soup, which strengthened her, though her stomach remained in knots. She texted Wanda to ask about Ned's funeral arrangements. Late in the afternoon, she changed into her dark blue jeggings, a green and blue flannel shirt, and her duck boots, and waited for Jacob. She pulled her hair into a ponytail and put on her diamond stud earrings. She didn't look like a killer.

It was almost dark when Jacob's red pickup truck turned down Rose Tree Road. Nobody was home, and Piper was glad for that. She sent a family group text, explaining that she had begged Jacob to take her to get some ice cream for her throat.

The hospital valet motioned for Jacob to pull ahead. He flicked his headlights to signal that he wasn't going to park. The afternoon had seeped into a smoky dusk.

Piper opened the truck door and the chilly air hit her. "Not chickening out, are you?" A cold front had pushed in while she was sick. A line of dancing leaves swirled across the hospital parking lot.

"No." Jacob handed his keys to the attendant.

She rubbed her thumb on the shiny chrome door handle. "Thank you."

"Right back at you, baby." He smiled and winked though his face drawn.

Piper wrapped her arms around her chest and walked through the automatic hospital doors into the bright lights of the main lobby and Jacob followed. The receptionist told her which room was Coach's and they headed that way. Passing the gift shop, she had a flash of déjà vu when she spotted another smiling, painted pumpkin. Piper's step quickened, as if she could outrun the numbness that had crept back into her soul. The tendrils of regret were knotted tightly.

They found Coach's room without a problem. It was empty, lit only by the blue glow of the TV. Jennifer must still be at work. Propped up on several pillows, Coach lay with his eyes closed, a Millington Valley pep quilt across his legs. The TV was set to Fox Soccer. A Liverpool and Manchester United game hummed in the background, punctuated by the bray of the heart rate and blood pressure monitors. Piper tiptoed across the room, sank into the recliner, and let her eyes adjust to the dim light. Coach's breathing was labored and he twitched and shuddered every few seconds. His angular features were sharper and his hair had turned almost completely gray.

It was dark outside now. Jacob went to the window and closed the heavy, industrial shades as if to hide the secret they were about to reveal.

"Coach?" Piper said softly.

Coach's eyes blinked and then focused. A weak smile. "What are you two doing here? Are Noah and Cooper here, too?"

"No, it's just us," Jacob said and went to his bedside. Piper stood at the end of the bed.

"Tell them to come tonight, eh?" His voice was thin and reedy. "We need to strategize about the Concord game. Our revenge is imminent."

"Sure, Coach. I'll make sure they drop in this evening," Jacob said.

Coach's eyelids fluttered. "I'm so tired. They drained some shit out of my lungs."

Piper circled around the bed. Up close, Coach was an even scarier sight. His complexion had yellowed, and tufts of his hair had fallen out. His collarbones pressed against his skin as if they might break through.

"Maybe now is not a good time. Should we come back?" she said.

"It's fine," he whispered. "I'm pumped full of morphine. Pretty good stuff. Fire away. What brings this fine lad and lassie here?" He pointed at the clock on the wall. "Seems to me you should be at practice, eh?"

"We need to talk to you," Jacob said. "It's important and it can't wait. There's something that's screwing up our lives." He looked at Piper.

She said, "Remember the night of Noah's birthday party? Not Labor Day, the night before. When we had the party at the quarry? You rode out to make sure everyone was okay to drive." Piper was talking too fast, but she couldn't help herself.

"Of course, I remember. I have cancer, not dementia." He laughed and then coughed.

Piper took a deep breath and forced herself to slow down. "You told us not to get in too much trouble. Not to do anything stupid." She tapped the bedside grab bar. "Well, we did something super stupid that night."

"It was an accident," Jacob said.

Coach hacked and pointed for the cup of water on this nightstand. Piper handed it to him and waited for him to settle. Then he gestured for them to move closer. "Go on." A shiver ran through his body and he shuddered.

Piper pulled up the Millington Valley quilt to cover his chest. Her voice cracked and she pressed her fingers between her eyes and then she told him.

The complete story.

Coach's stare became intense, alert, like he was peering into her innermost being. When Piper finished, he said nothing at first, motioning for the water again. He sipped it and then took a deep breath. "A terrible accident. A dreadful thing. But it is never too late to do the right thing. You must turn yourselves in. There will be a price to pay, but it won't be as bad as living with this secret." He paused and inhaled, his lungs rattling with the effort. "But wait until the season ends. Ned will still be dead in two weeks. It's selfish of me, but I want you guys to win." He reached for Piper's hand and then Jacob's. "We'll win and then I promise to help you make this right."

"Okay," Jacob said. Coach squeezed his hand, and then the blood pressure monitor buzzed and Coach's eyes fluttered. "Piper?" he whispered. "Agreed?"

"Yes, Coach."

Then another alarm sounded and Piper flinched. A nurse came into the room. "It's best if you leave him to rest." She pressed the reset button on Coach's monitor. "Don't worry. He's fine, just overtired."

As Piper backed out of the room, Coach opened his eyes and looked at her and whispered, "It'll be okay. Just take care of those bozos." He smiled weakly.

The nurse leaned over Coach as his head fell back. A doctor in green scrubs strode into the room. Jacob guided Piper to the door. The hallway was long and lonely as they made their way out of the hospital.

Sleep didn't come easily that night. Piper lay in bed, her mind unable to rest, worried about Coach. There was relief in knowing they had a plan, but there was an acute grief, too. She dozed off to sleep and at one point, woke from the brush of an icy chill along her arm. She kept hearing Coach say, "I'll help you." It took her a long time to accept that he couldn't make their guilt go away. He could only help them be big enough to admit it. It wasn't until the weak dawn light broke through the clouds that Piper truly realized that she had made a decision that would change the rest of her life. There would be no NYU. No dance scholarship—maybe no college at all. Her parents would be crushed to learn that she had hid her transgression from them. But that was okay because she felt something reminiscent of peace.

The next morning, Piper wore her heavy cream-colored fisherman's sweater over her shoulders, the arms tied around her neck. She felt stronger as she made her way through the crowded school parking lot with Jacob waiting for her in his truck. He smiled and popped the door lock. They were cutting today.

"Ready," he said as she slid inside. The cab was toasty and warm. Two cups of coffee waited in the center console, the scent filling the truck.

"Smells good. Toasty Buns Pumpkin Spice Latte?"

He nodded. "I thought you could use a shot of caffeine." He handed her a steaming Styrofoam cup. He was lighter, too. Relieved. They had made a decision. It was the right thing to do, even if they had to wait.

Jacob—his soft brown eyes, his gentle nature, his smile. Could it ever be the way he wanted—the two of them, a couple? She wanted him in her life. She sipped the coffee, holding the warm liquid in her mouth, savoring the cinnamon, nutmeg, and clove. Jacob was her friend—and if that's all she could be to him, she prayed he would be okay with that. Still, she set her cup in the holder and reached for his hand.

The verdict was still out.

He gently squeezed her hand, and she turned up her palm, exposing her naked wrist. She hadn't worn a Band-Aid. It had been five days since they had made up their minds to talk to Coach. There weren't any new burns.

"It's healing." He brushed his finger over her wrist with utter tenderness. "That's good."

Piper tucked a tendril that had loosened from her ponytail behind her ear and then swallowed. "I'm feeling better."

They rode to the funeral home in silence. It was time to say goodbye to Ned.

CHAPTER 39

"Better if we keep the truck here." Jacob nudged his truck into a spot between a white Toyota Camry and a blue Volkswagen Jetta in the most crowded section of the Boscov's parking lot. "My truck would stick out like a sore thumb up on Main Street," he said.

As they walked, the wind cut through the loose knit of Piper's sweater. "Hey, don't go so fast," she said. "I'm still in recovery mode." She tugged down her sleeves.

Jacob slowed and they popped into the grocery store to buy a bunch of white carnations.

"I should have picked roses from the garden," Piper said.

"Don't you think your Mom and Dad would have wanted to know why you were taking flowers to school?"

"Probably."

The cobblestone parking area aside the funeral home was empty except for Sheriff Mismo's squad car and three other vehicles, one of which was a hearse. Piper's heart sank, and she pointed. "You think we should let him see us here?"

"Does it matter? We're coming clean soon anyway. I want to be here for Wanda. It's the least we can do." Jacob waved his hand. "Plus, it doesn't look like anybody else will be."

"You're right, again."

They entered the building together and the funeral director, a vaguely familiar gray-haired man, guided them to the reception book. Piper counted only four other signatures. She wasn't sure what to do, but took the pen and signed her name. At the front of the room, Wanda stood next to an open casket, a crumbled tissue in her hand. There was one cascading spray of memorial flowers on the silver coffin and a large photograph of Ned in his army uniform hung above it. Piper recognized it as the one Wanda kept on her mantel. Soft classical music played in the background, and there was a scent of fresh lilacs in the room. Maybe they sprayed fragrance into the air. Two elderly women perched in the front row. Piper scanned the room for Mismo, but didn't see him. Wanda beckoned, and Piper and Jacob went toward her.

"Thank you for coming," Wanda said. Her eyes welled with tears. Piper handed her the flowers, offered her condolences, and hugged her. Jacob did the same, though neither one of them allowed their gaze to settle on Ned. Wanda dabbed her watery eyes with the tissue. "It's so wretched. That he died like this. You, young people talk about closure all the time. I guess I'll never have that." She gestured toward the empty seating area. "You know, he served his country in a terrible war. You'd think a few more people would want to pay their respects."

"Indeed," Jacob said. When did he start using words like indeed, Piper wondered?

"I am glad you two came." She moved toward the casket and placed her hand on Ned's cheek. "He used to call me The Great LaWanda. When we were kids, I wanted to be a magician and I forced him to be my audience." She smiled.

Piper peered over Wanda's shoulder. Ned's cheeks were hollow and his skin a gluey white. He was dressed in the same uniform he wore in the photograph. He looked lonely and small. Piper blinked rapidly, willing her tears not to fall. Jacob slipped his arm around her waist and pulled her close. Wanda touched Piper's shoulder. "It's okay, sweetheart."

Jacob pressed his fingers to his eyes and swallowed.

"I'm sorry," Piper said. "It's so—"

"Now, now, it's not your fault," Wanda said, her voice honey and sweet. "He's in a better place."

"We should get to school," Jacob said. Piper could tell that he was ready to get out of there. And she was, too.

"Yes, yes." Wanda adjusted her skirt. "Thank you for coming." She patted Piper's back and then Jacob's shoulder. "I'll be at the Concord game. It'll give me something to look forward to."

They made a quick exit from the receiving room, opening the door into the foyer. Sheriff Mismo looked up from the guest book, and Piper and Jacob froze.

"Hi, Sheriff Mismo." Jacob nodded and headed toward the door. Piper smiled and followed him.

"What brings the two of you here?" Mismo said to their backs.

"We're volunteering with the Visiting Angels for our Senior Project," Piper said, her heart thudding. "Wanda Walker is our match. We have gotten to know her and wanted to pay our respects."

"It's nice of you to come. I'm sure it goes beyond the requirements of your project. Sounds like A+ work." He cocked his head and raised his eyebrows. "It's best if you guys get back to school now. You don't want to break any laws."

Jacob pushed on the door handle and cracked it open.

"And good luck to the team, Jacob. I hope you beat Concord once and for all. It'd be nice for Coach O'Connell. A nice way to end things," he stopped himself. "End the season, I mean."

"I knew what you meant," Jacob said, the many unsaid implications hanging between them.

CHAPTER 40

A heavy frost capped the grass that morning, the front lawn a silvery, prickly meadow. No alarm clocks sounded. The pink and coral roses held their heads high, undaunted by the frosty, white crowns that landed in the night. Noah, Cooper, and Piper huddled at the kitchen table with twenty minutes to spare before they needed to leave for school. Nobody had slept well. Coach hadn't been at practice all week. They saw him last night and he was worse than the day Jacob and Piper had told him about Ned. He remained clear-headed, though, and pumped for the Concord rematch, insisting he'd be there. "I'd have to be dead not to make it." He wheezed and tried to laugh, but it came out a phlegm-filled gurgle. Nobody found Coach's constant death jokes funny.

"Mom called around 1 am. She was sitting with Jennifer until Coach stabilized." Dad poured steaming water from the teakettle into four mugs. "We'll have news soon."

With a fork, Piper pushed the Eggo waffle to the side of her plate. The syrup pooled in the dish's concavity and she swirled her fork in the sugary liquid, creating four little trails. She couldn't eat. This last week, her stomach had turned acidy and unsettled. Between the strep throat and the Ned-death-induced diet, she'd dropped ten pounds. She couldn't imagine having the strength to make it through Madame Sylvie's classes. Dance seemed far away.

Cooper folded his hands. "Maybe we should pray."

"Knock it off with that shit," Noah said. "Suddenly you're some religious freak. Like that's going to make everything okay."

"Leave your brother alone. If it makes him feel better, let him be."
Dad squeezed honey into his mug and then peeked at the window.
When he pulled back the drapes, Piper saw the tip of her mother's car.
"Here she comes." Dad tapped on the window.

Together, they went to the front porch. Many years later, Piper
would remember the sharp, cold cut of the morning air, the freshness,
and the scent of recently cut grass and wild onions, and the headlights of
her mother's white Pathfinder as it headed toward them down Rose
Tree Road. Mom parked next to the barn, killed the ignition, and stared
into space, lost in her own thoughts for a moment. Dad tightened his
robe's belt, as if that would fortify him against whatever news his wife
was to deliver, and he descended the steps. Noah hesitated and then
followed him. Piper and Cooper trailed behind, Piper's sneakers turning
wet with melting frost.

Their mother's eyes were bloodshot, and her face was drawn. Dad
slipped his arm around her shoulders, and rested his cheek against the top
of her head.

Mom looked at each of them. "I'm sorry, guys—"

"What?" Cooper rubbed the back of his neck. "No. No."

Noah placed his hand on his brother's back. Nobody spoke.

"They couldn't get his blood pressure regulated," Mom said as Dad
squeezed her shoulder. "He fought hard. His heart stopped three times,
but he kept coming back."

"He's—" Cooper gulped, "okay, though, right?"

"No, sweetie." Mom's voice quaked. "At 5:37 this morning, his
heart gave out for the last time."

Cooper wobbled, and Noah pulled him into his arms. A cold
pinprick exploded in Piper and her windpipe constricted as if invisible
hands pressed upon her neck. Noah's eyes were wet. Piper rubbed her
arms, trying to dislodge the icy blanket that covered her. Noah beckoned
her and she stumbled into their huddle as both of her brothers slung their
arms around her. Their parents' warm bodies pressed against their cluster.
The Rose family swayed in their driveway, arms entwined, tears running
down their faces. Piper's savior was gone. She would have to navigate
the truth on her own. Do the right thing. Coach told her to wait. So
she'd wait, but she would do it. She would tell the truth. For him.

CHAPTER 41

Swollen rain clouds sprinkled a fine mist on the Millington townsfolk, clad in trench coats and huddled under umbrellas, waited outside the funeral home. The line snaked around the building, in front of the United Church of Christ, and five hundred feet down Main Street. Cars jammed both sides of the street, the funeral home's lot, and overflowed into the cemetery. The jumbo orange mums that flanked the entrance were heavy with moisture and the stems separated under the weight. The soccer team was already inside.

With a disconcerting sense of having done this just last week, Piper sat in the front row with her brothers, Jacob, and Ethan, who had made an emergency trip home. The rest of the team was behind them, the folding chairs lined side by side several rows deep. Jennifer stood alone next to a silver urn on a thin wooden pedestal, greeting a long line of mourners. A poster-size photo of Coach in his New York Generals' uniform hung in the same spot that Ned's army photo had occupied a few days earlier. Piper counted fifty-seven flower arrangements, including an enormous memorial spray created with blue delphiniums, white roses, and a soccer ball that had been signed by each player and Piper. Coach was in that shiny vase, his bits of bone and ash. Piper twisted a rumpled tissue and wiped her eyes again. She had promised herself she would not cry, but she couldn't stop weeping. Coach dying wasn't part of the plan. Sure, he was sick. Deep down, Piper never thought this would happen. He would get better and help them make things right. The truth was a big and scary thing and without Coach; she felt unmoored.

Jacob's mother hugged Jennifer like she was a long, lost friend. She dabbed her eyes with her hot pink and aqua blue Lilly Pulitzer handkerchief, hiccupped, and broke into an exaggerated sob, leaning against Dr. Horn. It irritated Piper that Mrs. Horn acted like she cared. It was as if she wanted to make sure everybody saw her and remembered she had been sorrowful. Maybe then they'd forget she was the one who had gotten Coach fired with her nasty rumors, expediting his journey into that cold urn for eternity. Piper's gut clenched. She elbowed Jacob and gestured toward his parents.

"Why is she so distraught?"

"Piper, stop it." Jacob's eyes were full. "It's not like she wanted the man to die."

"Don't you think she's a little over the top?"

Jacob rolled his eyes. Ethan leaned over and whispered in his ear and they both rose and went to their parents and embraced Jennifer in a group hug.

The service passed in a blur. As team captains, both Noah and Jacob gave a quick speech, and then Jacob came back to sit with her. Principal Unger said a few words and Coach's boss from the battery company spoke. Cooper remained still, his hands clasped, and stared straight ahead. Piper tuned out; otherwise she was afraid she would fall apart. She rubbed her fingertips over the scabs on her wrist and fought the incredible urge to pick. Jacob slid his hand over hers, stopping her.

Then it was Piper's turn to speak. She rose, took three steps, and then turned around to face the crowd. Her vision blurred and she pressed her fingers against her eyes. She pulled the folded piece of paper from her pocket, took a deep breath, and read A. E. Housman's poem *To An Athlete Dying Young*.

The ceremony ended with Jennifer saying that Coach wouldn't want them to be sad and the best thing they could do was to live a good life in his memory. Then Queen's *We Will Rock You* was played. It wasn't the same as hearing it on the team bus in anticipation of a victory, but it lightened the mood. The receiving room was stuffy with the throngs of bodies and high humidity as people milled around after the service. Despite the crowd, Piper had never felt more alone.

"I've got to get some fresh air," Piper said to Ethan. They were waiting for their brothers by the rear door. Piper paused a moment, searching for the flutter in her stomach that being near him usually produced. Nothing. "I'll meet you guys at the car in a few minutes."

Outside, it was cooler, and the dampness was a welcome respite. Piper walked along the macadam path that led into the cemetery. Big oak trees canopied the lane and wet leaves gathered at the ridge where the footpath met the grass. Cars pulled out of the parking lot and headed down Main Street, their wheels noisy on the rainy road. The scent of moist dirt filled the air as she crested the small hill and began her descent toward the fairgrounds.

She froze.

The muddy outline around the freshly dug grave had smeared into the grass. The modest, temporary marker, square and flush with ground, read: Ned Walker, May 23, 1950—November 2, 2020. A pale pink earthworm stretched across the smooth surface. Piper stooped and gently plucked up the little creature and placed it in the moist muck at the base of the gnarled tree roots. "I'm sorry," she whispered to Ned. "I'll bring you roses from our garden."

She wasn't sure how long she stared at Ned's grave. At one point, she noticed that her hair was more wet than dry. The smack of heavy boots on the watery asphalt interrupted her reverie and she pivoted toward the sound. Sheriff Mismo wore a fancier version of his normal tan and brown uniform. Her throat tightened. Had he followed her here?

"Is something wrong?" he said. "You look like you just saw a ghost." He waved his hand and half-smiled. "Guess there are a lot of them around here."

"No, I'm fine." She hid her hands in her pockets. "It's a gloomy day."

"Paying your respects to Ned Walker, I see." He nodded and Piper's stomach flip-flopped. He studied her, waiting, as if expecting an explanation, and then he pulled his keys from his pocket and pressed the fob. His squad car's horn beeped and his siren lights flashed. "Had to park all the way down there."

"I needed some air. It was too gloomy and hot in there." Her excuse sounded weak even to her own ears.

"Sorry about Coach. He was my friend, too. Last time I saw him he was pretty doped up. He had some interesting things to say." He paused, as if challenging Piper to respond, and then he sighed. "Cancer's a bitch. Hopefully, the guys can win it all. That'd make him pretty happy."

"Piper!" Noah called from the top of the hill. Even from a distance, his face was filled with panic. "We're leaving now," he shouted.

"Got to go." Piper turned and started toward her brother, eager to flee Mismo. The church steeple, shrouded in mist, appeared to vanish into the clouds above Noah's head.

They piled into the Honda, all five of them: Cooper driving, with Piper in the front passenger seat; Noah, Ethan, and Jacob crammed into the backseat. When they got to the quarry entrance, Piper changed into her rain boots and donned her poncho. They hiked the path to the lake, stomping on naked, thorny wild raspberry branches. The trail was thick with fallen wet leaves, and Piper's boots grew heavy as the treads caked with mud. Still, with each footfall, she grew more determined, silently practicing what she planned to say. As they drew closer to the lake, the fresh scent of the water overpowered the raw, earthy musk. They found an outcropping of three big rocks on the stony bank and settled down.

"So why are we here?" Cooper said.

"We have something to tell you." Jacob nodded at Piper. She would take over now as they had rehearsed.

Piper stood. "Before Coach died, we went to see him." She paused and gave each of the boys her most serious look: first Ethan, then Cooper, and Noah. "We told Coach about what happened with Ned."

"What the fuck, Piper? Why would you do that?" Noah said, exasperated.

"We needed advice." She kicked her foot against the rock, and a clump of mud dislodged. "Keeping quiet isn't working." Her eyes welled with tears. "We took an accident and made it into a crime. Every day that we are silent, we commit the crime again. I can't live with myself and our silence, knowing our part in Ned's death."

Noah softened. "Hell, it's not been easy on any of us."

"Still, Piper, you promised to keep quiet," Ethan said. "And a deal is a deal."

Jacob rose. "Well, the deal is off."

"What? You've got the most to lose. You killed the fucker," Ethan said, his voice harsh. He picked up a stone and threw it hard toward the lake.

"Everybody, calm down," Cooper said. "You need to hear what Piper has to say."

"Coach agreed that the right thing to do is confess. We can't—I can't live—"

"I can't continue like this either," Jacob said. He placed his hand on Piper's shoulder. "It's eating me alive. I did something stupid and wrong, and I will gladly accept the punishment to clear my head."

"We're going to Sheriff Mismo. Coach was going to go with us, but obviously that will not happen now." Piper wrapped her arms around her chest, her poncho gathering in a wet clump. "But we're still doing it."

"The only caveat Coach gave us was that we would wait and not confess until after the last game of the season," Jacob said. "And we agreed."

"Are you sure you want to do that?" Noah said. "Once you say something, there's no going back."

"It doesn't matter," Ethan said. "It's three against two." He gestured to Noah and Cooper. "Our word against yours. It didn't happen. I'll tell Mismo that you just want attention because you're freaking out about not getting into Tisch."

Noah pointed to her wrist. "It's believable that you're mental. I mean, mutilating yourself? Mom and Dad are going to be so disappointed when I share that with them." His eyes were apologetic, but he wasn't backing down.

"Don't you dare," Piper said, her fury welling.

"I am not losing my scholarship because we made one poor decision. Not when I didn't even do it!" Ethan kicked a dead branch.

"Fuck you," Jacob said, turning a deep red.

"Just stay quiet and everything will be fine," Ethan said. "And if not, I think it sounds completely plausible that Piper's lost her mind. And Jacob is so in love with her he'll do whatever she says."

Piper's whole body clenched. Suddenly, Ethan was repulsive. And how could her brother—the guy who had helped orchestrate her Homecoming win, dressed up like a ballerina to cheer up Coach—be so cold-hearted?

"Coop?" Piper begged her little brother. "We should do the right thing. You know we should confess."

Cooper shrugged and pinched the bridge of his nose. "Man, I don't know. I've got to pray about it."

"Really, Coop?" Noah said. "Enough of this goddamn praying. The way you're playing, the D1 offers will flood in before the end of the season. You want to piss that away?"

Piper squared her shoulders and knew she had been lying to herself. She could never make the guys do the right thing. Still, she had to try. "Look, Jacob and I give you until the last game to make up your minds, whether you want to see the sheriff with us. I'd rather have you with us. But we are going to Mismo, and the evidence is on our side. Especially with Jacob accepting responsibility."

"Wrong about that," Noah said. "That gun is long gone."

"This is bullshit. You guys better keep winning and buy us time to talk sense into these two wackos." Ethan punched Noah's shoulder and tussled Cooper's hair. "Otherwise, war is coming sooner rather than later."

The ride home was silent, the tension prickly and thick. Nevertheless, Piper felt better than she had in a long time.

CHAPTER 42

The bagpiper marched in place at midfield. The doleful sound of "Amazing Grace" echoed through the valley. In the frosty morning sun, Piper was perched like a sentry next to Coach's Jeep, which Principal Unger allowed to be parked behind the Millington Valley bench. With the window open, Jennifer nestled under the same Millington Valley blanket that had covered Coach in the hospital a few short days ago. She watched the players warming up with a distant, empty stare.

"I think I'll go to Florida," Jennifer whispered. "I can't face the winter without him." Piper nodded, but didn't know what to say. Plus, her throat felt like a lemon was caught in it. She understood wanting to flee the valley. There were too many reminders here.

Coach's empty golf cart was parked near the goal that backed to Heartbreak Hill and had morphed into a makeshift memorial. Pots of mums were lined around it at the wheels, a Celtic FC jersey flapped from the open back, and a soccer ball lay on the seat, along with Coach's sunglasses, his umbrella, and a pack of Camel cigarettes.

The Concord coach contacted Coach Marky and offered to postpone the game a week to let the team regroup after Coach's memorial service. To Coach Marky's credit, he had polled the team to see what the guys wanted to do.

It was unanimous. They would play.

The bleachers were packed, and the sidelines crowded with lawn chairs and fans two rows deep. Piper located her parents huddled together on the top row of the bleachers, a shared blue blanket across their laps. Down below, Dr. and Mrs. Horn's lawn chairs were pushed close enough together that they held hands. Every fall sport team was there in uniform: the football players, the cheerleaders, the girls' soccer team, the field hockey players, and cross-country runners. Even the band was dressed, with instruments in hand. Sheriff Mismo stood off to the side by himself. Principal Unger and his receptionist sat in the first row of the bleachers. Mia settled on the ground, cross-legged in front of the fire trucks with a gaggle of drama students. She dabbed her eyes with a tissue. Ethan, being a former MVHS soccer star and captain, again had been given a ceremonial seat on the bench with the current players.

After warm-ups, the Concord players rose from their bench and waited at the sideline, their hands clasped behind their backs, their heads bowed. Before leading his teammates onto the pitch, Noah moved toward Jennifer. He wore a black armband inscribed in white with Coach's initials CJO. Mom and Dad had labored all night sewing the armbands. Noah hugged Jennifer and then walked over to the golf cart and tapped the hood. He waited at the edge of the field for his teammates. Jacob followed. Piper swallowed the lump in her throat as each player embraced Jennifer and then tapped the golf cart's hood. Tears streamed down Jennifer's face and Piper found it hard to breathe.

Then the two rival teams advanced, side-by-side to midfield. They parted and fanned into a circle around the bagpipe player. When the music stopped, there was a moment of silence and heads bowed. The wind blew, scraping the brilliant sun against their tear-stained faces. The moment of silence was broken as the bagpiper left the field playing *Scotland The Brave.* Then Mr. Franks led the band in a slow, mournful rendition of *The Star-Spangled Banner.*

With the shrill call of the referee's whistle, the game began—a game they'd waited for all season, maybe their whole lives. The boys of the Millington Valley soccer team stepped onto the field broken-hearted, aware that people get sick and don't always get better. Accidents happened. Life wasn't fair. There were no do-overs for bad decisions. They played as if their life depended on it, understanding that certain things were still in their control, certain things could be turned around, and that Concord could be beaten. They fought for redemption, and with the final whistle, they fell on their knees, their fists thrust skyward, tears on their faces, and victory on their side. The crowd erupted. As mad as she was at her brothers, Piper cried tears of joy. Coach would be proud. Deep in her heart, she knew somehow, she would convince them to do the right thing, but today she would let them have their victory.

The players signed the game ball and gave it to Coach's widow.

They had beaten Concord.

Finally.

For now, they had a reprieve. They could hold off the real world as long as they kept winning. Though she didn't admit it, this gave Piper some slight relief; she wasn't quite ready either.

CHAPTER 43

"Damn, Piper." Noah said curtly. "Can't you see that no good is going to come from turning ourselves in?" He knocked on the car window as he enunciated each word. "It's time to drop the self-righteous, sanctimonious bullshit."

"Wow, what a large vocabulary you have," Piper said as she studied Noah in the rearview mirror. She was done bowing down to him. He pressed his forehead against the glass, his eyes red-rimmed, his cheeks pale, and his normally well-kept buzz too long. The black CJO armband was wrapped around his bicep atop his long-sleeved, compression shirt. He pressed his fingers on the bridge of his nose.

"Cooper's got a lot to lose," Noah said. "Can't you think about anybody but yourself?"

"Like I don't have much at stake?" Piper gripped the steering wheel.

"Not like us. You already screwed up NYU."

She stole a glance at Cooper in the passenger seat. He was staring stoically out the window. It was a dark, chilly morning, and the fields they passed were a dull brown. Last night, the West Chester coach offered Cooper a full scholarship. Mom and Dad were stoked. If D2 schools were already making offers in Cooper's junior year, he was sure to end up with a full D1 ride come next year.

Noah sighed. "It's like we've been given a gift and you want to throw it in the trash. No good is going to come from being a martyr. Ned is dead. Nothing is going to change that. A fucked-up thing happened, but it's over, Piper. Trust me, it will all work out if you keep your mouth shut."

"Agreed." Cooper slumped deeper into his seat. "I don't feel like going to school. Should we cut?"

"Man, I'd be up for it," Noah said. "But I'm not hanging with our nutty ass sister."

"First, I'm not changing my mind about confessing. I was part of a coverup. Someone died, accident or not. And I played a big role in the decision to hide the accident. I wish I hadn't. I wish a lot of things. But my life is different now from what it was before that night at the quarry. Everything is covered in this slimy secrecy. It's destroying my life. And yours, whether or not you know it."

"Second, you guys have practice, which means you've got to be in school to attend after school activity." Piper turned on the radio and then added, "It's the last thing you can do for Coach. Win." Her voice hardened. "Plus, it'll buy you more time. Win a goddamn state title. So whatever happens afterward, you'll always have that."

"Somebody's got her estrogen on." Noah reached over the back seat and snapped off the music. "Coop, you've been praying lately. Anybody listening? We going to win a state title? By my calculations, we have a miracle due."

"Nothing yet, bro."

"What about the Concord win?" Piper turned onto Main Street. "Doesn't that prove something?"

"What? It doesn't bring back Coach." Noah tapped Piper's headrest. "Like Ned. They are both gone and neither of them have any influence in this world anymore. But you do. So keep your fucking mouth shut." He clamped down on her shoulder and squeezed.

"Knock it off." Piper wriggled. "What are you going to do? Beat me up?"

Cooper shifted in his seat to face Piper. "I think Noah's right. We have to drop this whole thing. We should stop talking about it. Let it fade. Maybe Ned's dying is a blessing. A message that we're supposed to keep our mouths shut."

Piper's grasp tightened around the steering wheel. "Is that what your God's telling you?" She took her eyes off the road for a moment to meet Cooper's gaze. "To not care that we left a dying man in the woods?"

"Hell no. But we didn't murder him. It was an accident." A plea for mercy and pardon flickered in Cooper's eyes.

"We didn't help him," Piper said.

Noah slammed his hand against the window. "Just shut the hell up. Everything is going to be fine." A raindrop splattered on the windshield. "I am so sick of hearing about this. Don't push me."

"Or what?" Piper flicked on the wipers and looked at Noah in the rearview mirror.

"Just don't test me." He peered out the window and quietly sang, "Once there was a little egg, that sat upon a wall. Soon he started to wobble, then he started to—"

Piper slammed on the breaks and they jolted forward. "Don't you touch Ernie's eggs."

Noah met her gaze in the mirror. "It's amazing that you care more about some stupid birds than you do about your own flesh and blood."

"Fuck you." She stared at him unsure of who he really was, but growing more certain of herself.

They drove in silence the rest of the way to school, the storm in Piper's chest about to explode. Pulling into the parking lot, Piper saw Jacob sitting in his truck at his regular spot. She tapped the horn twice. The rain fell harder.

"Damn." Cooper rummaged in the backseat. "Don't we have a goddamn umbrella in here?"

Piper rolled down the window as Jacob did too. "Wait for me, okay? I'm going to drop these two assholes at the overhang."

"Sure." Jacob gave her a weak smile.

Piper dumped her brothers at the curb where Mia was waiting. Noah wrapped his arms around her and kissed her forehead. He was a different person around her. Piper wondered what Mia would think of her boyfriend if she were privy to his nasty secret. Or maybe Mia knew. Piper shuddered.

She gently stepped on the gas, pulled away from the sidewalk, and headed toward Jacob. As she approached, he got out of his truck with a huge golf umbrella and popped it open.

"Thanks." Piper grabbed her book bag and squeezed underneath.

"You will not believe what happened," Jacob said as they let a school bus pass. "I got a text from the Shippensburg Coach. He wants to talk to me tonight. We scheduled a call for 8 PM."

"That's great." Piper sidestepped a puddle.

"My mom is excited." He stopped and looked deeply into Piper's eyes. "I figure I'll talk to him, but it changes nothing. About you-know-what."

226

"Let's not think about that for now. Just honor Coach by having a glorious end of the season. Make him proud. We'll worry about what we have to do later. Talking to the Shippensburg coach can't hurt."

"Guess you're right." In front of the school entrance, Jacob closed the umbrella. He touched the Band-Aid on Piper's wrist. "You're not doing that any longer, are you?"

"Eight days sober." She lied. Last week had been too much. Then she made a silent promise to herself that she wouldn't do it again and smiled.

"Good," Jacob said. He paused before opening the door. "I feel like, maybe, the worst is over. That things will work out somehow."

The soccer players walked the corridors as if in a thick haze, still shell-shocked from the emotional roller coaster of the last several days: Coach's death and memorial service, the incredible Concord win. Despite Jacob's optimism, Piper's cathartic rant against Noah, her bravado dissipated and she ambled through her classes, staying quiet and not interacting. Once again, a dull cramp of unease gripped her stomach.

Later at practice, Piper bundled in her down-filled Millington Valley parka, perched on the chilly metal bleachers. The rain had stopped, leaving the field soaked and rutty. A cold front was blowing in with a hint of winter. Coach's golf cart was parked on the far side of the field. The memorial had grown with flower arrangements, candles, and the football team had affixed a poster board to the front grill. It read *R.I.P. Coach O, MVHS Football*. The O was drawn to resemble a soccer ball. The world was emptier without Coach in it. The hollow sensation was everywhere.

Piper worked on her French for a while, but her mind wouldn't settle. The list she'd made, she carried in her phone case, folded into a small square. She dug it out from its neatly pressed position and unfolded it. Putting a little check mark next to a completed task made her feel better. She read through it again.

Be a good friend to Jacob (working on it)
Get back to dance (next week)
Focus on schoolwork. Straight As (trying)
Figure out Plan B for college
Write in my journal (makes me feel better)

Tonight, she would write to NYU, and appeal for a second audition. And then she'd fill-out the Goucher and Oklahoma college applications—both had decent dance schools. She scribbled Hunter

College on the paper. It was in New York and more affordable. She stared at the last item on the list:

NO MORE BURNS.

She didn't want to lie to Jacob anymore about her self–hurting. And she didn't want Noah and Ethan's claim that she was unhinged to be true. She had to stop.

JOURNAL ENTRY
FRIDAY, NOVEMBER 10

Things are microscopically better. Knowing we are going to come clean is giving me a touch of . . . I don't know . . . maybe hope? Maybe I can still make college happen? Or not. IDK.

I Googled, "How To Stop Self-Harm." The alternatives: Punch a pillow. Squeeze ice cubes. Draw on your body instead of harming. Strenuous exercise. When I dance so hard that I can't breathe, the urge goes away. But I don't feel like dancing. Maybe I should start running.

To stop, you are supposed to keep busy and not be alone. Also, stay away from any place where you self-harm. Other things to do: Throw away any self-mutilation tools. Aka: matches. Change your routine, add or remove ritualized steps.

Ask for help.

I'll write more later.

P.S. I did it. It was hard, but I called: 1-800-273-TALK and I didn't hang up.

CHAPTER 44

"You can't kick snow off a rope!" Jacob slapped Little Ryan's back as Little Ryan nailed a ball over the crossbar and it flew off Heartbreak Hill. "You couldn't hit a cow's arse with a banjo." He mimicked Coach's Scottish accent, making the A's sound the same. Since the chat with the Shippensburg Coach, Jacob seemed like a new man. Piper was pretty sure it was hope. Possibility.

"Why don't you try grabbing a salamander with Vaseline?" Little Ryan retorted in his best Scottish brogue, and they both broke into a hearty laugh.

In a flash, the team gathered around Jacob and Little Ryan, their moist breaths smoking in the cold air. Someone shouted, "You'll not play for me. You'll be with the fucking JVs the rest of the year."

"Aye, you've got to be the dumbest man I've ever met."

"Go for the jugular!"

Soon the entire team was shouting Coach's colorful colloquialisms. Piper watched from the far side of the field and smirked. Even Noah and Cooper had joined the messy, half-formed huddle, though they hung back and weren't as animated—especially Noah, who was downright stoic, observing the shenanigans with his arms crossed and a bemused expression on his face. Alone at midfield, Coach Marky blew his whistle and raised his bullhorn. "Hustle back. We got some serious work to do!"

The guys fell into position and practice resumed. On the car ride home, Piper was encouraged that her brothers had started to talk again in her presence. They hadn't spoken to her since Monday, when she wouldn't back down about confessing. They had come to a silent decision to agree to disagree—for the time being. She had decided not to bring up the Ned situation until after their last game, whenever that might be. So, they pretended everything was normal. Except of course nothing was.

"It might work," Noah said.

"No way." Cooper stomped his foot and the vibration rattled the floor. "Jacob can't play center mid. He's too freaking slow. Coach Marky ought to keep Coach's lineup."

"You're right," Noah said. "Stupid to switch now. You should be at center. Jacob ought to stay in the back on the right side. He's solid and tough."

"Maybe. He better not screw up."

"Hey, hey, hey. Whatever happened to win as a team, lose as a team?" Piper stuck out her tongue and made a silly face in the rearview mirror. She hadn't forgiven Noah, but for today she could pretend.

Noah almost smiled. "You look like you're taking one of those stupid fish-lip selfies." And then the corner of Cooper's mouth turned up and he expelled a little huff of breath. "I think we're going to win. I can feel it," he said.

Tomorrow was the first round of the district playoffs. That night Mia joined them for dinner. It appeared to Piper that Noah was falling in love. Perhaps that was more the reason that he didn't want to come clean about Ned. Piper enjoyed having Mia around. It was as if she had a built-in sister suddenly. Each day, the equilibrium regulated—the world felt more normal as if the status quo was being restored. But Piper knew this was an illusion that wouldn't last, that they were in the storm's eye and a person couldn't stay there forever.

"Do you think Jennifer will be at the game tomorrow?" Noah dunked his garlic bread in a puddle of marinara sauce.

"Maybe. I hope so," Dad said. "I'm sure it's been a tough week for her. Even if she's not there, you guys should seek her out. You don't want her thinking now that Coach is gone, that you don't care about her anymore."

Before Piper went to bed, she texted Jennifer: *Hope you are okay. It's been a sad week. District Championship tomorrow night. PR*

Piper woke early Saturday morning to Jennifer's reply:

Sorry, I can't make it. Leaving for Florida Sunday and I need to pack. Plus, well, it's just too sad. Sending my love. Coach is watching, I promise. Love you guys. I'll be back in a few months. Xoxo, Jennifer

The district playoffs were played in the Hershey Park Stadium. Millington was the first game at 11 AM. It was a weird time, but Noah said it was better to be the first game rather than wait around all day to play. The booster's club bought breakfast sandwiches for the team and, as team manager, it was Piper's job to pick up and deliver them. On Piper's drive into town, the valley glittered in the bright morning sun. The fields smoked and the mountaintops burst in bright patches of orange, yellow, and red. Since calling the TALK line, she hadn't burned herself, and she'd limited her hand washing to five times a day. Improvement. Small steps.

Toasty Buns' parking lot buzzed as cars swarmed in and out, their occupants racing into the café to snag a warm sticky bun to start the weekend. Inside, the place smelled like heaven—buttery fumes of crisping croissants, the sweet scent of baking yeast, cinnamon, vanilla, and coffee—oh, the coffee.

"It's ready to go." Mr. Dierdorf pointed to a box at the end of the counter, his baker's hat askew and his apron smudged with yellow paste. "I hate to miss the game, but there's no one to cover the shop on a Saturday morning. Wish them luck."

"Sure thing." Piper bounced on her tiptoes. "Where's the bill? I'm supposed to submit it to the office." The A-frame blackboard sign listed several yummy, gourmet coffees that make Piper's mouth water.

"No charge. Tell the boys when they win, I just want a photo with them to hang on the wall." He hooked his thumbs around the straps of his apron. "Order whatever you want. It's on me."

"Wow! Thanks." Piper gave Mr. Dierdorf a wide grin. "I'll try something new. How about the Toasty Café Mocha?"

"Coming right up."

From the takeout counter, Piper grabbed napkins, plastic forks, and salt and pepper packages and tucked them into the box next to the wax paper-wrapped sandwiches. She wedged the box on her hip and Mr.

Dierdorf handed her the lovely smelling coffee. "Thanks again," she said and turned to go, almost crashing into Mrs. Horn.

"Sorry, Piper." Mrs. Horn reached for the box. "Let me help you with that."

"I'm fine, thank you." Piper cringed, moving toward the exit.

"I'll get the door." Mrs. Horn stepped in front of Piper, blocking her escape. "Look, I know you're mad at me." Her shoulders hunched and she dropped her chin to her chest. "I've not had my proudest moments these last few months. How I treated Coach."

Piper didn't say a word. Instead, she stared over Mrs. Horn's shoulder through the glass door and into the parking lot. Her obnoxious BMW was taking up two spaces. Pathetic.

"You know, the Shippensburg Coach told Jacob that Coach called him just two days before he died to recommend Jacob." Mrs. Horn closed her eyes and took a deep breath. "It was so generous of him. Even after I—" Mrs. Horn touched Piper's forearm. They were near enough that Piper smelled Mrs. Horn's hairspray and saw the threads of the woman's pink lipstick bleeding into the fine lines of her upper lip.

"There's no excuse for my behavior. Coach's death has put things in perspective." She gulped as if she might choke on her words. "I'm ashamed of myself."

"You should be," Piper said in a shaky voice, a kernel of defiance in her chest.

"Jacob said you liked older guys and I let my imagination get the best of me. I'm sorry. You've always felt like a daughter to me—"

"It's probably better if I keep my mouth shut." Piper's bicep ached, and the coffee was burning a hole in her hand. "I don't want to be disrespectful to my elders." She held Mrs. Horn's gaze until the older woman looked away.

"I know, sweetheart. I hope you can forgive me." Her voice was clogged with emotion.

Piper's heart softened infinitesimally. "I'll try."

That morning, Millington Valley won the first round, 2-0. The following Tuesday, they advanced, winning 1-0. And two weeks to the date after Coach died, they played in the district semi-final winning 3-

2. For the first time in Millington Valley history, the high school would play for the district championship. Concord was making a parallel run for their district championship—maybe the two teams would meet again at States.

Noah and Jacob found a nice rhythm. Cooper refused to take off his armband. He not only wore it on game days like the rest of the guys did, but he also donned it with street clothing. Piper wondered if he slept in it. With each win, Cooper's praying grew more fervent.

"I'm giving God one more chance, that fucker," Cooper explained. "He let all this shit happen with Ned. He didn't heal Coach. He damn better give us that gold medal if he wants me believing in him."

"Maybe it's a woman," Piper said. "God. Maybe she doesn't walk around with a magic wand. Maybe it's not possible to pray your way to a state title."

But they won the district championship, and Piper wondered if Cooper's petitioning of the divine was working. The town's two fire trucks and Sheriff Mismo, in his squad car, met the victory bus at the corner of Rt. 664 and Pricetown Road, and escorted them down the hill and onto Main Street, Queen's *We Are The Champions* blaring through the windows. The lights flashed, sirens sounded, and the people of Millington Valley lined the pavement as the school bus made its way through town, horns tooting, cameras flashing, and souls healing.

The guys had bought themselves time, because Millington Valley High School soccer team was going to the PIAA State Tournament.

A first.

Only three games stood between MVHS and a championship cup.

CHAPTER 45

A pumpkin cut into a crude jack-o'-lantern was perched outside the post office. Its eyes and mouth had shrunk and it appeared to be melting. Piper cast a weary glance at it as she and Jacob traveled down Main Street. To step inside Wanda Walker's home, now that Ned was dead, filled her with fear. Neither she nor Jacob spoke. What would Wanda think of them if she knew they had left her brother to die? What were they doing, making her think of them as friends?

Wanda's limestone cottage was the last house on Main Street. The windows still had the original wavy glass, though the paint on the trim flaked and needed a thorough scraping and repainting. The frost had killed the flowers in the front bed, but weedy dandelions jutted through the thin mulch. It was as if she was seeing the place for the first time. Since she'd decided that she would confess, Piper saw everything with more clarity, her brain wanting to memorize details, fearing the world she knew would be stripped from her. Jacob went to knock on the door and Piper grabbed his hand.

"I can't go in." Piper tugged at her zipper.

"What? We can't stand up Wanda. She likes when we visit."

"Tell her I'm sick." Piper's stomach lurched, proving her point. "Actually, this total sham is making me ill. Until we come clean, I can't face her." She paused. "Do you think I'm a bad person 'cause I'm bugging out?"

"No, I get it," Jacob said. "You're a good person. And a beautiful dancer."

"What? Way to change the subject," Piper said.

"I thought I should tell you."

"Now? And how would you know—"

"I'm coming," Wanda called from behind the door.

Piper bolted. She scurried onto Main Street and the streetlight clicked on just as she passed the post office. Two hours later, she was back, sitting on the curb across the street waiting for Jacob.

"That was both terrible and great," Jacob said. "I was feeling pretty good, and then wham, she starts talking about Ned and it sucked. You're going to have to go back to get the service hours for our senior project."

"I know. Tonight, I just couldn't do it."

They cut through the fairgrounds and when they were deep within, Piper turned to Jacob and grabbed his arm. "How do you know what kind of dancer I am?"

"What?"

She studied his eyes, looking for a hint. The wind had picked up and Piper's hair blew across her face. "You've never seen me dance."

Jacob pushed a tendril behind her ear. "Yes, I have."

"When?" At his touch, a tingle sparked in Piper's stomach—warm and welcoming.

"You want to know?"

"Yes." She stared at him. The light from the rising moon caught in his brown eyes and even in the dimness she saw red creep into his cheeks, and her heart fluttered.

"Well," he stuttered. "I was at the *Nutcracker* last year."

"In Philly?"

He smiled, turning redder. "Yes."

"With who?"

"Myself." He looked away. "You were so beautiful and strong. I didn't tell you I was coming because I was afraid you'd think it was weird. I asked Ethan to go with me."

"And he passed?"

"Yes. But I still went." Then, shyly, he met her gaze and something electric shot through Piper. She froze, mentally checking and rechecking the physical current zapping in her body. It was real.

"Thank you," she said. Heat crept up her neck and across her face. She stared deeply into his eyes and their souls connected. *Ah, it's you, my love. The one I am meant to walk alongside.*

"I want to kiss you right now." He stepped closer. "With every particle of my being."

The feeling is mutual." She placed her hands on his chest. "But like you said, 'Maybe after,'" she said, but couldn't help herself from smiling. It was good to know how she truly felt. What she had always known deep down. Jacob.

CHAPTER 46

Boathouse row came into view on Piper's left side, and she forced herself to keep her eyes on the road. Mom and Dad had capitulated and allowed her to drive unaccompanied—probably just relieved she was ready to return to dance. Piper loved the colorful cottage-like houses perched along the Schuylkill River's edge, and how at night, with their perimeters strung with lights, their reflections glowed upon the water's surface. She took a quick peek as the Philadelphia Museum of Art appeared. Lately, the world blazed with extra details saying, "Take note; remember this." The sense of an ending was in the air—for soccer, dance, their childhood, and all that was before Ned. Piper was equal parts drawn toward and repelled by the impending conclusion. Her brothers were simply not talking about it.

Coach had died twelve days ago, but it felt like he'd been gone for months.

Last night, Millington Valley won the first round of States. The guys were confident going into the match. "Don't get too cocky," Noah said, breaking his usual morose silence from the back seat as they drove to school. In his best Scottish brogue, his lips turned up in a wee smile, he continued, "Underestimating your opponent 'tis thee kiss of death, I tell you. You must go for the jugular under all circumstances."

"We're seeded second." Cooper wore his CJO armband; he never took it off. "Shady Side Academy is the eighth seed. It's going to be a piece a cake."

And so it was.

Millington Valley won 2-0. The team gelled as if Coach was instructing them from the great beyond. There were no fouls, no sloppy play—just good, clean, technically sound soccer. Round one down. There were only two games to go to call themselves state champions. On the bus ride home, it came across Twitter feed that Concord won, too. There would be a rematch if both teams continued on this path. A divine settling once and for all. It was to be, because two nights later Millington edged out Parkland.

A state championship was on the line Saturday night.

Millington versus Concord.

A horn blared. Piper tapped the brake and checked her rearview mirror. An empty sensation swept through her chest. Funny, but she couldn't remember the last time she felt compelled to dance. She hadn't missed it the last few weeks. In her rearview mirror, she noted the guy drove a steel gray Audi A6. He hit the horn again and waved his hand, indicating that Piper needed to get out of the passing lane. She checked the odometer, which pointed to fifty-five, inched into the exit lane, and then navigated onto Broad Street. Despite the traffic, she found a parking space two blocks from the Rock School.

"Piper, dear Piper," Madame Sylvie scurried across the dusty floor to greet her. She caressed Piper's cheeks and kissed her forehead. "My darling, I'm glad you're back. It's terrible about your coach friend." She patted Piper's chin. "It's best for you to focus on your training. I've written to NYU. They will grant you a second audition, I'm sure."

Piper squared her shoulders and straightened up. "Thank you, Madame Sylvie." Then she took a deep breath. The studio's unique perfume was a comfort to Piper—the rosin, makeup, hairspray, sweaty tights and spandex, and Madame Sylvie's rosewater candles. She hoped it was enough fuel to move her forward. The six hours of class that stretched before her felt like something she had to endure. She paused. This was a weird sensation.

"Everything will be fine." Madame Sylvie swiveled toward the pianist and her long, chiffon ballet skirt lifted as Brittany entered the studio door.

"What was that about?" Brittany's hair was pulled back tightly against her head.

"Just the NYU stuff. She's trying to get me a second chance." They walked toward the changing room. "Truthfully? I don't know if I want to dance. I guess I'm not in the mood today." Piper leaned into the door with her shoulder, pushing it open. To sweat, to move, and to let the music fill her—that had pulled her through the horror of the last few months. This was an odd feeling. An unwelcome one.

Brittany dropped her bag on the bench. "You're reeling from the funeral and everything. You're spent. It's not like everything snaps back into place in a day or two." She wrapped lamb's wool around her toes and slipped her foot into her pointe shoe. "Let's go to Two Beans after class for coffee therapy."

Hours later, Piper and Brittany walked into the coffee shop, their coats zipped to protect their damp skin and sweaty tights and leotards from the November chill. A red maple leaf twirled across the sidewalk. This part felt good—she and Brittany, together again. Maybe next week, they'd ask Allison and Maya to join them. Perhaps the detachment—the root of the I-don't-feel-like-dancing-anymore—would evaporate if the foursome were restored. Possibly.

The bell jingled as Piper nudged the door with her shoulder. She inhaled the sweet whiff of baking muffins and freshly brewed java as they made their way to the counter. "I'll have the salted caramel mocha and the cranberry cheesecake muffin. Make it two. I'm starving." Piper waved her hand at the baked goods display case. "Get anything you want. I'm treating."

Brittany eyed the huge muffins, sprinkled with rock sugar, and the rows of flakey croissants and then ordered. "The same, but a coffee. Black."

Piper set her muffins on one of the up-side-down milk crates that dotted the café as makeshift coffee tables. She unzipped her coat, and sank into the beanbag chair closest to the big window facing Broad Street. Piper slipped off her Uggs and tucked her feet under her legs, shifting into a soft fold. "I could stay here all day. Maybe I should become a barista. Forget about New York, perhaps my contribution to the world will be to open a café on Main Street in exciting Millington Valley." She brought the steaming mocha to her lips, blew on it, and then took a sip.

"M. Sylvie put us through the ringer today." Brittany circled the thin stirrer around and around in her coffee.

"The entire class I was testing myself to see if I wanted to dance. My body went through the motions, but there wasn't that connection that happens with the music. It was sort of scary." Piper peeled the wrapped from her muffin and broke off a piece. "Do you ever get sick of it?"

"Not really." Brittany finally took the tiniest sip. "It'll pass. You're just in a funk."

"I hope so. It's weird to think about not dancing. It's been an important part of my life . . . one thing that hasn't let me down. That is, until Tisch, but that was my fault. Sometimes I question if I'm a good dancer."

Brittany stared out the window. A couple, dressed in coordinating black and yellow running gear, jogged by them. Piper glanced at them and then directed her attention at her friend. Brittany's upper lip quivered. "It's my fault, isn't it? The whole stupid American Ballet Theatre shit. Maybe you wouldn't feel this way if none of that happened."

"It's not you, Brittany. Trust me. It's definitely me."

"Well, we didn't talk for months after the ABT audition." Brittany blew on her coffee. "I'm not proud of the way I treated you. If I'm honest, I was jealous."

"That's not why. I'm sick of people expecting me to be perfect." Piper pinched her tear ducts. "Sometimes I hate myself." She pulled a clump of hair from her bun and twirled it around her finger.

"You are being way too hard on yourself. You're a brilliant dancer. And a good person." They were quiet and stared outside. Then Brittany pointed to Piper's wrist. "What's that?"

Piper laughed, the tears catching in her throat and turned her hand so Brittany could see it better. "I'm thinking about getting a tattoo. A rose." She had drawn a delicate flower, petals pink with a thorny, green stem over the purplish-red mark on the inside of her wrist. "Like it?"

"Cool. Looks like you might be allergic to the ink in the markers." Brittany touched Piper's hand. "I'm here for you. And I won't bail again. You know you can share anything with me, anything."

Piper paused. Every particle in her body wanted to tell Brittany all that had happened. The quarry. The accident. Ned's death. Mrs. Horn's rumors. The burns. Ethan. Jacob. Coach. Instead, she said, "Thanks, but I can't talk about it. Not yet, anyway."

Plus, she didn't have time. She had to get on the road and make it to Temple University before the heavy traffic hit.

CHAPTER 47

Ethan's dorm room door was ajar and the rat–a–tat–tat of the video game Fortnite reverberated into the hallway. Piper peeked inside and at first glance, thought Ethan was in the middle of a massive reorganization project. Every dresser drawer was pulled out and four sets of closet doors were open. Sweats, dress clothing, and cleats were strewn on the floor. Notebooks and textbooks lined the windowsill. His laptop was on his bed, and his PS4 perched on his desk, tethered by a tangle of extension cords and two controllers. A bowl of half-eaten Ramen noodles sat haphazardly on the bed next to a leftover pizza box. The smell was revolting: a nasty blend of mildew, dirty clothing, marijuana, and fermented beverages. The thought of dead skin particles, body oils, droplets of sweat impregnating the air made Piper's wrist itch and her heartbeat quicken. Before knocking, she dug into her bag, located her hand sanitizer, and expertly applied a cleansing glob.

"Piper?" He met her with an incredulous stare. "How'd you get in here?" He lounged in a grimy beanbag chair, bare–chested, red–faced, and sweaty looking like he had just returned from soccer practice.

"I smiled and followed a group in."

"Maybe the better question is, 'Why are you here?'" He fiddled with the controller and the clatter of machine gunfire echoed from the TV. "I thought we decided this can't happen." He pointed to himself and then to Piper.

"Don't patronize me. Are you afraid I can't keep my hands off you?" She stepped inside and closed the door. Then, looking around at the mess, she thought about sitting down, but reconsidered. "I came to give you one more chance to confess with Jacob and me. I think you'd come out a lot better in this situation if you went with us and told the truth. The last game could happen any day now. Time is almost up. We're going to do it."

"You guys are crazy. Just let it drop."

Ethan set the joystick on the ground. "We have a free pass. The old fucker is dead. Nobody knows what happened." He grabbed a shirt off the pile flowing out of his dresser drawer, smelled it, and put it on. "Doesn't it mean anything that you gave us your word to keep quiet? Why can't you leave it alone?"

"Because I can't. This would be something you don't understand. But I have morals."

Ethan moved toward her. "You're pretty hard to resist. Would we be terrible if we decided not to worry about Jacob in all of this? Me and you."

"I told you that's not why I'm here. Knock it off." Piper stepped back and bumped against his ramshackle bed, knocking a stack of odds and ends. An old flip phone clattered to the floor. Piper stooped. "What's this?"

"Nothing." Ethan lunged, ripped the device from her hand, and stuffed it in his pocket.

"It's a burner, isn't it?" Piper's eyes flashed. "It was you, wasn't it? You sent me an anonymous text the morning of my audition." For a split second, she felt relief it hadn't been Noah. "You're such a jerk. No, you're a coward. Like Coach said, people who don't sign their names are cowards with a capitol C."

"What the fuck are you talking about?"

"Don't play dumb. 'Secrets are safer,'" she sang. "Well, the game is over. I've always compared Jacob to you. I used to think you were better than him. Better looking. A better athlete." She smirked. "Hotter." She hugged her bag into her stomach, frozen in place, not daring to touch anything and praying that the horrible smelling molecules floating through the air couldn't permeate her clothing or her hair. "But you want to know the truth? You're a self-centered coward and that's disgusting."

Ethan looked as stricken as if she'd slapped him.

Her voice grew louder. "He's a better person than you are. He knows right from wrong. He's nicer. And he actually cares about me." She took a deep breath and composed herself. "Your brother is a million times above you. The truth is, this visit was an experiment. I wanted to see if you would do the right thing."

"What? Now you're testing me, Piper?"

"Yes, and you failed. There can never be an us. And it's not because Jacob is your brother. It's because I don't like you."

He reached for her elbow as she turned. "Don't be like that. Just because I won't throw away my whole future—your life, Noah's and Cooper's—and Jacob's most of all, you think I'm a bad guy."

"Yes, I do." She studied him anew, waiting, allowing him an opportunity to change his mind. When he didn't, she opened the door and said over her shoulder, "See you around the valley."

"You're nuts," Ethan shouted as Piper left. "Same tattletale that you've always been."

She stood at the end of the hallway, retrieved her hand sanitizer, and worked the gel down each finger, calming herself—it was okay, she would only scrub her hands this one time. She listened to the soft hum and occasional clanks emanating from behind the closed dorm doors. Then she rounded the corner and descended the steps, careful not to touch the handrail, her mind settled, and the bud of something new and beautiful sprouting in her heart. Its name was Jacob.

A half an hour later in the dark night, at a complete standstill on the Schuylkill Expressway with the river to her right, Piper marveled to see the boathouses strung with different colored lights. One building was outlined in red, another in green, and a couple in traditional white. As she waited for traffic to move, she rolled up her sleeve. There were no new welts, only the rose she had drawn, and this felt like an accomplishment.

That night, Piper completed the online applications for both Goucher College's and Oklahoma State's dance programs, attaching the hyperlink from her ABT summer intensive tape. There had been no word from Tisch about granting a second audition. And this was okay. She almost wished Madame Sylvie hadn't made the request. Piper also filled out the common application and submitted to Fordham University, Hunter College, and The New School as a regular student, no dance. Mom and Dad always said it was her choice, to dance or not to dance. And then, college might not be an option anyway, after she went to Sheriff Mismo. Piper hadn't done more research about what could happen, what the likely punishment would be. She didn't have a name to call what they had done—not Jacob, but the rest of them. But she felt proud that she wasn't trying to control the situation. And this was freeing in a bizarre way. But she wished Coach, with his bluntness and energy and generosity and wisdom, were here. Absolution was going to come at a high cost.

First, there was a state championship game to play.

CHAPTER 48

"This is it," Piper screamed, jumping to her feet. "Get forward!" Something was slipping away—something important. She pummeled the table. "Let's go!"

"Everybody up!" Coach Marky yelled, his voice wild with despair. At his side, Ethan hollered plays to his former teammates. The stands were loud and frenzied.

The last minutes of the title match were concluding in a frantic, impotent race against the clock. Piper imagined Coach red-faced, spitting venomous instructions from the ether. As the clock ran down, it flashed before her: the years her brothers played, the hours of practice, the constant bang of the ball against the barn wall, the English Premier games on the TV, the lumbering shadow of Coach's death, the jealousy, the victories, Mrs. Horn, the hope of what might have been. And what would come next with Ned. She wanted this win. For her brothers. Jacob. Her town.

The stars shone against the black night and the Hershey Park stadium lights cast a halo on the field. Piper's stomach whirled—this was it—the last game. Her heart raced and she felt as if she were falling with each Millington Valley shot that didn't go in the net. The guys hammered the Concord goal, but their attempts were denied by the Concord goalie, the crossbar, or maybe it was fate. Though the air was bitterly cold and Piper's toes were frozen, Noah was red-faced and sweat-covered, pushing himself harder than Piper had ever witnessed. Cooper, Jacob and the rest of the team were equally zealous and just as flushed.

A state championship game. Millington Valley was here. As providence would have it, Concord was too, and according to the newspaper, Concord was the favorite. But Millington Valley was holding possession and taking more shots. They were quicker to the ball on the ground and in the air. Play had stayed on their offensive side— they should have been winning. As regulation time expired, the bullhorn blared, the clock read 00:00 and the scoreboard 0-0. Next stop: two sudden death overtimes. The first team to score would win.

Piper was understanding why soccer was called the beautiful game. It moved in a fluid, continuous thread, more like ballet than any other sport. It didn't stop and restart like football, basketball, or baseball. There was an unparalleled aesthetic dimension to the flow and resulting unpredictability of the game; the crowd's hum a melodious accompanist. It was part craft, part magic—the line blurry between the two. It was also cruel and capricious. Soccer wasn't partial to favorites or care which team was supposed to win. You could play ninety minutes and still have neither team able to proclaim victory. You could battle through two sudden death overtimes, and still not have a winner. An entire season could be whittled down to five penalty kicks.

As this game would.

Waiting for the goalies to warm up and the penalty kickers to take their places, Piper scanned the stands, half-believing she would spot Jennifer. That she would have flown home to be at this game. Instead, she recognized Wanda Walker, bundled in a three-quarter length ski coat, her Millington Valley hoodie pulled over her head, wedged next to Piper's parents. Mia skipped sitting in the student section and took her position on the other side of Mom and Dad. Dr. and Mrs. Horn parked behind them—a quiet truce in place.

Again, the demarcation of blue and red in the stands gave a colorful visual of the rivalry. Both sides were subdued. Muted conversations took place and people milled about, making their way to and from the concession stand and restrooms. The energy was restrained, as both sides braced for what might happen next. And perhaps Concord was shocked that Millington Valley was making this game a challenge.

The referee blew his whistle, and both teams sent their five best shooters and their goalies to the field. Millington Valley's designated kickers stood together with their arms draped over each other's shoulders. In a penalty kick situation, the pressure is on the kicker; he has the advantage. The most the goalie can hope for is to read a clue by the way the shooter moves his hips and react fast enough to save the shot. Which is exactly what the Concord goalie did when Cooper took the first penalty kick for Millington.

Denied.

The blue and white fans deflated, and Cooper hung his head. The four other MV kickers slapped his back and Noah pulled his brother into the pack. Then Concord missed the first shot, too. Okay, still a tie—0-0. Little Ryan, the number two man and the only freshman, faked left and then rocketed his shot into the upper right corner of the net. The crowd exploded. Concord matched the goal—1-1. Jacob made his shot. But then Concord's third kicker whacked the ball and it went too high, sailing over the crossbar—2-1. Noah, the fourth man, walked toward the ball, picked it up, kissed it, and looked to the heavens. Then he drove his shot low into the sweet space in the back right corner. The stadium silenced, the score 3-1. If Concord fumbled the next shot, Millington would win—3-1. There would be no need for either team to take the final kick.

Concord missed.

Noah sprang into the air and then fell on the ground as Cooper and Jacob slammed into him. Little Ryan jumped atop the dog pile and the other guys followed. Coach Marky dropped to his knees and thrust his clipboard skyward as Ethan charged the field. The Concord side remained quiet while the Millington Valley fans erupted in joy. Mom and Dad were on their feet, leaning against each other, smiling, and Piper wasn't sure from the distance, but she thought they were crying.

Alone at the score table, Piper wept. This wouldn't repeat. Noah and Cooper would never play on the same team again. Coach was never coming back. But Millington Valley had won. That couldn't be taken away from them. Noah, Jacob, and Cooper would have that badge. Piper didn't know what they said to each other as they milled about the field after the game. She watched from the sideline: the pictures, the medal ceremony, the newspaper interview, and the bear hugs. Piper would let them have tonight to celebrate.

Piper waited at the score table, clothed in her heavy coat, transfixed. Jacob hadn't gone with the team into the underground locker room. He knelt at the goal post, his eyes closed, his forehead propped against the metal pole. His uniform jersey was wet with sweat, and even from a distance he appeared to be shivering. Piper took a blanket to him, but he refused it and told her to leave him. When Jacob finally lifted himself off the cold, wet turf, he pulled the black CJO armband from his arm and wiped his tears with it.

Noah, Cooper, Jacob, and Ethan were camping out at the quarry tonight. Earlier they had decided, win or lose, they would raise a toast in Coach O's honor. A tense understanding had been reached, and the lines drawn: Cooper, Noah, and Ethan on one side and Piper and Jacob on the other. In the morning, the unknown world would present itself when Piper and Jacob met with Sheriff Mismo. But until dawn, Jacob was their brother and friend. They would spend one last night as teammates.

CHAPTER 49

Showered and snuggled into her cozy flannel pajamas, Piper was at the kitchen table, sipping chamomile tea. The ancient herb was supposed to alleviate stress and soothe an unsettled stomach. So far it wasn't working. As the minutes ticked closer to morning and Piper's self-imposed deadline to meet Sheriff Mismo, she was getting sicker and sicker.

"I finally finished and painted your bookshelf." Dad smiled and set a Federal Express envelope on the kitchen table. "This is for you. Jennifer sent it. She texted, asking that I give it to you tonight after the game. And Mr. Dierdorf phoned. He's hosting a celebration brunch at Toasty Buns in the morning. He said it's his treat and everybody's invited. Text the team. I'll email the parents."

Piper lifted an eyebrow and reached for the package. It was late, and Mom was already in bed, and the guys, as they promised, were at the quarry, probably freezing their asses off. And now she'd have to wait a couple extra hours and endure the spontaneous championship breakfast party she didn't want to go to. Still, she was proud that she hadn't burned herself, and she'd only washed her hands two times since she'd gotten home.

"It was quite a win." Dad smiled. "Might be hard to fall asleep after all that excitement. The whole town is thrilled. I bet Toasty Buns is mobbed tomorrow morning."

"A night we'll remember, for sure." Piper quickly sent a team text and then picked up the Fed Ex package and ripped the perforated cardboard tongue on the back of the casing. "I'm going to bed after I finish my tea."

"Sweet dreams." Dad planted a quick kiss on the top of her head. "See you in the morning. It's been a rough season with Coach and all, but I'm glad you got to be a part of all this."

"Yeah, me too." She rolled the cardboard strip into a tight ball. "It's been . . . a life-changer."

She waited until she heard her father climb the steps and cross the floor, the creaky old boards announcing his every move. When all was quiet, she opened the parcel. Inside there was a sealed manila envelope and written across the front in a black sharpie, it said:

Piper,
Coach, my dear foul-mouthed, loving husband, made me promise to get this letter to you immediately after the last game. Remember, we love you and your brothers. I'll always be here for you.
Much love,
Jennifer

Piper's hand shook as she slipped her forefinger under the envelope flap and opened it. Inside there was a single piece of paper, folded in three. A message from the dead.

Dear Piper,
I'm sorry I'm not there tonight. I'll never know how this season ended, and that is my greatest regret about leaving so soon. No, not true. My deepest sadness is that I won't get to see you and your brothers head off to college, find your partners, decide on your careers, and start your families. Damn well pisses me off. Jenny and I could never have children, so when we met your gang, you guys became our kids. Thank you for welcoming us into Millington Valley. It's a tough town to crack. Eternity is approaching fast and I'm choosing to leave this world believing we're the PIAA State Champions. And somewhere along the way we crushed Concord once (or twice would be better).
Sports is a metaphor for life and I hope I've given you, your brothers, and the rest of the team a few lessons on the field that will help in the real

world. God knows I wasn't always an outstanding role model. Promise me, you'll never smoke or curse. And always wear sunscreen. Kidding aside, understand I had you and your brothers' best interests at heart. Trust me, I know I'm not always the most likable person. Hell, there are people who out right hate me (our dear friend Mrs. Horn, eh?). Despite how much that woman irks me, I convinced the Shippensburg coach to take a chance on Jacob. He's a good kid and deserves a shot. Keep in mind it's our differences that make this great world spin.

More than anything, remember there will be days when you'll be the underdog, the situation will seem hopeless, the bear will feast, but you still need to step on the field and give it your all. That's why we play the game. The winner is not predetermined. Always put your best foot forward and attempt to do the right thing. With that, I'm asking you for a favor.

My last wish is that you NOT confess to Ned Walker's accident. Know it was enough that you and Jacob wanted to do the right thing, and that you did the right thing when you came to me. I told you to confess after the final game, but that was only to buy some time and figure out how to fix this situation. After a lot of talking with Jenny, I met with Sheriff Mismo. I admitted to the shooting, explaining it was an accident. Noah gave me the gun and my fingerprints are all over it. Little Ryan was questioned and placed me at the quarry the night of the shooting. Sheriff Mismo has to do his "investigation," but the plan will be that he charges me posthumously. I've asked him to wait a couple days until after the team's last game so it won't cloud the joy you'll feel in victory or the time you'll need to mend if you've lost. And my sweet Jenny will stay in Florida for a few months until the talk calms down.

Piper, this is my gift to you, your brothers, Ethan, and Jacob. I've struggled with this decision. What you guys did was wrong, but you know that now. And I don't want you to ever forget. Let it be a part of you; let it guide you. There will be very few opportunities in your life when you get a second chance. My life is over. Let me take your guilt, shame, and your one bad decision with me. Your only burden is to do something good with your life. Find your purpose. Maybe it's dance and maybe it's not. Be true to yourself. And keep those bozos in line. You guys will do great things. Do not let me down.

Forever your friend,
Coach O

Tears fell from Piper's eyes onto the letter. Gratitude swept through her body, and then a quiet rage erupted. Noah knew about this. She grabbed her coat, the Pathfinder keys, and took off for the quarry.

CHAPTER 50

Piper ran like she had never run before. Jacob and Ethan's truck and the Rose Honda were parked at the quarry entrance, so Piper knew they were here. The frozen dirt broke under her footfall, and thorny, naked branches caught in her coat. The night was dark, and she held her phone in one hand, the flashlight bobbing against the black woods. The last five hundred yards she was in actual pain, sucking air. She smelled the campfire before she found them in the clearing and slowed down.

"Who's there?" Noah called.

"Me," Piper replied, plunging out of the woods, her hands up.

Noah wore his gold medal on the outside of his MVHS all-weather jacket. "What are you doing here? Is something wrong with Mom and Dad?"

"You're an asshole!" Piper punched his chest. "And a liar!"

Cooper jumped up and ran over, clamping his arms around Piper. "Simmer down," he said. Ethan and Jacob approached.

"You knew Coach was going to take the blame. That's why you weren't too nervous." Piper pummeled Noah's chest. "And you started sleeping again. Stupid me, I wanted to believe that you were coming around."

"What is going on?" Jacob said.

Piper thrust Coach's letter at him. "Noah talked Coach into confessing to shooting Ned." Jacob flicked on his phone's flashlight and read the note.

"Hold on," Noah said. "It was totally his idea. He called the night after you and Jacob did your stupid blubbering. He said he had a plan, a way to correct a mistake. That's what he called it. A mistake. Not a crime. Not a homicide."

"And you're okay with having Coach take the blame for something he didn't do? That's how you want him remembered?"

"God, Piper," Ethan said. "Look, Ned is dead. Coach is dead. Just let it go."

"You act like we're in some video game. And there are no real consequences for anything. When we left that quarry, we killed a man. What we meant to do doesn't matter. Every crime is a mistake, isn't it? Doesn't it mean anything to you guys that Ned was alive when we left him? Are you sociopaths? Can you live with that the rest of your life?"

"What good will come from telling? Seriously? I'll lose my scholarship." Cooper tugged at the medal around his neck. "They're right, you know."

Jacob handed the letter back to Piper and looked at the guys. "Look, I'm the one with the most to lose. It's not okay to let Coach take the blame. Plus, he was so drugged up, I don't think he was thinking clearly."

"Just shut up." In one quick movement, Noah tackled Jacob, throwing him to the ground, and punched him in the nose. Piper jumped back and stumbled. Then Cooper lunged to pull Noah off Jacob.

"You and your goddamn self-righteous bullshit," Noah hissed, his arms flying.

Jacob bucked and flipped Noah onto his back, pinning him. The two guys were equally wild and mutually furious. Ethan grabbed Jacob from behind and tugged to no avail.

"Stop it. Stop fighting!" Piper shouted.

"You just want to get into my sister's pants," Noah said as he hit Jacob's back. With that, Jacob kneed Noah in the crotch and Noah shrieked. Jacob rolled off Noah and collapsed. White-faced, Noah groaned, turning to his side. His eyes were squeezed shut and his hands covered his groin. Jacob wiped the blood from his nose.

And then it was over.

"Shake it off," Cooper said and reached for Noah's hand. He jerked his brother to his feet.

Noah stood and winced. "Asshole," he muttered to Jacob.

Piper crouched on the ground next to Jacob. "You okay?"

"Fine." Jacob's voice hitched.

"It's best if you get out of here," Ethan said to Piper and Jacob. "Everybody needs to cool down. And you two need to wake up. You're right, Piper, this isn't a game. It's our fucking lives."

Piper slipped her hand under Jacob's arm and lifted. He easily stood up and wiped his coat sleeve across his nose again. "Let's go," she said softly.

"Whatever else you want me to do, Piper, I'll do it." Noah called after them, his voice contrite. "But not this. We made a mistake. A bad one, and we're sorry. We're sorry! Please let it go."

Piper and Jacob made their way back to the quarry entrance. "They can ride home together in the morning." Jacob opened the Pathfinder's passenger door for her. "You're brave," he said, and chuckled. "Like Wonder Woman and Black Widow on steroids."

"What do you think?" Piper said. "Are they right?"

"No, I don't think so. Ned's blood is on my hands and I can't live knowing that. I can't think about their scholarships. I can't even think about mine. But honestly? It's up to you. I trust you to know what's right. I'll do whatever you want. I don't want to ruin your life."

She leaned against the car. "Let me sleep on it," she said and looked at Jacob. He wasn't the little boy she'd grown up with, and it was as if she saw him as another girl might. His curls were charming in a crazy, sexy sort of way with a big lock falling across his forehead, and his eyes were a soft, honey brown. Just a little taller than she was, he was solid, his chest heavily muscled like his legs, a rock—a solid, secure boulder. She felt the little shoot that had sprouted in her chest bloom and grow, stirred to life by his pure intention. He loved her, and she knew this, and this more than anything was a balm on her soul. In all that was wrong, if they walked forward together and did the right thing, she knew they would be okay. Somehow. She didn't want to wait until after.

So, she took his face in her hands. Startled by her touch, he cocked his head as if to ask what she was doing. Then she traced his jawbone and ran her fingers over his lips, never taking her eyes from his. Little electric snaps fired through her body, stronger than anything she'd ever felt with Ethan. When their lips met, Piper tasted his sweat and blood and knew she was coming home. He pulled her into his chest and his hand slid behind her back and rested above her tailbone, both heavy and soft, reassuring and exhilarating.

When Piper's breath caught and she was about to lose herself, Jacob stopped. "Not now. When this is all over." He smiled, his face full of adoration and devotion. "I've waited so long for you. Let's make things right first." He gently placed his hand over hers and turned her wrist to face his lips and then he kissed the burns that were slowly morphing into a single, fierce rose.

Piper dropped Jacob off at his place and drove home. Before she went into the house, she rummaged through the barn and found the super long extension cord and the floating pond deicer. The air was unfriendly and cold; the moon high and bright. The cygnets were due to hatch any day and she couldn't chance the water turning too frigid. She dragged the cord across the yard, attached the deicer, and placed it in the black water. Bert snorted and glided across the glassy surface. His opalescent feathers gleamed in the moon's shimmering beams.

"Big things coming," she said to the majestic bird. "For all of us."

She feared what tomorrow would bring, but she didn't need the night to think about it. She knew what she had to do. Accepting responsibility for what had happened would be the only way she would ever get over this. The only way she could ever be free. She sent a group text to the guys.

Tomorrow after breakfast. 12 PM meet me at the Sherriff's. I'm going with or without you.

She hit SEND.

CHAPTER 51

The next morning, from her third-floor bedroom window, Piper watched the driveway with a crater in her stomach. The bookshelves' fresh paint smell was strong. She checked her phone again, a new sort of nerves revving in her gut. Noah's text was time stamped 1:17 AM.

Ur on ur own.

A heavy frost covered the yard and a thin layer of ice collected at the edge of the pond far from the heater floating in the center. Ernie perched on her nest twitching side to side and Bert waddled back and forth on the bank like he was nervous. And then a tiny gray cygnet stumbled out of the nest. Bert headed to the water. The baby tottered and slid into the pond, following its father.

A sign.

Mom and Dad left to decorate Toasty Buns so Piper had the house to herself. She walked through each room, letting her mind pause on certain memories. Glimpses of Christmases. Sunday dinners. Horseplay with her brothers.

At 9:50, when Noah and Cooper still hadn't shown up, Piper retrieved Madame Rosemary's blue ribbon and tied her hair into a ponytail with it. Then she left and drove through the valley. The brilliant sun turned the muddy autumn fields a deep chestnut brown and the leafless mountains black against the blue sky. Cruising down the hill, she spotted the overflowing Toasty Buns' parking lot—the whole town was there. Mr. Franks conducted the marching band as they swarmed the sidewalk, joyous music thumping from their instruments. She found an open spot on the street and scanned the mob scene until she located Jacob. He motioned for her to jump into his mother's BMW. Only then did Piper let out a breath.

Of course, he was there. He would never let her down.

"When we're done here, we'll head over to Sheriff Mismo's office," he said. His swollen nose looked tender, and purplish rings shadowed his eyes. "You ready?"

"I think so." Coach's letter was tucked in her pocket for later. "Are we doing the right thing? Our brothers will never talk to us again."

Jacob looked at his watch. "There's no turning back now." For the first time, she saw doubt, or maybe it was fear, in his eyes. As the parking lot grew fuller, they waited together, both silently hoping and looking for their brothers, the heat blowing, their fate hanging, Eventually, Jacob said it was time to go and he opened his door, but before he exited, he extended his pinky.

"The Rose-Horn secret handshake. Whatever happens today, I will always love you."

Piper linked her little finger in his. "We've got this."

They walked across the pavement, and as Jacob was about to push open the door, a horn blared. They turned around. The Rose's black Honda flew over the top of the hill, followed by the Horn's red truck. The vehicles slowed and swung into the packed lot. Ethan busted out of the truck, headed straight for Jacob, and wrapped his brother in a hug. "I'm with you, Buddy."

Noah slammed the car door. "We win as a team and we lose as a team, right?"

"What?" Piper said with astonishment. "You changed your minds?"

Cooper hugged his sister. "We fought about it all night. Admitting what happened is the right thing to do. Let's hope the big man has mercy on us."

"We can't let Coach take the fall," Noah said. "I fucking hate to admit it, but you're right. This shit is going to eat us alive if we don't do something." He tenderly knocked her shoulder. Then he slung his arm around Cooper's neck. "And this guy is trying to beat you for Goodie Two Shoes of the family. His moral compass is pointed fucking due north."

"I couldn't pretend any longer," Cooper said.

"I knew it." Tears welled in Piper's eyes and her heart swelled. "Deep down, I knew you'd come around."

The five kids walked into Toasty Buns, brothers and sisters, friends and enemies. Their parents, teachers, fans, friends, and teammates cheered as they entered and, with the scent of coffee and the possibility of redemption, something uncoiled in Piper. All smiles, Mr. Dierdorf shuffled people to tables and raced around refilling drinks. Mom and Dad sat with the Horns just like old times. Every table was packed with standing room only around the breakfast bar where Principal Unger and Coach Marky were stationed.

"Hey, hey, hey," Little Ryan said and slapped Cooper on the back. "I saved you guys a table." He pointed to the booth by the window. They maneuvered through the throngs of well-wishers. Noah spotted Mia and waved her over.

"You sit with the team," she said and kissed his cheek. "I shouldn't leave my parents." She pointed to the far corner where her mom, dad and little sister sat donned in MV blue and white. "We'll catch up later." She hugged him. "Congrats, again!"

Piper slid out a chair festooned with blue and white balloons at the head and the guys slid into the booth on either side. She wanted Coach to be here—today—to bask in the glory of this moment. The feast began and they stuffed themselves as if it were their last meal. Thick French toast. Maple syrup. Eggs Benedict. Hash browns. Sticky buns. Freshly squeezed orange juice.

It had been a waiting game—this lying season—and she had won. The guys were going to do the right thing, and this was all that mattered. Piper sipped her coffee and glanced at each of them. Jacob first, then Noah, Cooper, and Ethan. They were trying to be good, decent human beings. They had decided to come clean. They were accepting responsibility, and that meant something. Whatever it was had snapped and fallen toward justice. And in that moment, she decided this was enough.

She couldn't do it.

She could not destroy their lives. Plus, it was what Coach wanted.

One life had been lost. The tally was too high already.

Touching her wrist, she ran her fingertips over the smooth welts and sent up a silent promise to Coach. She was understanding how much he must have loved them. And she would give that gift to the guys.

She pulled out her phone and typed. She held up her cell, tapping the screen, and raised her eyebrows, indicating they should check their devices. One by one, each of the guys retrieved their cells and read her message.

That u decided to do the right thing is ENOUGH. The secret stays with us. Congrats state champs. MVHS rules! Love u, P

"What?" Jacob said thunderstruck. "Is that what you want?" Before Piper could answer, Coach Marky clinked his fork against his orange juice glass. The recently appointed twenty-four-year-old coach rose and the crowd shifted to face him.

"Attention, attention," he said as he raised his glass. The room quieted. "This is a glorious victory. A time of celebration." His voice cracked and he paused. "It's been a pleasure to lead these fine young men, especially our seniors." He nodded toward Noah and Jacob. "The truth is, we wouldn't be here today if it weren't for one man. Coach Christopher O'Connell. Rest his soul. He made us believe we could win. That anything could happen. That Concord wasn't invincible. I can hear him right now, 'Sometimes you eat the bear and sometimes the bear eats you.' Well, we ate the bear last night." He raised his glass a little higher. "That's all I've got to say."

The fans applauded and there were echoes of hear, hear and then Ethan grabbed Piper's arm. "Do you mean this? You're not going to turn us in?"

"I'm not. Coach wanted us to make something of our lives. To do good. That can't happen if we're in juvy or jail. Do you think you bozos can do that?"

Noah looked at Piper imploringly. "But are you serious?"

"More serious than I've ever been." She touched Jacob's shoulder. "You too, forgive yourself. No good will come from more destruction. We can't undo what has been done."

Jacob nodded solemnly. "You're right. You're always right, Piper."

The relief was palpable. Noah pushed his plate aside and placed his fist in the center of the table. "Do good," he said and squeezed his eyes so the tears wouldn't fall. Ethan laid his palm atop Noah's knuckles and struggling to speak, uttered, "I promise, Pipe. Thank you. And . . . I'm sorry."

Then Cooper reached across the fold, added his hand to their huddle, and bowed his head. "Thank you," he said softly.

Jacob's was last, and his fingers trembled as he set his hand upon the pile. "I love you guys. Man, I'm sorry."

Piper's future flashed before her, unfettered.

Maybe there would be another Tisch audition. She looked at her parents; they were so happy, laughing and enjoying the morning. She would make them proud.

New York was possible.

Plus, there was this new thing with Jacob.

And dance. She wanted to dance again.

She couldn't wait to get home and see if the two other cygnets had hatched.

For the first time in months, hope bloomed in Piper as she lifted her hand to add her flesh to their covenant—their vow. The clatter of cutlery and the jolly chatter of victory seeped into her marrow.

It was then, through the big storefront window, she saw Sheriff Mismo's squad car followed by two more police vehicles crest the hill— their sirens whipping red and blue in the radiant morning. The din in the café faded to a hum as her every sense sharpened and the room grew still. Her mind processed the situation in slow motion—each tick of the clock elongated and delayed—until the blare of the sirens crashed down the hill and exploded in her head.

The guys' heads jerked toward the street. A shocked what-the-hell look crossed Noah's face and Ethan paled. Cooper shut his eyes and prayed, silently. It was as they watched Sheriff Mismo walk from the parking lot that Jacob reached for Piper's hand.

"You can't undo what has been done," he whispered. Then even softer, he said, "I told Mismo last night. I thought it would make it easier for us today." His breath brushed her ear. "No matter what, I will always love you." He kissed her softly.

Again, Piper turned to look at her parents, the flashing red and blue of the police lights in their faces. They would be disappointed—shattered, betrayed—and this pained her more than anything.

Still, as Piper stared through the window, she permitted herself one last fleeting possibility that she was misinterpreting everything. Her fingers tightened in Jacob's and her heart thundered in those few moments as Sheriff Mismo unclipped the handcuffs from his holster, pushed open the Toasty Buns' front door, and their futures rushed in.

THE END

ACKNOWLEDGEMENTS

This book was inspired by my brothers' soccer coach, Ronald J. Carruthers, who died as their team made a deep run into the 1989 Pennsylvania State Tournament. Ron was a friend to our family and impacted my life in ways that have reverberated through time. Like the fictional Coach O, Ron Carruthers was loved by some and hated by others. And like Coach O tried to spare Piper and her crew from the consequences of their actions, the real-life Ron tried to steer me away from a future he suspected held heartache. Young and headstrong, I didn't heed his warning, and it took many years until I was able to understand his predictions. The irony is that in writing this book and revisiting Ron's legacy, my lying season ended, and with it, a reckoning of my past. Still, I wouldn't trade the journey. I wonder if Ron watches our days—my brothers', my sister's and mine—and if we have made him proud.

Thank you to my mother, Suzie Christie, who is perpetually convinced that her kids are just about to make it big. "It's not over yet," she still tells us and we half believe her. Thank you to my late father, David Christie, who was my first reader and gave me the confidence to keep trying. I miss him every day. Thank you to my sister, Tara, for her steadfast and enthusiastic confidence in this story. Thank you to Rich— Ron would be tickled to know you produced four soccer-playing sons. And to my brother, Jamie, how lucky that we were born into the same family and walk together in this life. You are my rock.

Thank you to my writing friends, Kelly Coon, for reading an early draft. And to Lisa Mahoney for her tireless help in revisions. My creative world wouldn't be complete without Amy Impellizerri, who began as a business client over a decade ago, and who has grown into a dear friend both on and off the page. She has taught me to always choose hope. I am endlessly grateful to my mentor Sandra Scofield—first my teacher, then my editor, and now my writing partner and friend. Many thanks to my non-writing tribe for their constant support of all my ridiculousness: Sandy Barber, Haley Lawrence, Valerie Mackey, and Amy Rothermel. Many thanks to my publishing team at Black Rose Writing, including Reagan Rothe, David King, and Justin Weeks.

To my readers, without you this writing wouldn't make sense. You complete the creative circle. Thank you for reading my work and for reaching out to tell me when I've hit the right note. To my muse, thank you. And finally, to the two greatest gifts of my life—Cali and Cole—it is all for you. Someday, you'll understand your mom was young once upon a time and she had dreams, too.

Good luck and Godspeed to *The Lying Season*.

See you farther on up the road.

Love,
Heather

READER'S GUIDE
The Lying Season

Discussion Questions

1. If you were to find yourself in the same dire situation as Piper, Jacob, Ethan, Noah, and Cooper, would you have gone to the authorities immediately? Why or why not?

2. Discuss how each of the characters handled the guilt and how it affected their lives. Who is the moral compass of the book? Is it Piper or Jacob or even, Noah? Make an argument for each one. Why does Jacob confess to Sheriff Mismo without Piper?

3. Should Piper's parents have more aware of their kids' subtle behavioral changes? If they had noticed and addressed the emotional shifts in their children, do you think it would have impacted how Piper, Noah, and Cooper handled the situation?

4. Discuss Piper's romantic feelings for both Ethan and Jacob. How does she mature throughout the book and how is this reflected in the evolution of her relationship with the Horn brothers?

5. What effect did Coach O have on the team, the individual families, and the community? Describe his strengths and weaknesses. Discuss his decision to pin the accident on himself, knowing he was dying. Does this make him a hero? Why or why not?

6. Discuss the following themes found throughout the novel:
   - You can't undo what has been done.
   - A quick decision can change the trajectory of your life forever.
   - Soccer is a metaphor for life
   - Sometimes you eat the bear and sometimes the bear eats you.

ABOUT THE AUTHOR

Heather Christie is the award-winning author of the novel, *What The Valley Knows*. Her essays have appeared in *Salon*, *Writer's Digest*, *Scary Mommy*, and *Elephant Journal*. She holds an MFA in Creative Writing from Pine Manor College and can be reached through her website at www.HeatherChristieBooks.com.

Note from the Author

Word-of-mouth is crucial for any author to succeed. If you enjoyed *The Lying Season*, please leave a review online—anywhere you are able. Even if it's just a sentence or two. It would make all the difference and would be very much appreciated.

Thanks!
Heather Christie

Thank you so much for reading one of **Heather Christie's** novels.
If you enjoyed the experience, please check out our Recommended
title for your next great read!

What the Valley Knows

"A taut, compelling family tale."
—Kirkus Reviews

CPSIA information can be obtained
at www.ICGtesting.com
Printed in the USA
BVHW031214240721
612471BV00001B/7